COACHMAN

SUE MILLARD

Jackdaw E Books, Cumbria, 2022

COACHMAN

Second edition published in Great Britain 2022

Paperback ISBN: 9781913 106249

JACKDAW E BOOKS
Daw Bank
Greenholme
Tebay
Penrith
Cumbria
CA10 3TA
http://www.jackdawebooks.co.uk

COACHMAN

Sue Millard

Procession of Mails on the King's Birthday, by John Sturgess (fl. 1864-1903) published in *The Coaching Age* in 1885.

CHAPTER 1.

Stony Stratford, April 1838

"You up there! Wake up."

George heard the voice, but his eyelids refused to lift. Surely he could doze for a few minutes while the coach changed horses? Now that the roof-top seat was still, oblivion was sucking him into its delicious depths, so that he was back in Carlisle with Lucy, saying goodbye in the firelight, wrapping her in his arms while dawn filtered through the shutters.

In his half-dream she was repeating, "Go…I'll follow you as soon as I'm better. Go now. Go." And he didn't want to, but he'd applied for the job and if he didn't keep the appointment…

The voice spoke again at his elbow: "Coachman!"

The title roused him, but then he remembered he wasn't the driver, only a very weary passenger on the Albion, who'd travelled all yesterday and half today. And he'd left Lucy behind at the Blue Bell. Damn it, he should never have set off without her. He should have waited till she was well.

"Come on, boy. Are you fit to drive us?"

He dragged himself out of sleep, and saw the grey-bearded guard balanced nonchalantly on the tread half-way up the coach side, waiting for him to answer.

His driving whip had slipped towards the passenger next to him. He retrieved it, and adjusted his hat against the spring sunshine.

"Where are we?" His lips and tongue were clumsy with tiredness.

"Stony Stratford, the Cock Hotel. Look, I need a coachman. I've told 'im 'e mustn't drive but 'e will, unless I put someone on the box pretty quick."

George struggled to understand. Down in front of the coach, a team fretted at the restraining hands of the ostlers.

"He's never been this bad afore," said the guard. "The Guv'nor will dismiss the both of us if I let 'im drive – and if I don't, I'll have to drive, and then we won't get up to Town this side of dark. Then I see'd your whip and I thought, ah, there's a coachman, so maybe we're in luck."

The body of the coach shuddered. Something very heavy must be loading, to disturb its massive springs. A hat, a head and shoulders came up, fell back, and reappeared. They were followed by a body wrapped in a greatcoat, a body that chuckled and rolled as the stable men pushed it upwards, that heaved itself belly-first onto the driving-seat amid a gust of brandy fumes, and then lost its hat. George woke up fully, all his driving experience shouting outrage.

"He isn't going to drive, is he? That barrel of lard! He's paralytic."

A bonnet poked out of the window below and screeched, "Coachman! We are five minutes behind time! Be pleased to start!"

The driver roared back, "Immee-jusly, Madame! Throw me the reins, boys, tally-ho." He accepted his hat from a stablehand and placed it on his head with a royal disregard for its orientation.

"I'll have the devil's own job to get him off the box now," sighed the guard. "Hurry up, climb forrard, or he'll drive us all to Kingdom Come."

"I think I'd better," said George, and the guard slapped his arm encouragingly and jumped down.

As George scrambled over the lazy-back onto the passenger side of the box, the driver saw the whip in his hand, and reached out towards it. "Oh, now there's a useful toy – have to borrow that – y'see, Thetford pinched mine!" George drew it away, and the fat groping fist fell instead on his elbow.

The guard shouted from below, "Get off the box, Anderson, and sit behind."

"No, s'my place and I'll keep it, he-hee. Fetch another brandy, and not too much bloody water."

The screech from inside the coach demanded, "Coachman! Guard! Are we to start or will you gossip there all day?"

It was the ostlers who decided the matter by throwing the reins up to George's side of the coach. As he caught each one and slotted them between his fingers his tiredness vanished. He made his adjustments by feel, so practised that he didn't even have to think about it. This was a challenge – an excitement he hadn't foreseen. What would these horses be like? They were fresh, a daytime team – not likely to be the "three blind 'uns and a bolter" he might get at night – but the lead horses were half-rearing, far too anxious to go. He couldn't tell how much humouring they would need, and if the drunken driver wouldn't get off the box, he'd have to drive them from the near-side, too.

A shout came from below. "What are you doing, boy?" It was the yard porter, disturbed from his routine by the delay.

"What's it look like?" George shouted back, jerking a thumb at the barrel of lard.

"Oh! Ah! Well, he's been in the tap-room all morning. You'd better drive on!"

"I will! What kind of a team are they? Whip or voice?"

"He's got heavy hands – hit and hold on – so they've got hard mouths and they don't listen too well."

"You ought to give me a refund on my fare!"

"Ah, fight that out with Mr Chaplin, it's none of my business."

George laughed. The yard porter couldn't know that it was Chaplin he was travelling to see. But what a way to arrive, driving one of his coaches.

"Drive on," ordered the porter, "drive on! I've another coach due any minute."

George sang out, "All right behind?"

The screech from inside said, "And high time – !"

Her voice was cut off in turn by Anderson roaring, "Get on!"

The leaders jumped forward, the bars jerked and the wheel-horses were dragged with them, the collars halfway up their necks. The traces snapped taut and the coach rocked into motion.

"We're off, boy," crowed Anderson, waving a leather flask at him. "By God we're off!"

The man on the roof seat behind cried, "You're not in control of these horses. This is outrageous!"

Isn't that the truth! thought George, as he fought to balance the power of the team. The wheel-horses were galloping crammed up against the hindquarters of the leaders, out of time with each other, snatching the pole from side to side so that the coach began to sway left and right like Anderson's flask of brandy.

The man behind shouted, "Give them back to their proper driver!"

"Aye, give 'em to me," said the barrel, grasping suddenly at the reins. "I'll pull their back teeth out."

George drove him off with an elbow to the face. "Go to blazes!"

Anderson collapsed with an oath and a gust of brandy, and the horses bolted.

They galloped down the road with the coach thundering behind them and pebbles rattling off the body like grapeshot, the inside passengers wailing while outsiders cursed and clung to their benches. George sang, "Ste-eady, ste-eady, woo boys, ste-eady…" but the horses seemed to hear nothing but Anderson's blasphemies and fled like a herd stampeding from wolves.

In that first mile a dozen panicked carriages scattered in front of the coach. George's face was a grinning mask of concentration. Hard mouths? Their jaws are made of wood! His give and take with the reins made as much impression as beating on the door of an empty house. He just had to do his best to keep the coach safe until the horses outran the terror that drove them.

Pray to God everyone else would hear the guard's horn calls, and stay out of the way!

"Woo boys, ste-eady… woo boys, ste-eady…"

He was watching for the horses' necks to lower, their flattened ears to relax. They would come back to him eventually, and he could ease his grip. Thank God it was a straight road! It was another wild half mile before he felt their necks soften; another quarter before their heads lowered and their jaws began to give to the reins. Within another hundred yards they dropped from gallop to canter, and he had them under control.

The moment the coach was running in a normal fashion the man behind rediscovered his courage and poked George between the shoulder blades.

"You're not authorized, young man! Not authorized to drive this coach!"

"That's as may be, sir," said George, still grinning from the excitement of the runaway. "We'll be good and early at the next change, so you'll have plenty of time to complain."

"I shall report you to the proprietor!" exclaimed his passenger, and poked him again.

The guard shouted over the luggage on the roof, "That's all right sir, you do that. Mr Chaplin will be thankful that he's sober."

Prompted by the word "sober" Anderson struggled upright and wagged a blood-smeared finger under George's nose.

"Listen. When they tell you they're wore out, they ain't. All you have to do, is to remember the short Tommy. Know what I mean? Thetford has it tucked in the basket back there. Hit 'em hard enough and they'll go all right. There now."

As though this pronouncement had been a swan song, he sagged back into his driving seat. George bawled over his shoulder, "Guard!"

"Yes, Coachman!"

"Your driver's falling asleep! And I need directions."

"Pull up then. I better lash him down so 'e don't drop orf."

George persuaded the team to a trembling halt, and with grunts and oaths and a length of cord the guard secured the driver to his seat. Then he roughly wiped the blood off his face, folded up the reddened handkerchief and stuffed it back into Anderson's coat.

"Better not frighten the lasses along the way," he said.

The passenger spluttered another protest but the guard said calmly, "Was you wanting to make a complaint, sir? If so, me and you are going to fall out, cos if this young man don't drive, you'll have to put up with me handling the ribbons, and I'll tell you, as a coachman I make a bloody good carpenter. Unless you're wishful to drive yourself? They ain't a team for a beginner, now are they? Thank you kindly then, we'll carry on as we are. Coachman, he won't bother you no more," he added, not distinguishing between Anderson and the passenger. "Now, it's a straight run to Dunstable. I'll blow for you in plenty of time, so the horses'll be out in the road waiting for us and we'll go on grand. Don't you worry about going into Town, neither. I'll direct you. They're real smart horses there – a real pleasant team to drive."

"If I get that far without falling asleep," grunted George. "You might have to lash me down, too."

CHAPTER 2.

Carlisle, October 1837

Lucy first saw George strolling into the Blue Bell, seeming to bring with him all the sunshine of the crisp autumn afternoon. He stood his whip against the bar and doffed his smart hat to her most politely, and when he asked for ale his smile was so firm and handsome she had to stop herself hurrying, in her eagerness to serve him.

After he'd taken the edge off his thirst he didn't wander off to find a seat like most coachmen did. He unfastened the buttons of his driving coat to take in the warmth of the inn, and leaned his elbow on the little counter.

Lucy seldom bothered to question her customers, but there was something steady and restful in his face, and something very appealing in his warm brown eyes.

"Have you come very far?" she asked.

"Oh, around," he said. "Liverpool, Manchester, Buxton, all over."

"Buxton? Oh aye? I've heard it's popular to take the waters if you're poorly. But it must have done you good. You look quite healthy." She gave a hint of a smile, inviting him to laugh, and he did.

"I wasn't taking a cure, saucy. I was driving a coach."

"As if I couldn't have guessed." She flicked a finger against the whipthong that hung like a coiled white snake from its stick. "Was it good work?"

"Not bad. I drove the manufacturers, and the commercial gents, and their wives and families. It was nothing fancy."

This time she laughed, not believing him. "Oh, I'm sure it must have been."

"Well," he said, "it was a business, just like yours, I suppose. If you can give your passengers something useful about the scenery or the places they should visit, they remember you and give you a good tip."

"And you had plenty to tell them, I suppose?"

He only smiled a little. "They're manufacturers – the new rich – people who want to move in society. I don't care so much for them because they don't care how I drive – and that's because they don't know how it should be done! But if I had *you* on my coach, I'd find all manner of things to tell you."

"Oh, I couldn't move in society," she said. "I've lived here too long! But if you have a new way to stop the customers fondling me, I'd be glad to hear of it."

"Impossible," he said, "unless you could put on a hundredweight of flesh and about forty years! And that would be a dreadful waste."

She had no time to answer before Mr Farrimond shouted, "Wench! Fetch us brandy, will you?"

She excused herself and carried brandies to the fireside for Farrimond and his friend Armstrong. She considered her new customer. He seemed a bit cagey about his background but she couldn't fault him for that: she knew what it was to need defences. Too many men had come and gone through the doors of the Blue Bell, and the other houses where she and her mother had lived.

When she came back he was looking into an empty mug.

"Shall I fill that up for you, sir?"

"George," he said. "Davenport. But you can call me George," and when she reached for the mug he wouldn't release it until she'd repeated his name.

While she poured the ale she found it easy to go on talking. "Why did you leave Buxton? Didn't you have a good place?"

"It's the end of the season. They call them butterfly coaches, you know, because they go to bed as soon as there's a hint of autumn. Now let me ask you something, my lovely judy. You're too pretty to be called Wench. What's your name?"

"Lucy, sir."

"Ah-ah – George, remember?" His smile warmed her again and she smiled back, and then to her own astonishment, found she was blushing. She busied herself wiping down the bar. She still had to ask two very important questions.

Keeping her eyes on the cloth, she rubbed the little curved counter top, paying far too much attention to the detail of its rounded edges. She knew he was watching her. She asked without looking up, "So, do you have a place now in Carlisle?"

"Yes."

"And will you be staying here long?"

"Just until the spring."

She felt a pang of disappointment. As though he understood, he leaned towards her and said gently, "But this looks like a snug place to spend a winter night. I don't want anything fancy, only a bed to myself – then y'see, whatever I find in it, I've only myself to blame, haven't I?"

She looked up to find him so close that she could hear him breathe.

"Do you have a room for me? Go on, fix me up, Lucy my darling." He took her hand and pressed a half-crown into it, folding her fingers inside his own.

She wondered, for a moment, whether he thought he was buying her. That would have ruined everything. But she judged that his eyes were sincere.

Then her mother had come in from the kitchens and started to discuss terms for his lodging.

"A single room? There's only one that's empty. Most o' t'coachmen shares, two or three to a room. Oh! well if ye insist, ye'll have to find the price ..." Mrs Hennessy paused as if waiting for a response, and he drew out a handful of silver and looked at them both with that half-smile. Lucy knew that for her mother ready cash was a powerful lure. "Very good, in that case, ye'll be welcome – sir. Should I send Michael to fetch your bags?"

"He won't stay," said Ma, in the kitchen. "Too high in t'instep. Too free with his cash."

Lucy kept her face expressionless.

"He'll do as he pleases, I expect," she said.

"Aye well, they all do," said Ma. "Men. Trick is to make 'em pay for what pleases 'em. You make sure you give him nowt unless he pays for it. He's just a customer."

Lucy said nothing. She had learned very early in life that it didn't pay to contradict.

Ma repeated, "Aye, nowt but a paying customer. Never mind his pretty ways. Hard cash is what we deal in here, remember."

Lucy still said nothing. If she had tried to speak, her mother and the cook and the kitchen boy would have known she was on the verge of tears. She was disgusted by her mother's dismissal of George as "a paying customer," though not at all surprised, because Ma Hennessy had seen so many men come and go, here at the Bell or across the city in the Lanes, that she had stopped treating them as human. Ma had almost brainwashed Lucy, too, into thinking of men as a separate species, to be managed with a few basic words as horses were – fed and sold plenty to drink and never trusted too far. Lucy had never cared for any of them but she had learned to smile and flirt just enough for them to give her tips, and as they seldom looked higher than her breasts they didn't notice that the smile never reached her eyes.

George Davenport was different, though. In that moment at the bar counter, he had got past her defences. She was no longer merely a servant girl who avoided the hands of obfuscated coachmen. She badly wanted to see him now, to know he would be around, and she wouldn't smile mechanically or flirt with him for his money. He was young enough talk to, and if he preferred silence she would be content just to look at him. Her mind was so full of the warmth of his eyes, his young strength and confidence, that she was awake and glowing and restless, confused by emotions she had never had before. She was angry with herself. She didn't know whether she could trust those feelings. But one thing was certain: George mustn't think of lodging anywhere else but at the Bell.

In fact, he had stayed.

In the first few weeks, George would come in from his afternoon coach, change his wet clothes and come down to eat, and then go out to walk before dark. Some nights he persuaded Jem Walker and Robert Lloyd to accompany him to the little Theatre round the corner, and then he required his shaving water early and dressed like a gentleman. Other evenings, he laughed and joined in the banter and sang, Lucy thought, very well – the rough comedy of the tavern as well as rustic ballads or sentimental songs such as 'She wore a Wreath of Roses,' or the music of the 'Beggar's Opera.'

She disregarded the men's coaching talk, which was mostly of horses and harness and coaches; roads, foul weather, jokey recollections of mishaps and lucky escapes. Armstrong tended to dwell on bad turns revenged or opportunities seized, and Farrimond, who had recently been to a Chartist meeting about Equal Representation, would bring up the rights of the working man. Such political arguments only ended when the brandy put Armstrong to sleep. Lucy was intrigued, however, by the way George listened and smiled, as though their attempts at adult conversation amused him. It was a strange expression, one much older and more superior than his youth should have worn.

When the winter came, with the geese honking overhead to the Solway coast, there was far more snow than usual, and George stopped walking out after his day's driving and hung around watching her, teasing while she worked. It seemed to her that when he wanted a maid to serve him food, to bring hot water for shaving, take his boots to be cleaned or replace the candles in his room, he asked for her more often than for Mariah. She tried not to hope. She told herself that she was mistaken, but Mariah's spiteful comments soon proved she wasn't. Lucy absorbed the spite and said nothing. She had learned very early in life that if she reacted, her mother would blame her and support her opponent, and her only defence had been silence. But now, with George breaking the pattern of her servitude, she began to think of escape.

She asked him first to tell her about the aristocratic customers he had met and interesting places he had seen. He was willing enough to talk of them. But when she asked about his past, he gave her a half-smile and began to voice the thoughts of the beer mugs and plates she was clearing from the tables. He was equally likely to hold a conversation with the cat on the hearth, so long as it deflected her curiosity. She didn't know what to do with him, and yet her heart seemed to stop every time she saw him.

He continued to be generous. That snowbound Christmas he gave a Christmas-box to Ma Hennessy, to Mrs Carruthers the cook, to Mariah, to Michael the porter and sometime waiter, and Petey the pot-boy. According to Mariah, George had only given them a shilling each, the same as Mr Farrimond or Mr Armstrong, so Lucy didn't reveal the fact that he'd given her two half-crowns wrapped in a blue satin ribbon.

There was no mistaking that message.

She had tied her hair with the ribbon that night, before she tiptoed down the stair to scratch at his bedroom door. It was not his money or his gifts she craved. What she longed for was to slide into the warmth of his arms, to confirm that someone as brave and kind as George could want her. She didn't believe he would fall in love with her in return, but if she pleased him, when he moved on he might take her with him.

CHAPTER 3.

Carlisle, March 1838

George woke to Lucy shaking his shoulder. He clung to sleep, but she twitched the bedclothes off him.

"Come on, love. Get up."

When he began to stir, she stepped back and lit his candle from her own, and the dark wood-panelled room wavered drunkenly behind her twin shadows.

"Damnation, woman…" He sat up.

"It's twenty minutes to seven! The Mails are out already. I've asked Mrs Carruthers to make you a bacon sandwich." She hurried soft-footed down the stairs.

He began to dress.

He was used to getting up before sunrise. Until last week, he'd been driving the New Times stage coach from Carlisle to Kendal. By now he would already have been a long way south, driving his fourth team of the day out of Shap towards the snowy heights of the Fell, his lamps the only moving lights on the road. The Newcastle Mail was a recent promotion for him and its seven o'clock start should have been easy.

But this was the first time Lucy had stayed with him all night. When she got up for work he'd fallen into that early morning sleep that was the most luxurious of all... it was a good thing she had come back to wake him.

He pulled on his boots, and clattered down to the kitchen with his greatcoat flying out behind him. Lucy was waiting, rather nervously, with his sandwich.

"Here," she said. "Hurry – I'm supposed to be – well, I don't want Mam to catch me here."

"Oh, be damned to your mother." He snatched a kiss and the sandwich, and dashed out. He called back, "I'll see you tomorrow, I expect..."

The four Mail coaches were lined up in St Cuthbert's Lane, from the corner of the Crown and Mitre on English Street to its inn-yard at the rear. The Post Office, and the Blue Bell, were on the other side of the street.

A thin rain drifted through the light of the coach lamps and laid a mist over the horses' woollen rugs, and over the sacks protecting the stable boys, and over the oiled coverings of the mail bags that the men hoisted onto the coach roofs.

An ostler walked down the lane carrying a lantern, and stopped beside each coach for the driver to check the horses' harness. When he moved on, the light slid across the gold paint of the letters V R, and the names of the cities on the doors: Edinburgh, Port Patrick, Glasgow and finally Newcastle. When he reached the end of the line, George was leaning in through the coach door, wrestling a bale of newspapers into its place under the seat.

"Morning, Joss." George stood up and put his hat straight and took another bite of his sandwich.

"Thou's got up late, eh? Give thyself more time tomorrow. Remember it's nobbut luck thou's got this job."

George, his mouth too full to speak, only grinned at him and carried on with the daily routine. This team must take him over the first ten miles of his route, and the speed required by the Post Office left little time for breakdowns along the road. By the light of Joss's lamp, he checked the traces and pole chains, and the reins and their settings on each bit, while the horses stood quivering under their rugs and their shoes clicked on the cobbles.

"What sort of a team are they, Joss? They look smart enough, but then, they're a city team."

"Aye, looks isn't everything. Johnnie Yates complains they dun't ga fast enough to keep theirselves warm… Is thy harness right, now?"

"Good as it can be. I'll get Barney to change anything that needs it."

Joss nodded satisfaction, and walked back up the line.

George pushed the last piece of bread into his mouth. Breakfast on the run, and Joss's warning, were small penances for last night… Lucy loving him, wrapping him in physical pleasure and at last sleeping curled in his arms. When she got up for work, she had knelt in the firelight, replaiting her fair hair with those quick, intimate fingers… He supposed that as the day went on Lucy's serenity would fade just as his own did, but those pictures, those sensations, would carry him through a lonely night in Newcastle and bring him back hungry.

Passengers began to arrive, from English Street, from Blackfriars and from the Coffee House, gathering in little groups to show their tickets to the coach guards and pay the balance of their fares. He buttoned his coat and gloves, took the reins and climbed to his driving box. Once he was wrapped in his coach apron he considered himself on duty, wearing the everyday mask of politeness. Behind him on the roof seat, two men greeted each other in a businesslike way that suggested they were regular travelling companions.

“We have a fresh coachey, eh? Is he any use?”

“Better ask him.”

A hand on his shoulder. “Can you drive this team, boy?”

George, still basking in Lucy’s calm, felt none of the irritation that the word “boy” normally produced. Over the last six years he had moved steadily up from one post to the next, one town to the next, until he’d achieved this place on the Newcastle Mail. Although he was only twenty-two, he was far from being the novice that the question implied, and he believed he’d got the post on merit.

“Davenport, sir. If you please.”

“Oh, very well! Davenport. Can these horses do the times?”

“Yes, sir, of course.” If Johnnie Yates had been driving them, they would be too scared not to do their best. Whether that would be enough, he would soon find out.

Here was Mr Dixon, a local mill-owner, climbing to the box-seat beside him.

“Good morning, Davenport.”

“Morning, sir.” George knew him reasonably well. They were much the same in looks, both tall and dark. Dixon was the older of the two, but almost as trim a figure as George. There the similarity ended. George was poised, handling the reins with easy precision, while Dixon sat enthroned like a God of the Weather under a large black umbrella.

“I shall be with you as far as Hexham,” Dixon informed him. “I hope we shall have a good run.”

"I'll do my best for you, sir." George had driven for most of the Dixons over the past few months and although he had little interest in the family's cotton trade or their politics, he'd been polite to them and found they tipped freely. He had better pay proper attention.

He could feel the tremors of the coach body which told of Barnes, the guard, jumping up to his little iron seat, the thump of his foot on the locked boot-lid. It was nearly time to go. The horses knew the sounds and began to paw the cobbles, and his nearside wheeler would have stood on her hind legs if the boy hadn't caught the rein to keep her down. Yes, Johnnie Yates had made them anxious, all right.

Above the stamping horseshoes and the chimes of city clocks, a bell struck seven. One after another the guards on the four coaches blew their horns for the "Start." The boys stepped back from the line of horses, the ostlers pulled off the rugs, and Dixon braced himself and took hold of the seat rail.

George called to his passengers, "Sit tight!" And to the horses: "Trot on!"

The departing Mails filled the street with a joyful rhythm of horseshoes and iron tyred wheels. The noise and movement thrilled through his bloodstream. From now on this coach was his business, and he answered to no man, except his Post Office guard. He commanded six different teams, stage after stage, to ensure that the Mail, the guard and his passengers made ten miles an hour en route to their destinations.

George was proud to be driving a Mail, trotting north through Carlisle every morning. He discounted the fact that his coach was badly-built and heavy, and the only paintwork that wasn't blistered was the new V R in gold. He took very little notice of the weather. It didn't matter to him that the Mails had fewer seats than the stage coaches. A Mail coachman's job was to make fast driving appear easy, and that required great skill. His customers were quality and appreciated quality driving, which made their tips proportionately bigger than the ones given by stage passengers, so it pretty much balanced out as far as cash was concerned. He had no doubt that a Mail coach was what a man should drive if he wanted to be acknowledged among the best.

There were crowds of men and women coming in through the streets to work. By law, the Queen's Mail had right of way, and when the post horn blew "Clear the Road" it was up to the workers to get out of the road as best they could. George knew very well, though, that drivers who knocked people down tended to lose their jobs. He held his team in line behind the Glasgow Mail.

Beside him Dixon was looking down into the crowd, acknowledging greetings from some of the people who George assumed must be heading for the Shaddon mills. The rest clumped through the slush with collars and shawls pulled up. Once again George realized how lucky he was to do work that he loved. Horses were an endless delight to him, and even the challenge of getting difficult ones to work well was deeply satisfying. As the traces swayed and tautened, as the reins flickered and fed back the rhythms of the horses' movement, he already felt that he and the team were learning each other's ways. When he'd driven them for a month or two they would almost read each other's minds.

The four Mails trotted through the Scotch Gate, and across the twin bridges of the river Eden that was flooding grey-brown and angry over the Sands. George forgot his pity for the workers. Once the coach had crossed the river the team hit Stanwix Bank and began to feel the full weight of the coach, and he had to give them their heads in order to pull up the hill. The horses threw themselves into the work, haunches sinking powerfully, hooves digging hard. He checked them only for the swing right towards Brampton, in case the momentum of the turn upset the coach – it wouldn't do his reputation any good to throw the Mail wrong way up in his first week, and especially not with Dixon sitting beside him. The three Scottish Mails held their course northwards, and with the turn safely negotiated the Newcastle Mail headed eastward on its own.

By the time they passed the last of the houses, the wind had grown strong enough to push Dixon's umbrella against George's driving arm. It was one of the regular annoyances of coaching and he had learned to put up with it, so he was pleasantly surprised that Dixon at once let go of the seat rail and shifted the umbrella to his outer shoulder.

"Thank you, sir! You'll notice we've arranged for the wind to be behind you."

"Too kind," said Dixon. "I appreciate what you've done with the clouds, so I need not squint into the rising sun, but permit me to point out that it's also raining. I feel that is excessive attention to detail."

"I didn't expect you to sit outside, sir. I thought it would be just the railway engineers. For me, they deserve the rain."

"You're biased."

"Ah, they're only going to Gilsland. They won't melt in that time. Now at Hexham, sir – you are going to the station? Not to the White Hart?"

"Yes, to the station," said Dixon.

"Then I hope you'll be warm enough, sir, until we get there."

"Don't worry, Davenport. I shall not be much colder up here than inside, and it will make the railway journey seem positively tropical."

"Mind the engine doesn't set fire to you," said George. "That would be warm enough, I dare say!"

Dixon laughed. "I'm not fool enough to travel in one of those open wagons."

"I still wouldn't fancy riding behind a boiler, sir. It might go off at any minute."

"Hush," said Dixon, leaning closer, "don't tell that to the engineers. Poor fellows. They don't realize the dangers they face."

One of the men behind gave Dixon's umbrella a smart tap.

"Are you a sceptic about steam?"

The mill-owner lifted the umbrella and turned sideways to talk.

"Indeed no! I power my mill with a stationary steam engine. But I doubt our coachman cares much for steam."

"I do not, sir!" agreed George. "I dare say that in your mills, steam must be a big improvement on water power. And I'm sure the railway people think they can beat the coaches, but I don't believe they can do as good as job."

The man behind exclaimed, "The company is risking a good deal of money, young man, so I hope very much to prove you wrong!"

George replied over his shoulder, "The day they send a steam engine up Shap Fell, gentlemen, I'll hang up my bars."

The engineer buffeted him on the back. "You may have to, my boy. Railways are going to be ten times faster and safer than coaching."

George just smiled and said to the horses, "Trot on, boys."

Dixon nodded to the other two men, and sat facing forward again. The Mail had covered another mile before he asked, "I take it that you are satisfied with your position here?"

"Maybe. I like to drive four horses, and the Mails are the toughest test of your timekeeping. But I doubt whether this job will still be here next year."

"I think you have no need to worry. Even if the Mails were to go to Newcastle along the railway, there will still be work for good men like yourself, in private service. And as it happens," he added, as if the idea had only just occurred to him, "I am in need of a coachman."

George glanced sideways, not sure whether he was being teased. "Really, sir?"

"Yes," said Dixon. "Really. Specifically, I keep two carriage horses, a cob for the dog-cart, and three saddle horses. We're out in the country, of course. I don't spend much time at Tullie House."

"I see. And is there a cottage, sir, or does your man have to live in?"

"Oh, he lives in. Everything is provided – livery, meals, laundry. The cook has a soft spot for handsome young men. Would you be interested?"

"In the cook, sir?"

Dixon chuckled. "She might be a little old for you! I believe my man would speak well of the place. If you felt you could improve my stable, I would give you a free hand to buy anything you thought suitable."

George nodded. He wondered what sort of budget would be available. He could see possibilities – excluding the cook – though the cob was probably a heavy, rough-legged sort that he would prefer to get rid of. He'd buy a decent pair of horses that could take turns in the dog cart or match up as the wheelers in a team of four.

"Do you drive your own horses, sir?"

"Very rarely. I'm not much of a horseman. I prefer to employ someone who is."

Well, that would be interesting: a chance to school a team exclusively to his own preferences. Of course private service, wearing a family's livery, would be quite different from driving a Mail. He wouldn't be the autocrat he was here, where gentry and aristocracy asked keen questions about his technique and conversed with him on equal terms. He would have to trim his manners and sit in lonely state, and if he was allowed to make any remark at all he would have to preface it with, "If you please, sir," or "I hope I'm not overstepping the mark, madam, to suggest…" A lot depended on the master, and the mistress.

He asked bluntly, "Why is your man leaving?"

"One of my neighbours has been trying for years to poach him off me," Dixon replied, with a chuckle. "When he heard our fellow wanted to marry, he offered him a cottage, and he took it like a shot."

"Do stop all this chit-chat," interrupted the man behind. "The coachey has work to do here and now! Don't be late for that train, boy! We have business with the railway company."

George said, “The last I heard, sir, the farmers still set their clocks by the passing of the Mail.”

“Then look to your off leader,” advised the railwayman. “The other driver gives them a smack all round – he’s got a whip that fairly rattles them. What’s happened to him?”

For answer, George drew a deep breath and shouted, “Duke!” The horse that was slacking took up his share of the work without needing the whip.

“Was that what you wanted, sir? As for Johnnie Yates, he’s laid down on his sick bed. This cold weather’s done for him.”

“I am not at all surprised,” said the other. “I would rather have had an inside seat myself, if you had not already been full.”

Bastard, thought George. The railwayman had no concern for Johnnie himself, only for the whip-power that he believed was missing.

He remembered how sympathetic Lucy had been, even though she only knew Johnnie as a customer at the Blue Bell.

When George told her he’d been promoted to the Mail in Johnnie’s place, she’d asked at once, “Is he poorly?”

“Yes, very.” George had pulled a face. “He wouldn’t have given up his coach if he could sit upright and hold the reins.”

“Poor man,” she said. “It’s going to be very hard for his wife.”

“Poor kids,” he echoed.

“You’d better make sure you wrap up properly before you go out.”

How she loved to take care of people! She was a fine warm-hearted lass. He wondered how she would react to Dixon's offer of a position out in the country that, clearly, could only accommodate a single man.

CHAPTER 4.

George came back to Carlisle the following day in the same condition as he had for the past week: almost wet through. In the stables of the Crown and Mitre he pulled off his last pair of gloves and eased his scarf away from his neck, and draped his rain-soaked apron over the partition of an empty stall. They would all very likely still be damp in the morning.

The steamy fug of the stables and the mealy smell of straw reminded him of his grandmother's kitchen on breadmaking day. When Joss Elliott came through the doorway George half expected to see him in a flour-dusted apron, with fingers coated in bread-dough, but by the grey light from the window, he saw that Joss had a sweaty horse-collar and harness hanging from one shoulder and a bridle and reins in his other hand, and the fancy vanished at once.

"Ah, George," said Joss. "Mr Teather left word that he wants to see thee."

"All right, I'll just put away my whip."

"No, he said soon as may be, so go now. Tek it with thee, or he'll likely not remember what thou's there for."

"Well, what does he want me for?"

"Maybe thou's been chasing the maids? Catched one, for owt I know."

As George set off for the yard, Joss called, "Eh, thy wheel-hoss, Daisy, she's got a nasty cut on her hock. What's thou been doing?"

"She lost her footing at the bottom of Stanwix Bank. She was damned lucky the wheel didn't go over her."

"Just tek a bit more care, eh! We're short enough of hosses after this winter."

"Give me a coach that doesn't load so heavily – tell the lawyers not to write so many letters! Is the Guv'nor in the office?"

"Go in and ask Mr Cowan."

Across the yard in the coach office, George hailed the clerk.

"Joss says the Guv'nor wants to see me. Any idea where he might be?"

Mr Cowan put up a silencing hand. The booking clerk was a deity not to be annoyed, and his attention was fixed on the customer buying tickets. George moved away towards the fire. He thought about that nasty business on Stanwix Bank – Daisy's scrambling fall, and the efforts of Violet, the other wheel-horse, to hold the coach back on her own. He hoped the old mare hadn't strained anything – time would tell, he supposed. He hoped too that Daisy's injury wouldn't take long to heal.

Through the doorway he could see the rain cascading off the eaves, undercutting the heaps of snow at the road-sides and gathering in stippled puddles along the gutters. The daily forage wagon was turning into the inn-yard, loaded with hay for the stables, the horse rain-streaked and resigned, the driver hidden under sacking. George watched with sympathy, but it was a long time since he had escaped from that level of misery – and, God willing, it would be a long time before he descended to it again.

At the Blue Bell he would change into dry clothes, and Lucy would serve him something hot and tasty, and at the end of the evening he would drag his mattress off the bedstead and onto the floor in hopes that she would share it.

"Well, George," said Mr Cowan, at last. "Barney brought in your fares, and he paid your fine, too. It's not like you to be late."

"I had a horse go down," said George, reluctant to move away from the fire. "Barney had my share of the fine."

He didn't mention the short-distance fares, paid "over-the-shoulder," that he and Barnes had split between them and which more than covered their penalty for lateness. He knew this was an area where even Mr Cowan was accustomed not to enquire too closely.

George asked, "What does Teather want with me, d'ye know?"

The clerk stared back at him, an Olympian unimpressed. "Mr Teather didn't disclose any reason. He is above stairs with Mr Gray, but whether he is free to speak to you, I cannot say." He closed the cashbox with a click, and this time, turned the key. "Go up, and I daresay you'll find out."

George shrugged, and ducked out into the rain and ran the short distance to the front of the Crown and Mitre. He went up the stairs two at a time, but he straightened his hat and coat and made sure the whip-thong was coiled tidily before he knocked at Mr Gray's door.

"Yes!"

Teather and Gray were sitting at a table beside one of the sash windows. The rain beat on the glass, and an unlit lamp stood among the papers, ready against the fading of the afternoon light. Teather, a weatherbeaten man in his thirties, was a local contractor for both stage-coaches and Mails, and Gray was the landlord of the Crown and Mitre, which contained the Coffee House and the Assembly Rooms and was a centre of culture as well as one of the major coaching inns of Carlisle.

George took off his hat, and waited, noting that the office fire was much bigger than Mr Cowan's.

"Davenport," said Teather at last.

"Good afternoon, sir. I was told you wished to see me."

"How long have you been driving for us?" asked Teather, lifting a couple of papers off the table as though searching. "Not just the Mail – altogether?"

George, who knew that his employer was only play-acting, said, "Five months, sir."

"Passengers tipping well?"

"Nothing outstanding, sir," said George, though he knew that Teather, like his father before him and indeed like all the proprietors George had ever worked for, was fully aware of his coachmen's "perquisites." They turned a blind eye because a man who drove skilfully and looked smart would attract business that covered the rake-off. Gray spread his hands on his knees and chuckled at George's evasion.

"Like the work?" asked Teather.

George was surprised to be asked. Any proprietor knew that a coachman – even a bad one – considered himself an artist at the profession, and thought that any less glamorous work was not worth doing. Both men were watching him, so he replied, "I like the Newcastle run, thank you, sir, but those long drags over Shap Fell were cruel on the horses."

"You had no accidents." Teather almost sounded disappointed.

"I'll arrange one if it would amuse you," said George, straight-faced. The suggestion was a kind of double bluff, gambling that Teather wouldn't yet know about Daisy's fall. He saw both employers raise their eyebrows, and added, "Sorry, sir."

"I should think so, man," said Gray. "It was a poor subject for a joke."

With an air of getting down to business, Teather said, "I doubt that Yates will be back to drive the Mail."

"Yes, I heard that, sir. Very sorry about it." Accident or bad weather might disable a coachman at any time, but George was young and could make a sport of risks. Johnnie Yates, by contrast, was the far side of forty, and had a wife and family depending on him.

"We were discussing your suitability as his replacement. It's between you and Longmire."

"Whatever you decide, sir," said George. He held the solemn face he'd put on about Johnnie, and hoped it concealed his interest. He'd driven all the Newcastle teams now, and was getting the measure of his work.

"The customers seem to like you," said Teather. "Have you had difficulty making the times?"

"Everyone has, sir, this past month. When the weather's against us we're hard pressed to keep up the pace without killing the horses. Especially over Shap."

"George Eade has managed it."

"Yes, sir. He would." The proprietors of every staging inn between Carlisle and Kendal complained that Eade exhausted the teams they supplied. But Eade was very deaf, and with each complaint, his deafness got worse and his driving remained the same.

"You're not a family man, are you, Davenport?" asked Gray. "Or attached in any way?"

George thought of Lucy, but he said, "No, sir."

"Good," said Teather. "Then we'll put you back onto the New Times, and Longmire can look after the Mail."

"Sir." God damn it! He'd guessed wrong. "Would you compensate me, sir, for changing back?"

"Well, I'll be blest! You have a high opinion of yourself! Why should I pay you more!"

"I'm sure you could let me have half a crown more, sir. I admit I'm sorely disappointed. And I know what you pay Johnnie Yates for the Newcastle run."

Teather said reluctantly, "You can have a shilling for your cheek. This week only, mind!"

"Don't waste it." Gray lifted his glass of ale with a smile.

Recognizing the unspoken question, George said coldly, "I can find better uses for my wage than pissing it up the wall. Sir."

Gray laughed, saluted him, and drank. "Improve his trade, and he might pay you next week, too."

George walked back to the inn-yard, fuming. Damnation to early starts and Shap Fell and having to wring the last ounce of effort out of his horses! Damnation to rain and snow and that particular evil of Shap, high winds! And when Teather had put him onto the Newcastle Mail, George had reckoned it was safe to pay off that comfortable room in Kendal, so damnation to finding somewhere to sleep – again! And his spare coat was still in Newcastle. It was all a bloody mess.

The empty forage wagon was pulling out into St Cuthbert's Lane, the horse struggling to make a start over the wet cobbles. The carter whipped it, and George said sharply, "Oi! Leave him alone. The poor old sod's about buggered."

The carter spat at his feet. "Ah's got fower mair loads to fetch and tip yet. Git on, Blackie." And with another smack of the whip he drove away, hunched under his sack, the picture of a man to whom virtue meant getting the day's work done and nothing more.

George gripped his own whip tightly, and glared after the carter's retreating back. By now he would have been glad to punch someone. The ostlers guessed his temper and stayed out of his way, and the only person who looked straight at him was Joss Elliott, upright on a hard chair by the harness-room fire, an almost-dead pipe his only concession to relaxation. The lads cleaning leather kept their heads down.

Under Joss's critical eye, George swallowed the anger, and relayed the news of his demotion as calmly as he could.

"Aye, well," said Joss, "thou looked the boy all right, all dressed up in the Queen's scarlet. Thou'd best leave yon coat for Tim to brush-off. If thou wants to cut a smart figure for the girls, thou'll just have to visit a tailor."

He knocked the remains of his pipe into the bars of the fire, and went out to supervise the next coach.

George pulled off the scarlet coat and slung it over a harness rack, and looked for a rag to wipe his whip. Back in October deaf George Eade had told him he was "soft" because he wouldn't hit his horses with the "short Tommy," a thick, vicious weapon that needed strength but no accuracy. He had ignored the old fellow's scorn, but today he could happily have used such a whip on Teather. A true coaching whip was too long and too delicate for the brutal hacking he wanted to do. However Teather's plans might develop, George knew he wouldn't get back onto the Newcastle Mail. If he didn't want to spend his days flogging horses over Shap Fell, it was time to move on.

As he hung the coach whip beside its fellows, Joss came back in, carrying another wet collar and harness. George put on his old greatcoat and took his leave. Damned if he wouldn't accept that post with Dixon, after all.

CHAPTER 5.

Inside the Blue Bell, Henry Farrimond and John Armstrong drew back their feet and let George through to the fire. They were big men, further thickened by driving in the cold for mile after mile with interludes of hot brandy-and-water. Their coaches had come in an hour earlier, so both had changed into dry clothes, and dined, and now with glasses in hand they and their coat-tails occupied most of the space on the two settles.

"Now then, Geordie," said Armstrong.

"Afternoon, John. Is this weather wet enough for you?"

"I'm glad to see the back of that frost," said Farrimond. "My horses all stayed on their feet today, thank God."

Armstrong swallowed brandy with the air of a man warming up for a long and argumentative evening. "I'd rather have dry cold than this rawness."

George was intent on absorbing heat from the fire. "We had a horse down. And there was a miserable bloody railway man who kept grumbling that I was late!"

"Their timekeeping's a joke," said Farrimond. "Did you know – when it was frosty back in January, anything that went by rail for any part of its journey was late? Some of 'em an hour or more. The only London mail that kept time was the one from Holyhead. And for why? Because it goes all the way by road and doesn't touch the railways."

"It doesn't surprise me," said George. "The first day I was out with the Newcastle Mail, when I put my passengers down at Hexham station the engine was still steaming-up. I was nearly at Corbridge before it caught me."

"It's slipshod. They're never going to take our work, not at that rate."

"They're going to build dozens of bloody lines, though," said Armstrong moodily. "All these bills going through Parliament. Waste of money if you ask me."

George said, "I wish they could take the timber wagons and the cattle off the roads. It wouldn't matter if those were an hour late!"

"Might as well build a railway to the moon," said Armstrong. "They'll never replace the coaches."

Farrimond said, "What, John, you mean you wouldn't give up your coach to go navvying?" He winked at George.

"At my time of life?" retorted Armstrong. "You can morris off."

"You can always do with another string to your bow," said Farrimond, with a knowing look.

George laughed, rather sourly, and said nothing about his own disappointment. The landlady came hurrying by and he trilled a whistle at her, but she only gave him a sharp glance and said, "Oh, it's thee."

"It is, Mrs Hennessy." He was careful to give her the remains of his smile. "Were you expecting another admirer? You'll have to be very very kind to me or I'll be jealous."

"Less of thy sauce." She was snatching up empty tankards from the tables. "If thou wants to see Lucy, she's not here."

"I was thinking of coffee," said George, automatically hiding his real thoughts from her. "Or tea. I'm not fussy."

"Tea-caddy's locked," she said.

"I bet the key's hanging in your petticoats. Would you like me to look for it?"

"Get away." She flapped an exasperated hand at him.

He could see Lucy in the shadows, with a finger to her lips, nodding towards the back door. He faced her mother with his best innocent expression. "In your own good time, Ma, of course. You know we all adore you."

The landlady turned to George, her hands full of tankards. "So what's thou want? Coffee or tea?"

"I'll just go and make room for it." He made sure he was the other side of Armstrong's thick legs before he added, "I'll have cocoa!"

In the back porch, Lucy's cold little hands met his.

"Ooh, chilly paws. Slip 'em in here and get warm!" How could she be cold, in an apron, a woollen bodice, and a heavy skirt underneath which he knew she was wrapped in petticoats?

"Don't be cheeky," she said, but she slid inside his coat all the same, and stood on tiptoe to kiss him. It was more than a welcome – it was a homecoming. He put his hands round her waist, so slim and straight that he could almost span it, and the dim rainy yard vanished in the warmth of her lips. He could feel her fingers stroking him through his waistcoat, and was ashamed of having denied her to his employers.

"Are you ready for your dinner?" she asked. "There's ham, or beef, or brawn, or a fine mutton pie."

The effect of her hands was almost painful. He stifled a gasp. "Mutton pie."

"I'll tell Mrs Carruthers. And now you tell me what's happened."

"What?"

"I could see when you talked to Mr Farrimond that you were cross. It's the way you hold yourself. What is it?"

"Well, I had a horse come down and damned near break a leg. And now Teather's taken me off the damned Mail! He's put me back onto the New Times over Shap."

"Don't swear. I know you hate having to push the teams over the Fell."

"If that's all Teather thinks of me…"

"And you'll still be away every other night."

"Not for long, love! It's time to look for something else. I had the High Sherriff's brother on the box-seat the other day – you know, one of the cotton men. He offered me a job."

"Oh! You mean the Mayor? Mr Dixon?"

"Do I? He's a Dixon all right but I don't think he's the Mayor."

"Then it must be the other one," she said. "The Mayor's brother."

"He said I would have a free hand to buy matched horses for a team. Well, it couldn't have come at a better time, could it!"

"But he doesn't live in Carlisle."

"No, he doesn't."

"Well – would you go?" Her voice trembled a little.

"I might. Would you miss me?"

"I might," she echoed. He felt her stiffen as she gathered her courage. The hope in her voice was damped down, cautious, but it was hope all the same. "If you do, will he give you a house to live in?"

"No." He realized his answer would disappoint her. "I'd have a room over the stables, I suppose."

"Oh. Well!" she said, letting go of him and dusting her skirts. "I don't know why thou troubled to tell me, then. I don't suppose thou'll miss me."

She was normally careful to speak in a ladylike fashion, so he knew the slip back into dialect meant she was seriously upset.

"Lucy…"

She snapped, "Go on, follow thy hosses, see if I care."

"Lucy, I don't want to leave you. You know that. It's only that – well, the railways are closing in on Carlisle, you know. There may not be any work for me, not good work, not a Mail. It'll be hole-and-corner stuff, or hard heavy work like driving over Shap Fell."

"And why does thou think Mr Dixon's work will be enough of a challenge for thee? And will his wage be good enough for thee? Thou's too used with taking perks off all and sundry." She shook her head. "It's not like thee to mistake the cash value of a job!"

"We didn't talk money," he said. "For heaven's sake, lass, we were on top of a coach in the pouring rain with two railwaymen breathing down our necks! No gentleman is going to discuss terms in that situation. I only said I would think about it. Not that I will take it."

"And didsta include me, in that thinking?" she asked. "Or only t'hosses?"

"Of course I thought about you. You're always there at the back of my mind. Haven't I been a good-tempered fellow these last couple of days? What do you put that down to, eh?"

"I put it down to thee thinking wi' thy breeches instead o' thy brains."

"Lucy! I was pleased that Mr Dixon asked for me. And now that Teather's pushed me back onto the New Times… it just seems a good idea to make the change. But if you don't like it, well, I don't have to. I could find something better. I've driven in Liverpool and Manchester – I can handle a team on busy streets. So I could move to Newcastle. And think how much mail goes south. There must be endless work in London…" He grabbed her round the waist and swung her, using the movement to wheedle her. "Lift the hem of your petticoats," he murmured, "and see how far south I can get."

"George…!" She giggled as she slapped him off. "Behave yourself!"

He caught her hands, though as the dialect was back in its box he guessed her temper was under control.

"I'll behave if you will!"

"But you have to go?"

"If I don't look sharp I'll be driving over Shap Fell until Kingdom Come."

"Then wherever you go, I'll go with you."

He held her still. "Truthfully?"

"I mean it," she said. "I can't stand it here much longer."

"I know you don't get on with your Ma, but is it that bad?"

"You haven't been here long enough to know the whole story. I'll tell you one day. But when you go, wherever you go, I want to go with you."

He tested the idea, not having thought of it seriously before. Well, why not? If he got a really useful post, perhaps on a London coach, he would be able to afford rooms. Their own little paradise – no creaking single bedstead, no Ma Hennessy to worry about. What fun that would be! So in a rush he made the final jump, and said, "But we ought to marry, my beautiful, before we go."

"Oh George!" Her eyes filled with tears. "You're so lovely, and such a fool! We can't marry here. Everybody knows me, and they know I'm not of age. And if Mam found out she would never agree."

"We're only a few miles from the Scottish border."

"That's no better. Gretna would be the first place she would look for us!"

"We'll run away to a big city then, and get married where nobody knows us."

She looked at him the way his mother used to – as though he was a small boy desperate to be among the horses in the inn-yard, and she feared he would be trampled.

"We'd have to lie," said Lucy. "I won't tell lies before God."

He cocked his head at her, puzzled. "Would you rather pretend we were married? How is that different? We'll do it properly – even if we do have to tell some fusty old cleric that you're twenty-one. Once we've exchanged our vows and signed the paper, I wager your mother won't think of annulment. I'm not asking you to run away with me and jump the broom. So there – say it – say you'll marry me."

Her fingers gripped his, and she said shakily, "Yes. I will."

"That's my lovely girl. I know you only said Yes to get away from your mother, but I'm going to hold you to it!

Now isn't that worth a kiss?" He pouted theatrically. "Just there, please."

"All right." She stood on tiptoe, and laughed when he didn't help her. But then he laughed too, and swept her into a tight embrace and kissed her.

She kissed him back wildly, as though he might vanish the moment she let him go. And when at last she drew away, she whispered, "I love you. I think I always will."

"So you ought," he said with a chuckle. He felt brave and slightly tipsy and ready to conquer the world. "I'm going to drag you away from your mother's clutches. That alone deserves your devotion. I just have to get a job where she can't find either of us."

She said, "Oh you! You play at everything except your work."

"There's nothing wrong with that. Work is important. It makes me what I am."

"Your work's a disease," she said, "called horses."

CHAPTER 6.

Carlisle, March 1838

By the quality of the light between the shutters, it must be early morning.

Last night – Saturday – he'd eaten his meal and drunk only a couple of pints of ale as he looked forward to Lucy slipping into his room. But late in the evening, she had whispered that he must excuse her. The cardinal was visiting, she said, and he must sleep alone. He wished now that he'd drunk brandy, whisky, sherry – anything to dull his brain. It had been very late before he fell asleep.

The inn was still quiet this morning, or as close to it as it ever could be. There were light footfalls past his door, maybe a night-girl leaving – a temptation he'd always avoided, never knowing who was clean and who was not. He heard skirts brushing the panelling as she slipped by, and Ma's voice shrilling up the stair.

"Get out – your sort should ha' been gone hours ago! Go on, child, shoo!"

He didn't trust Ma Hennessy. Even without Lucy's anxieties he could well believe the rumours about her unsavoury background. She certainly had a double standard, that knew the traffic for what it was, and tucked Lucy away on the top floor. It occurred to him for the first time that perhaps Lucy herself had chosen to sleep there, safely out of reach.

I wish she'd been with me last night.

He went to the window and swung back the shutters. His room, on the top floor of the Bell, looked onto St Cuthbert's Lane and the back of the Crown and Mitre Assembly Rooms. Slivers of morning sunshine picked out chimneys and gable-ends of tall town houses, Abbey Street and Castle Street, and above them all the Castle and its sandstone keep stood brilliant against the northern sky.

Breathing in the crisp air, he considered what to do with the day. What he wanted was to take Lucy out walking through the meadows beside the Eden until, at dusk, hunger drew them back to the city's taverns. But, what with the cardinal, and her work, and her mother's severe eye, he supposed there was no point in asking.

He washed, viewing his face critically in the little mirror. His family history looked back at him. John Davenport's slightly over-strong jaw, Emily LaRue's dark eyes and hair, even the arrogant tilt of the head that his grandfather LaRue had, in the miniature portrait among his mother's few belongings. By rights that miniature should have been sold with the rest of the estate, to pay the old man's gambling debts – and she sometimes threatened to sell it herself when Davenport's drinking left them short of housekeeping money – but somehow it never happened.

As he dressed he wondered whether Lucy ever saw her mother in the mirror. It was a relief to him that she hadn't inherited Ma Hennessy's looks. Perhaps those cold eyes and discontented mouth only came with time – with an absent husband and a trade that induced disillusion. He'd make sure Lucy didn't have cause to develop them.

His tug at the bell-pull was eventually answered by a rapid mouselike scratch at the bedroom door.

"Come in, lovely!" he called, and there she was, Lucy herself in her coarse "brat," her cover-all morning apron, with her bright hair hidden under a twisted rag. "Ooh, you're irresistible in sacking." He caught and kissed her, but when he tried a squeeze she drew back.

"Don't, George, please."

"Sorry, lovely. Aren't you well?"

"I told you, it's the cardinal on a visit. What did you ring for?"

"Bring me some hot water to make myself kissable."

"You shaved last night – and you're dressed!"

"Damn good excuse though," he murmured into her ear. "Has your mother put breakfast on? Or is she still chasing the light-skirts off the premises?"

"She's in the kitchen," said Lucy. She kept her head down, and her hands busy with the linen of his shirt.

"So you ignore them. Very sensible."

She looked round the little room, apparently running some kind of mental check. "George, I want to ask a favour. Will you attend church with us this morning? Mam wants to go to the Cathedral today, so she's feeling dreadfully proper."

"Church! On a Sunday! What an innovation!" he cried, inviting her to laugh.

She remained serious. "She's run me ragged all morning but she says if I get all the breakfasts done and the tables cleaned, you can sit with us."

"What!" He was genuinely surprised by Ma's boldness in attending the Cathedral instead of St Cuthbert's. And he was angry at the old harridan for using him as bait to screw more work out of Lucy.

"I hate the way Mam twists things," she went on. "She says you don't go to church and you ought to, and then she pretends that's why she doesn't like you paying attention to me. There are times I could kill her!'"

He chuckled. "Now there's a prayer if ever I heard one!" For a moment he considered the idea seriously – a dozen devils flitted through his mind with ways to drown or burn Ma Hennessy, or best of all to chuck her off the coach over Shap – he pictured her frowsy underwear flying one way, cap and grey hair the other, her stout body trundling down the fellside and scattering the sheep. The chuckle grew and consumed him until he had to give way to it, and Lucy giggled too and began to smack him. He fell backwards onto the bed and pulled her with him, both of them laughing. Maybe she'd take pity on him after all? She lay soft across his chest, little ripples of laughter running through her. But when he reached for her skirt-hem she folded like a spider and cried, "No!"

He let her get up, and sat grinning while she straightened herself and re-fastened her head-rag.

"Do I have to come to church?" he asked.

"It means a lot to me. Please."

"I haven't been to church since I came here."

"The day Mother turned to Jesus was the best day of my life. And look – we have to make her think you're going to stay here. Pretend! You're good at pretending! Come on – I'll help you find the psalms. Please!"

“Well… ” It might be amusing to sit thigh to thigh with Lucy and distract her from her prayerbook and the cardinal. And if she thought it might fool the old hag too…

He said, “Yes.”

CHAPTER 7.

After breakfast he ran back upstairs for his new broadcloth coat and tall hat. When he came back down, he was accosted by Jem Walker and Robert Lloyd, the coachmen of the Glasgow Independent and the Newcastle True Briton. Jem and Rob had accompanied him during the winter to several musical evenings and plays.

"Geordie!" said Rob. "Just the man. Come and persuade your landlady that we're upright citizens." He gestured at Ma Hennessy who stood hands-on-hips at the doorway to the bar.

George asked, "What are you two jesters doing here? It's too early for morning visitors, you know! Is she throwing you out? You're not foxed already?"

"On a Sunday? Chance would be a fine thing. And to prove it, I must inform you that she is so ungracious as to object to us collecting charitable subscriptions."

Jem laughed at the tongue-twisting phrases, but George asked, "Why, who's died?"

"Poor Johnnie Yates, God rest him."

"Ah," he said. "So soon."

"And there's Molly left with those three lads and the oldest of them only seven."

"I'm just going out. Come with me, eh?" Ma Hennessy had snapped that Lucy still had work to do, so he planned to go for a walk before attending the Cathedral. "I don't want the old bat to see how much cash I keep on me." Out in the street, he gave Rob a half-sovereign and two half-crowns. "There. That five bob is for what's-his-name – the oldest boy – Jackie. Let him choose to give that money to his Ma."

"I will, ta," said Rob, looking at him with some curiosity.

"I was just that age when my own Da was killed."

"Ah, I see," said Jem with sympathy, and punched George's arm. "Bad luck. But what the devil was he up to?"

"He was drunk. A wheel-horse started to fuss when he was fixing the traces, so he lashed out, and got kicked in the head for it."

"I don't believe a word of that," said Jem. "Those old time horses were too worn out to lift a foot if they didn't have to. Thanks, anyway."

"Aye. Pleased to have seen you, Geordie. We're going to St Cuthbert's to tell the vicar, and after service we'll try the Coffee House. We'll have Thurnam's print some handbills tomorrow, and we'll put your name down as a subscriber."

He said, "Tell Mrs Yates, I'm sorry about Johnnie."

Left to himself, he turned towards the west Wall of the City, and followed it to the Irish Gate. The west wind blew cold and fresh from the Solway marshes, but as it came it picked up the coal smoke of the terraces, the sugary reek of the brewery, and the lint of the Shaddon Mill, whose vast brick chimney stood up in the sun above the rooftops of the industrial quarter.

Across the street, below the Castle wall, was the workhouse. George turned away. He knew only too well how children feared to be separated from their parents, confined to meagre food and uniforms and regimentation designed to make poor relief as unpleasant as possible. He understood why, when constables threatened, the beggars vanished from the prosperous streets into the back-alleys and yards of the Lanes. But when they re-settled like a flock of ragged starlings he had to walk past their clutching hands, stiff with the effort of keeping his mental balance. "Fought against Boney, lost a leg at Waterloo, sir." "Our mother and father died, sir. Spare us a penny for bread." He couldn't deal with them, couldn't be generous as he thought a real gentleman should, considering the workhouse a convenient solution to the problem of poor aid. If he gave to every beggar, where could he ever stop? It was no good priding himself on his mother's side of the family, the reckless grandfather and the lost estate. He was reminded, every time, that the ungentlemanly side of his nature had the upper hand. He mentally reserved another crown for Molly Yates, with her hard-driving, hard-drinking husband dead of pneumonia.

He met respectable families chattering their way to early service, and whenever he recognized a customer he smiled and raised his hat. Perhaps they guessed that he didn't worship in any of the churches of the city. He didn't much care. Here was Castle Street, home to the older members of the Dixon family. It was hard to get away from them in this part of the city. He walked on.

Dixon's comments about railways had nagged him throughout the intervening week, and he welcomed them now to take his mind off the ghost of Johnnie. His own remark to the engineers, that people set their clocks by the passing of the Mail, had been no more than truth. The sub-contractors, drivers and guards combined to run the Road more reliably than clockwork. Dixon and the railwaymen might be convinced that steam would give the coaches competition, but how could little stretches of rail-road, unconnected to each other, possibly compete with coaching's established network? Farrimond and Armstrong of course had persuaded themselves that it would never happen. George wasn't so sure, but all he knew was that by training and profession, he was a commercial coachman. A very gentlemanly occupation… George smiled wryly at himself and walked on, along the strip of wall that led to the Scotch Gate, then past the crowded openings of the Lanes. It was too early for most of the whores to be about but there was one pretty lass, wrapped in a shawl, sitting on a doorstep. She looked very young, but tired, as though she hadn't yet been to bed – at any rate, not to sleep.

"Hello Charley," she said, with the resigned smile of a girl who knew he wasn't going to buy. And although the reminder of all that he'd missed last night provoked a definite stirring, he told himself he wasn't interested. He winked at her and kept going, back through the market and along St Cuthbert's Lane to the stable yard. He needed to get back in touch with his own roots, with the quiet noises of the stables, the chestnut, bay and grey horseflesh, the sharp animal smells and the rhythm of teeth crunching hay – and once there he sighed, as he did every Sabbath, with pure contentment.

Joss Elliott put his head round the door. "Oh, look out boys, here's Lord Muck and his new coat. It must be Sunday. Mind where you tread, your Lordship." The bricks of the stall-way were shining clean as always. For answer, George flipped Joss's cap off his head, caught it and threw it under the nose of the nearest horse. The horse flinched, but Joss spoke a quiet word, and the horse nudged the cap and picked it up in its teeth. Joss sidled into the stall to take the cap gently and smoothed a hand over the gelding's body as he sidled out again. The horse looked round after him, then returned to its hay.

Joss settled the cap back on his head and grinned at George. "I could learn that'n to play whist, though first I'd have to learn him not to eat the cards."

"Another fortnight should do it, then! Everything all right with my horses?"

"Thou knows that as well as I do."

"How's Daisy? Will that hock mend?"

"Ah, she's coming right. I meant to ask, did the new gelding behave himself, that they gave thee at the White Ox? Thou said nowt, so I forgot. He didn't kick? Good. Thou's tactful with hosses, George, for all thou makes 'em work. I wish I could say the same of every driver I've met. What else is fresh?"

"Not much. You'll have heard about Johnnie Yates?"

"Yes, poor fella. I give a bit to the subscription for Molly and the boys."

George nodded, and said, "So did I. D'you think Johnnie has left much for her?"

Joss shrugged. "He did all right. Every coachman does – there's plenty of perks – but he drank a sight more than thee, boy. Said it was to warm his chest, o' course, but it didn't stop his chest killing him, did it? No, I've no idea what he'll have left her. The subscription'll see him buried decent, and keep them for a while, but after that – who knows? If Molly's lucky she'll marry again afore that money runs out. If she won't, thou knows the odds."

George nodded, frowning. "What about the boys? The big ones are old enough to work. When my Da was killed,

Granda put me to work in the stables. I didn't have to go into a mill or, God forbid, a colliery."

"God? Ah! Well, there's many a widow with bairns has to rely on Him." Joss spat, careful to aim at the stable drain. "She's not well herself, thou knows, but she'll work her fingers raw stitching shirts for a few pennies a time, and maybe end up walking t'streets. Anything rather than see them starve. Oh," said Joss roughly, "thou's fair spoiled my Sunday. Making me think of that. Get away. Take thy fancy coat out of here. I've work to do before we go to church."

"Turning me out, Joss?"

"Hasn't thou any young women to bother? If thou must hang about here, put a pinny on and help. No? Then thou's had all the buttering-up thou's going to get, so away with thee."

CHAPTER 8.

Later in the morning, George strolled back along the west Wall towards the Cathedral precinct. He went through the Abbey Gate, and scanned the ingoing congregation for a sight of Lucy.

It was Mrs Hennessy that he spotted first, in a dress and cape of drab dark green. Beside her Lucy wore severe grey. She had a pale blue bonnet as a token splash of colour, but its brim defended her face like blinkers on a horse, and he didn't like it much. Both women had their backs to him, no doubt expecting him to arrive from the Coffee House, so he was very tempted to creep up and catch Lucy round the waist to make her squeal. However, her nun-like appearance among the sober churchgoers daunted him, so he only murmured a deep "Hul-LO," against the side of her prim little bonnet.

Lucy gasped, and Ma Hennessy turned like a ship in full sail, slowly, and with Sabbath dignity. He took off his hat to her in exaggerated deference, which didn't impress her at all.

"Well, Mr Davenport," she said, "I doubted thou'd make the effort to come, let alone arrive early."

"It is Mr Davenport's business to be punctual," said Lucy. Her mantle brushed his sleeve, rousing in him as she always did in public a mixture of desire and irritation at the need for self-control. "Let us go in, shall we?"

Hat in hand, he followed Mrs Hennessy and Lucy through the main doorway, and accepted a prayerbook with at least the appearance of respectability.

When they reached their seats, nimble footwork and Lucy's unspoken collaboration steered Mrs Hennessy first along the row. Both women knelt, folded their hands and closed their eyes, so he did the same. He discounted Ma's religion as a front – a token of respectability rather than anything deeper. He wasn't so sure about Lucy. *The day mother turned to Jesus was the best day of my life.* Who could tell what that meant? The bulk of her petticoats seemed provocatively close, but perhaps he was imagining that.

When Lucy resumed her seat, he got up and looked around at the rest of the congregation. Solid, devout Cumberland families filled the nave; robust young men in coats and trousers, shiny-faced girls hiding like Lucy in the newest styles of bonnets; mothers and fathers and grandparents, whose attention to fashion declined with their increasing years. There was a flutter of hushed conversation as they waited for the service to begin. Seeing those serious faces all turned resolutely towards the altar, he knew he had better settle himself.

Lucy nudged him and whispered, "What are you staring at?" She shifted nearer so that her petticoats pushed against his thigh, and instantly his attention veered back to her. Out of his confusion he managed to say, "The window," whose colours were sparkling in the mid-morning light, "and the draperies on the lectern. It's very handsome, isn't it, purple. I ought to buy you a dress that colour."

Lucy's hand came out from under her mantle to pat his arm. "It's the colour for Lent," she whispered. Then he felt her foot, decidedly not imaginary, pressing against his. From then on, he could only make a pretence of turning his thoughts to higher things. The next hour was going to be less tedious and far more of a torment than he had expected.

To his surprise, though, as soon as the clergyman appeared Lucy turned her shoulder. She kept a proper distance while she listened attentively to the preacher's resonant voice reading St Paul on justification by faith, and joined the psalmist in begging God to wash her from her iniquity. George refused to connect the request with his own behaviour and sang cheerfully of "forty days and forty nights, tempted yet still undefiled."

The sermon began and his attention wandered. Among the parishioners he saw none of his customers, or at any rate, none that he recognized in their Sunday clothes. They seemed mainly tradespeople – the class who, if they travelled by coach at all, climbed nervously up the ladder to the roof. Meanwhile, Lucy kept her face steadily towards the pulpit, and her bonnet hid everything except the tip of her nose.

When the little clergyman finally bowed to the altar and processed out of church, George was so close to bouncing with relief that he turned to Mrs Hennessy and thanked her for inviting him. Lucy looked grateful, but her mother only tossed her head in scorn.

"Reverend Goodenough's sermon were too short. Nivver tell me thy thanks are sincere."

George smiled and stepped out of the pew, and bowed to the ladies to precede him, since that was safer than leading them like his belongings and perhaps in the wrong direction.

"The Reverend Vansittart would have given us an hour," sniffed Ma.

"Well, Missus, it must be his busy day," he suggested, as she rustled past. "Sunday and all."

Mrs Hennessy merely stared at him.

Now, when he could look around freely, he realized what a strangely imperfect building this was. A colonnade of pointed arches looped along one wall and vanished, incomplete, into another. The fantastically carved choir stalls lacked their hanging finials, and niche after niche stood empty of saints. What ought to have been the longest of the cathedral's four arms seemed to have been amputated, and the whole church turned back to front. God might, perhaps, have power, but religion and its trappings were second-rate.

One of Ma's friends paused to exchange the time of day with her, so as soon as the two widows were comfortably tattling George hissed into the side of Lucy's bonnet, "What a pantomime!" She gave a soft, breathy giggle, but wouldn't answer.

A heavy hand fell on George's shoulder and he spun around, half expecting a reprimand. But the heavy hand turned out to be a friendly one – Mr Dixon, escorting his mother, who was puffed up with petticoats and the same friendly dignity as her son.

"Good morning, sir," said George. "You startled me. How are you?"

"I'm well, thank you," said Dixon. "How pleasant to see you here. Mother, this is the young coachman I was telling you about."

Polite introductions followed, George keeping a straight face as he presented "Miss Hennessy." Mrs Dixon offered a kindly nod to Lucy, but gave Ma only a hawk-like stare.

"Do put up your hat, young man," she said, turning back to him. "I think we haven't seen you here before. Do you usually attend another church?"

"Yes, Ma'am," said George, his face from long practice as innocent as a child's. He just hoped she wouldn't ask which church.

"Well, it's fortunate you've worshipped here today," said Dixon. "I have some good news for you. I would have told you in the morning, as I'm bound for Newcastle again."

"I shouldn't see you, I'm afraid, sir. I won't be driving the Mail any more."

"Ah. Promoted, eh? You are too good for us! However – if the ladies will excuse me?" Dixon strolled gently away from the door into the sunshine, and George, with a slight bow to the three women, followed him. Once they were out of earshot, Dixon said, "You are on another coach, I hope?"

"Yes, sir, the New Times, bad luck to it."

"Sore point, eh? Are you sure you won't come to work for me?"

George hesitated while he considered what to say. So far he had told nobody about his engagement to Lucy and their plans to elope, because Joss, for instance, looked in far too often to the Blue Bell, and Jem and Rob's open speech would have betrayed them to Ma Hennessy a hundred times over. However, Dixon was unlikely ever to be a customer at the Bell so he was probably a safe ear for George's future plans. Confiding his hopes would somehow make them more real and the whole business would feel less underhand. It was even possible that Dixon might make practical suggestions.

George said, "Thank you, sir, I'm quite certain. I'll stick to the Shap run while I find a position in London. And in confidence, sir – the old lady doesn't know it yet –I intend to take Miss Hennessy with me."

"I see," said Dixon, with speculation in his eyes.

"We intend to marry, sir, as soon as we may."

"Well, then, I understand why you are steadfast in refusing my post. But is Miss Hennessy of age to marry? If Mrs Hennessy doesn't know, I doubt she will give her consent."

"I doubt it too, sir, very much! Our wedding may have to wait until we reach London – where I understand these things can be arranged."

"Oh yes – there are ways around legislation, if you are determined." Dixon gave a tight, understanding smile.

That glimpse of the canny tradesman both startled George and reassured him. He glanced towards Lucy, who stood demurely beside Mrs Dixon senior, only her bonnet signalling the swing of her attention between her mother's conversation and this one.

"I am quite determined, sir."

"Well, then, to our muttons. I was in London this week on business, and I put up at the Swan with Two Necks. Next day I ran across the proprietor and we got talking. Mr Chaplin – you'll have heard of him?"

"My word, yes, sir. There's no man has more power in the coaching trade."

"Mm. Oily sort of fellow– soft-spoken, you know – but sharp as a tack. Something in his manner rather put me in mind of a collie dog, the kind who just might nip your heels." He gave a little chuckle. "He has quite a litter of pups, too – a baker's dozen at least."

"He has my sympathy, sir," said George, and they both laughed.

"Well, Chaplin has four or five coaching inns… though the railway lines have split the City until you can hardly recognize it. Slum tenements coming down, Houses of Parliament going up – it's all build, build, build. Anyhow – coaching – the Post Office is soon going to send a good deal of the London Mail by the railways. Chaplin thinks they will give him serious competition." Dixon nudged George's arm. "I would say it's going to happen in all the major cities, in the next five years – ten at the most. Do you still think commercial work is going to be better than running my stable?"

George glanced across at Lucy, and took a deep breath. "Yes, sir, thank you all the same."

"Very well! If London's really where you want to work, why not go to the top? Go to Chaplin. I would be happy to recommend you. Of course, you must understand there is no guarantee that he will take you on."

George's wits leapt through question after question and his heart pounded against his ribs. The opportunity was there, after all! Sooner than he hoped! Was he ready? He would need maps. He must ask at Thurnam's. And Lucy must be prepared to leave at a moment's notice. He realized that Dixon was waiting for him to say something.

"That's most kind of you, sir."

The mill-owner lifted his shoulders, delicately.

"My clerk will simply draw up a letter that you can take to Chaplin. It is no trouble to me personally. Of course, it would be useful if in return you could find me a coachman."

CHAPTER 9.

On each journey over the next few days George imagined that William Chaplin, a coachman born-and-raised, sat at his left elbow and criticized his driving. He was able to forget him while he was weaving through the town traffic, between phaetons and gigs, cattle and sheep, timber teams and coal wagons, but where the roads were clear and the work routine, he had time to become self-conscious about his own skills. Was he really any more than a hayseed with an inflated idea of his own abilities?

Chaplin would test him. He was probably the best in the country at his trade. He had built a business that owned thousands of horses, that dealt with half the Mail out of London and carried trade to all points of the compass.

But what if George gave notice to Teather, and then said something so stupid that Chaplin wouldn't take him on? There were a dozen ways he might make a fool of himself. He knew very well that everything he'd done, even driving in Newcastle, was likely to be very small beer compared to driving in London, which everyone said was the greatest city in Europe, perhaps in the world.

He went to Thurnam's, which provided him with Cary's "New Plan of London and its Vicinity" and he spent hours each evening poring over it, even carrying it with him in his overnight bag. With the map, he began to study the geography of London's coaching inns. By Thursday night he knew parts of the city as well as his own face in the mirror. Chaplin's headquarters, the Swan with Two Necks, stood in

Lad Lane, close to the General Post Office in St Martin's le Grand. Sherman's, the old Boulogne Mouth rebuilt as the Queen's Hotel, was even closer. Although George knew that nothing could prepare him for the reality of London, the visualization gave him a measure of calm.

On Saturday Lucy teased him, "You're off your feed. Are you pining for somebody?"

"I'm lovesick," he said, catching her round the waist. "You haven't visited me for over a week. Why don't you bring a pie to my room, some time around midnight?"

She freed herself, with an anxious glance round at the half-empty room.

"Behave, you great softie."

"All right then, lovely," he said. "Take this to your Ma, and tell her I want you for an hour." He held out two half-crowns.

"I'll do no such thing," she said, and flounced away to the bar.

He got up then, and put the money down in front of her. "Ma can chaperone you. I need a letter written, and I want you to write it."

"A letter! Well! You can write it yourself, I suppose."

"I can, but you'll ask to know what's in it, so you might as well write it."

As he expected, she was intrigued. She folded her cloth and, telling him to wait, disappeared into the back offices. He took his five shillings to the table again. Farrimond, by the fireside as always, glanced over at him and said something to Armstrong, and they both chuckled.

When Ma Hennessy appeared, she came straight to the table, with Lucy following uncertainly behind her.

"All reet, young man. What's thou up to? Demanding her time, indeed!"

He repeated his explanation. "I want Lucy's help and I'm willing to pay you for it. You can sit there and watch us if you want." He laid the five shillings on the boards again. "I want paper, ink, blotting paper and a good pen."

He could see Ma dithering about setting a precedent if she allowed Lucy to sit down when she ought to be working – and at the same table as a customer.

Greed won. She picked up the coins and glanced at the clock. "One hour. Lucy, fetch Mr Davenport what he asks for. Michael! Come and clear these tables!" And to George she said, "I'll have an eye on thee, mind."

He sat back in his chair, and gave her his most devastating smile.

Ma said fiercely, "She's to sit at opposite side o' t' table," and bustled off.

When Lucy came back with the writing materials she glanced round again. Farrimond and Armstrong were nursing brandies by the fire, and four customers sat under the window, absorbed in a game of cards.

"Mam's not settled," she warned him. "She's polishing things." But, after a moment, she sat down and opened the inkpot.

"That's my girl," he said.

"Who shall I direct it to?" She straightened the paper and dipped her pen.

"Mr W. J. Chaplin."

She looked up quickly, excitement in her eyes. "Mr Chaplin the coach proprietor?"

"Hush! Yes. Now then..."

He showed her Mr Dixon's letter of recommendation.

Dear Chaplin

The bearer of this, George Davenport, is a coachman very well known at the Carlisle office of your subcontractor Mr Teather. Hearing that on completion of the Railway between Newcastle to Carlisle the Newcastle Mail Coach may soon be discontinued, he is desirous of obtaining a driving position with you nearer to the City of London. He is 22 years of age. I believe him to be a sober, steady man, deserving of a responsible situation.

Yours truly

To W. J. Chaplin

Geo. Dixon

He sat smiling while she read it. She asked in a low voice, "Is this what you were discussing with Mr Dixon?"

"I couldn't tell you," he said. "I didn't dare, not in front of your mother. Mr Dixon's clerk sent this round the next day. If it turns out as I hope, we're on our way to London."

She let out a faint squeak of delight, and at once clapped her hand over her mouth; then, controlling herself, looked down at the paper with a perfectly blank face, and dipped the pen again.

"I shall be ready," she whispered.

"That's my girl." He winked at her. "Now, you'd better pretend to be angry with me. Loud as you like."

She blinked back at him, in case a nod gave her away, and said loudly, "This is very unkind, Mr Davenport. I had a high regard for you, until this minute. How dare you pay my mother, and ask me to write such a letter!"

By the fire, Farrimond and Armstrong glanced round, and her mother straightened and stared.

"Keep going," said George under his breath. "You're doing grand." He leaned back, and said aloud, "Well, I have to go to London sometime, y'know. I can't prove that I'm the best till I'm among the best."

"But what will you do then?" she snapped. "Once you are the best. Where else is there to go?"

He shrugged. "I won't know till I get there, will I?"

"Oh, Mr Davenport!" cried Lucy, with a perfect note of tragedy in her voice. She put down the pen, and hid her face in her apron.

He held out a hand towards the paper. "Well! If you can't perform this little service for me, I shall have to ask your mother to give me my money back."

"How is she taking it?" she muttered, from behind the fabric.

He muttered back, "Can't see… but I bet her ears are burning."

"Please don't do that!" wailed Lucy. "Only give me a moment to compose myself!"

She put the apron to her face again, and only George could hear the little snort that she muffled behind it. He was astonished at how well she was playing up to him. She might be laughing or crying – and even from across the table, he wasn't quite sure which. Ma Hennessy, at the other side of the room, would have no clue at all. She'd be forced to rely on what he said in return.

"Now don't take on, lovely – you've been deceiving yourself, that's all, and I'm sorry for it – but it won't mend matters to burst into tears!"

"Oh Mr Davenport! I shall miss you that much! Oh dear – I mustn't cry over your letter…" Lucy made loud sniffling noises behind the apron. "Give me a moment! Let me compose myself – oh, I do hope I haven't spoiled it!" She kept her head down, and took up the pen once more.

"That's the ticket, my dear! Now, when you're ready – *Dear Sir, Acting on the advice of Mr George Dixon – from whom I have a letter of recommendation* – two Ms there, please, my lovely …'

Ma Hennessy returned to her polishing, her grim mouth twisted with satisfaction.

CHAPTER 10.

A week later, George and Lucy were sitting on the mattress in his room, gazing into the fire.

"Well, come on, tell me," she said at last.

He drew a letter out of his pocket. "Mr Chaplin has agreed to see me."

Sealed with a plain oval of wax and addressed in a businesslike hand, the letter suggested that Mr Davenport should attend the office of the Swan with Two Necks and bring with him his character references. In a slightly less neat hand, it was signed, *"I am, Dr Sir, Yours truly, W. Chaplin."*

"He's being very polite, isn't he?" she said.

"Your handwriting must have impressed him."

She looked up at him with eyes that struck him as feverishly bright. Was she ill? He pulled the blankets protectively around them both, sharing a little tent of warmth.

She said, "We'll have to go very soon, won't we?"

He pushed aside his unease and agreed, "I've given Mr Teather my notice. I can go as soon as he's replaced me on the New Times. I expect he'll put Tom Mounsey onto it – he was looking for work the other day. Can you be ready?"

"My clothes have been packed since you wrote to London! Which way shall we go? The Mail through Manchester would be fastest, wouldn't it?"

"Yes, but that leaves here in the evening and your Ma's likely to be about. No matter whether she believed what we said the other day, if she sees you leaving with me she'll do her best to stop you. I think we ought to go as passengers on the New Times – there's a joke on me, if you like!– but Tom Mounsey's a good fellow, so if I tip him the wink he won't tell your Ma. The main thing is, it leaves early enough for us to get out and away before she notices."

"Well," she said, the paper quivering in her hands, "it's a good thing we are both early risers."

"We'll go right through to Liverpool, and take the ferry over the river, then from Woodside we can catch the Albion to London."

"You're sure that will work?"

"Didn't I help the Albion change horses every day on that road, and the Woodside Mail too? I was brought up there. I know that route as well as I know the New Times."

"I'm sure it would be better to go with the Mail through Manchester."

"Don't fret, lovely. You wouldn't get any rest at all on the Mail." It wasn't like Lucy to be stubborn without good reason, and he began to worry again. "Whichever way we go it'll be a devil of a journey! Will you manage it? Maybe we ought to break our journey – we could stay for a night with my grandmother at Eastham, and you could rest properly."

"We could, but that would waste time. Mr Chaplin writes that you're to attend at your earliest convenience. Never mind me. I'll be sure not to hold thee back."

He saw now that she was shivering, and he re-arranged the blankets around her.

"I'm sorry," she said. "I can't seem to get warm." She wrapped her arms tightly about her knees. "Mam shan't force me to stay. I'll be ready, even if she locks me in my room."

"I wouldn't trust the old bitch as far as I could throw a horse, but I'll have the door down before I let her keep you here."

"Oh George," she said, "I do love thee! And I'm being a goose. Mam can't lock me in – the bolt's on the inside."

She giggled, rather shakily, and he laughed and hugged her. Then he dug in his waistcoat pocket, and brought out a little gold ring set with two turquoises. "Why don't you put that on?"

She took it very carefully, as though it might break if she were too eager, or perhaps she didn't quite believe it existed. It pained him to see her try the ring without success on one work-reddened finger after another.

"Look," she said proudly, "it fits my little finger. Thank you, pet."

"I thought you'd like to have it, to wear when we're on the road."

"I'll keep it safe till then. I'll treasure it. Only I daren't wear it before we go. If Mam sees it, she might guess – and she mustn't stop us."

He snorted. Ma! In their last encounter she had stopped only just short of charging him a fee for the past few months of what she called "Lucy's services." It would be as well, he thought, not to tell Lucy how low her mother had valued her. It had left a nasty taste in his mouth.

***

In the small hours, he woke to hear Lucy breathing harshly and rapidly, and when he lit the candle he saw that her face was wet with perspiration.

"What is it, lovely? You're frightening me."

"I'd better leave you to sleep. I'll go to my room."

"You won't," he said. "Stay under the blanket, and I'll mend the fire. Has anyone been ill, that you've met in the last few days? A customer, or any of the servants or the tradesmen?"

"No. But there was a woman with bairns came asking after you…"

"Molly Yates, yes. You said she came to thank me for the subscription I gave when Johnnie died. What about her?"

"She had a cold."

This didn't look like a cold to him. It occurred to him, chillingly, that Johnnie Yates had died of a fever and a cough that he had thought was only a cold.

"I must go back to my room," she whispered.

"There isn't a fireplace in your room."

"I'll be all right."

"You won't. It's no damn good to you without a fire."

"But Mam…" she said.

"Be damned to the woman. I'll tell her you're in no fit state to work. Lie there and keep warm."

***

He ran down and galvanized the kitchen staff. He knew Mrs Carruthers and Mariah both had a soft spot for him, and although it was early, he had no difficulty in persuading them to look after Lucy. Ma, appearing at the doorway, sniffed at finding him on the premises.

"Sick, is she? Thou'll have brought it on her, no doubt. And you'll be gone and leave her to it, I suppose. No more'n I expected."

He was aware of Mrs Carruthers' shocked intake of breath, and of Mariah stifling a terrified giggle. But he stood his ground. "Enough of that, Ma. She's taken the influenza."

"Well? What does-ta want me to do about it?"

He looked at her jutting chin and downturned mouth and resisted the urge to smack one into the other.

"Behave like a mother! Feed her and let her sleep! She can sleep in my room, with the fire. I'll go and sleep in hers." He managed a scornful laugh. "Don't worry, Mrs Hennessy. I shan't charge you for it!"

CHAPTER 11.

Whenever Mrs Carruthers came puffing up the stairs with a bowl of broth, or Mariah looked in to exchange the chamber pot for a clean one, Lucy knew where she was. She dreamed at times that she was downstairs serving endless lines of coachmen, Farrimond, Armstrong, Mounsey, Johnnie Yates, Brydon, Lloyd, Walker, their guards, their passengers. George was always at the far end of the line, waiting, smiling, unreachable. She knew she should be looking after the ring he had given her, the one she mustn't wear in case her mother saw it, only she couldn't remember now why it had to be secret, and she didn't know where he had hidden it, and she couldn't drag herself out of the sagging bed in order to look.

Only once, when her mother's face swam in front of her, was she back in that house in the Lanes, scolded as a burden, forced to earn money. She struggled against horrible images, hands that held her down, arms that carried her away, doors that were locked and had no keyhole or key. "Jesus, save me. Oh Christ, save me." Her only shield was to pray, over and over, repeating the same words until her mind grew numb and blank, and she slept.

Some time in the small hours of that night, she woke, coughing, and found George at her bedside.

"Hello there," he said.

"Hello thyself," she whispered. The firelight leapt on the walls, but the terrible images were quiescent, perhaps waiting for him to go away so they could surround her again.

"You know I'm here, then."

"Aye." Her voice rasped in her throat, painfully, and she coughed. "Thou shouldn't be waking," she said. "Thou'll oversleep and be dismissed."

"Don't fret. Everything's all right, and you're making more sense that you have for days."

"I'se had some right bad dreams."

"I know." He didn't pursue it. "Do you want a drink?"

When she nodded, he helped her to sit up, and gave her water, though the glass wobbled in her hands and he had to hold it steady for her. That's how weak I am, she thought.

"How long have I been ill?"

"Three days."

"What day is it?"

"It's Easter. When even the dead get out of their graves and walk."

"Don't blaspheme."

"Don't frighten me again, then." She heard his voice tremble. "You've been badly. Mrs Carruthers and Mariah, and me and even Petey, we've all done a turn looking after you."

"Not my Mam?"

He pulled a face. "I don't know why you even ask."

***

She woke again to a grey light, and through the lattice window that faced the Castle she could see the clouds racing away, and a little patch of primrose coloured sky opened, then closed, like a cheeky winking eye. She turned her head, and there was George, dozing in a chair by the fire. It did her heart good to see him.

Mrs Carruthers had come in – it was the click of the door latch that had woken her – bringing bread as well as broth.

"Supper's here, lad. Will ye take it for her?"

George roused, yawning, to take the tray.

Lucy knew, by the way Mrs Carruthers gave a quick nod and hurried out again, that trade was busy downstairs and her mother was bullying the staff.

She tried to sit up, intending to put a pillow against the wall so she could lean on it and look at George more comfortably, but she was shocked at the weakness of her arms.

He put the tray on the chest of drawers and came to help her. "Do you want the blankets round you, or are you warm enough like that?"

It was on the tip of her tongue to say everything was all right, but she knew it wasn't. "Blankets, please." It was a voiceless croak, frustratingly lacking any of the emphasis she wanted, but he made her comfortable, and put the tray across her knees. She whispered a grace before she began to eat.

In a rush, as though he had to force the words, he said, "I hate to tell you when you're still poorly, but I'm going to have to leave soon."

I, not we.

She bent her head, feeling that the scar on her heart would begin to bleed once more.

"I hate to go," he said, "but you need to be much stronger before you can stand the journey." He waited, but she had gone back into silence, her ancient defence. "I've already stayed a week later than I meant to. I can tell Mr Chaplin I had to work my notice, and he may excuse me on that account – but I can't stretch the time much longer. If I do I'll lose the chance, and I can't live without work."

She was afraid he would leave at once, sure that he would be relieved and thankful at his escape. She must master the need to cough. Perhaps she could whisper. "Well then, thou must go."

"You'll follow me as soon as you can, won't you?" He clasped her hand.

She was dismayed to find herself weeping. She knew that weeping, like arguing, was disastrous – throughout her life, when she cried she had found herself alone. She had no faith that George would still want her when she was too weak to get out of bed, let alone travel. Why should he? Now he really would go away.

In fact he laughed, and stood up, which convinced her she must be right – but all he did was to remove the tray carrying the soup and put it back onto the chest for safety. She was so overwhelmed with love and gratitude that she sobbed outright. He gave her a handkerchief.

"Don't cry, lovely," he said, "it isn't the end of the world. We'll manage. Come on, dry your eyes." The linen wasn't clean, but it comforted her because it smelled of him, of horses and leather and his working gloves.

"I'm sorry," she croaked. "I don't know what's the matter with me. I'm not usually such a wet goose."

"You've been ill! Of course you're a bit vapourish! Look," he went on, "I'm going to give you five sovs – here. You're going to use them to follow me the moment you're well. I shall be waiting for you."

He pressed the gold into her hand, gently, just as he had on their first meeting.

"I wish I didn't need them," she whispered, tightening her fist on the coins. "I want to travel with you. I want to be out of this. I don't trust anyone except you."

"I'll slip Mrs Carruthers a bob or two. She likes you well enough anyway, but it'll jog her memory when she's being run off her feet downstairs. You just set your mind on getting well."

"I'll try."

"You'll be up and about in no time and then you must simply make a run for it. I'll write to tell you where to find me. You'll be better by then."

Lucy nodded, feeling more able to face the task he was setting. She must recover as quickly as possible, and she must pretend to be broken-hearted over George's departure, because if she didn't Ma would guess their plans and never let her out of her sight. Still, feigning heartbreak wouldn't be too difficult at the moment! She would keep her clothes packed for the run to London, and perhaps one of the coachmen, or a guard, might buy her ticket without alerting Ma… She must keep all her money very safe indeed.

"Put the sovereigns in the drawer," she said. "And what did I do with your ring? I can't remember…"

"It's in the drawer, too. But have you anywhere secure in your room?"

"Yes, there's a secret place behind the chest. I keep my tips there, and your brooch."

"Good. Now promise me you'll use the money to buy an inside seat. The roads will be dusty before long, but if you're inside you won't have to breathe so much of it. And remember, even the Mail takes thirty-six hours to do the journey. Don't try to do it without stopping. If you get no rest you'll make yourself ill again. So promise that you'll book a ticket that lets you sleep somewhere overnight, then catch the next coach."

She nodded again. "I promise."

"I wish I didn't have to leave you to travel on your own."

"I don't mind," she whispered. "I don't mind anything, if I know you'll be waiting for me."

"That's my lovely girl," he said.

CHAPTER 12.

London, April 1838

The day was dying in a blaze of light, red, salmon, amber, yellow as George drove the Albion into London. The city lay under a smoky veil where the light of sunset was replaced by strings of yellow gaslamps and echoed by the small stars of candles. To his right, distant hills swallowed a scarlet sun, and ahead the new-lit lamps of the night coaches came at him as they climbed out of London.

Familiar though he was with cities like Newcastle, Liverpool and Manchester, he was astonished by the size of London. What riches must be here, to have thrust up the endless spired and towered buildings in front of him. Even the horses on this final stage were far better quality than he had handled before, and seemed unspoiled by the previous handling of the coachman snoring in a drunken lump beside him.

He was driving on his nerves now, back and shoulders burning with tiredness. Thetford, the guard, had supported him all the way, keeping him on the right road, calling fresh teams out from the inns, shouting to him to stop while he fixed the brake-shoe before steep descents. When they came down into the city itself the streets were thick with evening traffic, country-bound coaches going out, City-bound coaches ahead of him and behind, town-chariots, gigs and phaetons, cabs, wagons and omnibuses, handcarts, people. The smells of refuse, foul drains and horsedung were as strong as anywhere he'd been – for a moment a mouthwatering strand of roasted mutton made his belly grumble – then coal smoke bit the back of his throat, and he coughed, and the mutton was gone. The closer they got to the Thames the more often everything was submerged in the river's own muddily obscene stink.

Now Thetford leaned forward over the luggage and parcels, crowding the back-seat passengers as he called directions and commented on the oncoming traffic.

"That's the down-coach, see it? That's Pigott driving. He must be making good time, a-cause we don't usually meet him till further into the city."

"Or are we late?"

"No! You're managing just fine."

Between the sooty cliff-faces of stone and brick and stucco, the Town horses quickened their pace, telling George, "Not far now! Nearly home!"

As the smart bays strode through the traffic George realized he was almost too tired to do them justice. Over the rooftops the great cathedral dome was lit by the setting sun, and they passed the classical portico of the Post Office, smart inside its railed yard at St Martins le Grand, then the Queen's Hotel, new but rapidly becoming as sooty as its neighbours. Thetford called his directions more urgently. The passengers on the roof began to gather their belongings and sit tense and quiet, while Thetford's instructions and horn-calls became a constant flow.

"Steady, steady, you're nearly there. You'll turn left in a moment – look for Milk Street." He blew "Near Side" and a lad with a handcart waited out of the way of their turn. "Steady, boy! It's narrow going into the yard, and so twisty as a serpent. I'm a-going to sit down now. Don't scrape anything off."

George knew it would be safer and easier and much wiser to bring the team down to a walk, but his professional pride scorned such a timid arrival. He could hear his grandfather's advice, *Keep the leaders out of draught. Hold all four steady, tap the whip on the inside wheeler's flank to keep the pole straight, don't swing the leaders till their chests reach the turn.* The tyres ground over the cobbles in graceful arcs, Thetford blew "Clear" and the Town horses trotted through the gateway of the Swan with Two Necks.

George called them down to a walk, suddenly aware of how much strength he had needed over the two days of the journey. He was grateful to the horses, at one with them and their dust and sweat and thirst, and he let them stroll quietly to the end of the yard, keeping to the rear of a stage about to leave. The Royal Bruce's lettered sides announced its destination as Manchester, and it clattered away heavy with bags and full of passengers.

Thetford let go a gusty sigh of relief.

"Strewth, boy, that was some drive."

George threw the reins down to the ostlers, and they began to unfasten the traces and pole-chains. He was taken aback when they led the horses towards the booking office and vanished down an underground passage.

The stillness of the coach seemed to get through to Anderson, who began to twitch inside his ropes. George reached across and loosened the knots, and he was just turning to get down when a little grey-haired man rushed at the coach, climbed over the front wheel, grabbed Anderson by the sleeve and coat-lap and tumbled him onto the cobbles. George was sufficiently alarmed to jump down at his own side of the coach and peer underneath, but there seemed no harm done. The driver rolled over, limp and chuckling. The fall which might have injured an active man had done no more than wake him and he was pulling himself into a sitting position, feebly wheezing, with his cheek against the wheel-hub.

"Cheerio, Guv'nor."

The Guv'nor shook him. "Anderson! What did I tell you last time?"

"Ask the cush-tomers for a tes-timonial. They won't complain, he-hee. Slep' like a baby aaaall the way."

The passengers were dismounting, the outsiders groaning as they climbed down the little iron ladder. Thetford held it steady, reassuring them, "Only one more step, nearly there, yes, there we are, thank you sir, thank you – "

The Guv'nor's tirade thundered out from the other side of the coach.

"Get up! Get up, I said! Well, if you can't stand, I won't have you driving my horses. Collect your dues from the office. You're dismissed. Take your money and go."

George, fuzzy with tiredness, forgot his usual prompts to departing passengers and only woke up to the fact when the bonneted lady handed him three shillings. He remembered then to tip his hat to the complaining outsider, who gave him a florin along with a reluctant nod.

The Guv'nor came round to speak to his customers, and left Anderson lying. His manner became softer, almost obsequious, and even the Kentish accent – which George thought was Cockney – transformed into something more universal as he handed them over to the housekeeper.

"Good evening, ladies, gentlemen. Welcome to the Swan. If you're staying with us now, please follow Mrs Baring. She will show you to your rooms. Thank you, sir. Thank you, madam."

Anderson rolled off the wheel onto his hands and knees, got up and tacked across the yard towards the office.

A porter had gone up the coach-treads of the Albion to unload boxes and trunks from its roof, so George retrieved his whip from the box-seat and looped the thong tidily while he waited for his bags. Having gone into the boot first they were bound to be the last unloaded, and he'd only just retrieved them when the coachbuilder's man came into the yard with his pair of stout horses and hitched up, climbed onto the box-seat and drove the now-empty Albion out and away into the dusk. The yard men had begun to line up Mail coaches, side by side, ready for the evening departure. Among them George spotted the Port Patrick Mail, an old friend that looked naked waiting for its rooftop load.

His attention was drawn back to the Guv'nor, who was demanding of Thetford, "How could you let Anderson drive in that condition? He's a disgrace."

"I didn't, sir. I told this young man 'ere to take the ribbons. He brought us in." He winked at George, and the Guv'nor gave them both a sharp look.

"Very well. Finish your work. See me in my office tomorrow morning at eight. And you, young man, come with me, now."

When he added, "Leave that whip in the booking office," for a moment George was almost befuddled enough to obey, but then he pulled himself together and said, "This is my own, sir. Anderson's whips may have gone with the coach."

The Guv'nor stared, and for a moment they stood under the gas-lantern, assessing one another. George became conscious that his chin bore a day's stubble and his clothes were dusty and crumpled. Too late, he recognized the features of the man before him, exactly as his fellow-drivers and Dixon had described them – the keen eyes and halo of badger-grey hair, the practised politeness of manner overlying a collie-dog obsession with business. If George hadn't been so stupid with lack of sleep, he would have known at once that "the Guv'nor" was William Chaplin.

"Very well," said Chaplin, with a tight smile. "Coachman. Come with me, and bring your whip."

CHAPTER 13.

In the office, Chaplin leaned back against the edge of a heavy table and left George standing. "Well, go on. Tell me what happened today on the Albion coach."

"Sir," said George. "We couldn't make anything of your coachman. Thetford took his whip away, but he wouldn't get down off the box, so the men gave me the reins, and off we went."

"Did Anderson make a nuisance of himself?"

"Not deliberately, sir. He nearly dropped off a few times, but he seemed to think it was a good joke." George didn't mention bursting his nose, nor Thetford roping him on. "He offered to share his brandy."

Chaplin walked over to tug the bell-pull, then perched against the table again. "Ever driven in London before?"

"No sir."

"Did you manage all right in the traffic?"

"Yes, sir. After we got onto the stones, Thetford directed me." George was mesmerized by Chaplin's delicate face, which seemed to grow larger and smaller, and to jerk in and out of focus.

"What pace were you going when you came into the yard?"

"A short trot, sir."

"Damage anything, hey?"

"No sir."

"Hm. Lucky for you. How long have you been travelling? I mean, before you joined my coach."

"I started yesterday morning from Carlisle on the New Times for Liverpool. I boarded the Albion as a passenger last night." Scarcely two days. It seemed like forever.

A maid arrived, and Chaplin ordered, "Tea, cold beef and plenty of it. And the lamp." When she had gone, he continued, "Why didn't you come by the direct route? You could have travelled all the way from Carlisle on the Port Patrick Mail."

"Well, sir, by taking the stage I had four hours' rest in Liverpool, instead of only an hour and a half through Manchester." It seemed ridiculous now to think that he had planned to relate childhood memories to Lucy, to take her across the Mersey on the ferry, to point out familiar landmarks and stay the night at the inn at Eastham where he'd grown up. All that had vanished with her illness, so there was no need to mention it to Chaplin.

"I had time at Liverpool to wash and dine, and have forty winks before I caught the Albion. I paid the boot-boy to wake me."

"And that, in a nutshell, is why we struggle to make the Mails pay." Chaplin drew forward a chair and waved George to it. "Sit down. I'd like to know your name."

George hesitated, wondering hazily whether he was being made fun of. He put his bags in a corner and with owlish care stood his whip behind them before he fumbled open the pocket of his greatcoat.

"I have a letter, sir," he said, "three letters. A recommendation – a reference from my former employers – and the one you sent me."

Chaplin accepted them, and carried them to the window to read. After a moment he repeated, "Sit down, Mr Davenport."

George obeyed, uneasily, and only because of the direct command. He could only hope that what Chaplin was reading would impress him. He knew the reference from Teather said much the same things as Dixon's letter of recommendation, though Teather had not seemed much disturbed at receiving his notice.

Chaplin put the papers on the table. "I know Teather. He's subcontracted to me on the Port Patrick Mail. Who's Dixon?"

"He's a cotton man, sir, family of the High Sheriff and the Mayor of Carlisle. He was one of my regulars on the Newcastle road. I believe he stayed here before Easter. He said he met you."

"Quite possibly. And what were you driving in Carlisle? A pair coach? A short stage?"

"Four-in-hand, sir, between Carlisle and Kendal. And a spell on the Newcastle Mail."

Chaplin nodded. "Very good. Plenty of the spirited class, I suppose?"

"Sir?"

"Good perks? Of course, once the railway is completed to Carlisle, your Newcastle coaches will be worth nothing. It's the same with the Birmingham line. Horne has already given up the Woodside Mail contract. I dare say Teather was happy to let you go? He'll have plenty of men to spare! And so shall I – when I take my northern coaches off the road I'll have long-coachmen coming out of my ears. So tell me, Mr Steady-and-Responsible, why I should set you on." He tucked his chin down, and pinned George with a very sharp gaze.

As George began to answer, a young woman's voice outside the office said, "Is that for Papa? Thank you, Maggs, I'll take it in. You bring the lamp."

"You have the devil's own luck, young man," said Chaplin. "This will give you a moment longer. Sarah?" he called. "Is that our tea tray? Come along in, there's a fellow here expiring for want of a cup."

Sarah came in, holding the door open with her hip in order to manage the tray. "He ought to be more than satisfied then – I've two cups here! Mrs Baring seems to have sent bread and beef, and pickles, too."

George got to his feet, determined that Chaplin should see his best manners. Sarah urged her father out of her way, and set down the tray with a cheerful rattle. "Now, who is it who is dying for this cup of tea?"

The maid put down the lamp, and left. As Sarah unfastened her bonnet George saw her clearly for the first time. She was taller than Chaplin, slender, with the same dark hair and eyes and delicate face, and she appraised him with the same confidence as her father. A subtle relaxation of her shoulders showed that when she recognized him for a coachman he became less interesting, not an equal. He wiped all expression from his face, and she smiled just a little, which gave her an air of authority despite her youth. Soberly dressed she might be, but she was the employer; he, the servant.

Damn the girl.

Chaplin said, "Sarah, this is Mr Davenport."

George made her a brief bow, stiff and almost insulting. "Miss Chaplin."

"Oh no," she said at once. "You should call me Miss Sarah."

He blinked. He was too tired to grapple with the niceties of social address. Chaplin, however, came to his rescue. " 'Miss Chaplin' means Eleanor, my eldest daughter. Sarah is my next eldest, and too dashed sharp for her own good. My dear, Mr Davenport has brought the Albion up safely from Barnet –"

"Stony Stratford," said George.

"Anderson was rolling drunk on the box." Chaplin exchanged a look with Sarah. "Please pour for us, and hand Mr Davenport the beef."

"Anderson will have to go, Papa. The customers were complaining of him just now."

"I dismissed him."

"Good," she said.

She poured a cup of tea for George, and set it with a plate and cutlery at the end of the table. Although his mouth watered at the smell of beef and pickles, he held back, because he wasn't sure he should be sitting down in the office, eating, while the Guv'nor and his daughter were on their feet.

"Eat! Eat!" said Chaplin, seeing his hesitation. "This is only my thanks for driving the Albion, so don't assume Anderson's post is yours. Tomorrow you may go hungry, so sit down and eat!"

George obeyed. Over his head, Miss Sarah talked to her father. "Mamma asked me to remind you that we have Mr and Mrs Horne supping with us, and Mr Mackeson, and you promised we would be home in good time. Eleanor is helping her to entertain."

"If Mr Mackeson is there, I'm sure she is," said Chaplin, and Sarah gave a small chuckle.

George wondered whether Mr Horne might be the coach proprietor whom Chaplin had already mentioned but, embarrassed at eavesdropping, he kept his head down and drank tea. He found it had no sugar in it, but he was too thirsty to make any fuss. Besides, the bowl lay at the other end of the table beside Miss Sarah and he was doubly damned if he was going to ask her to hand it to him.

"Simpson brought me over in the carriage," she told her father, "so we can leave as soon as you have seen the Mails off to the Post Office."

"I hope Simpson's keeping out of their way," said Chaplin. "Davenport, you were about to furnish us with reasons why we should employ you. Go on with your beef while you do so."

George looked up from his meal and found Miss Sarah watching him. Far from leaving the men to their discussion, she had pushed aside the tea tray and picked up the three letters. Chaplin seemed perfectly at ease with her reading them. Well, if Miss Sarah was trusted with business, George had better be quite sure he talked sense.

"I applied to you before Easter, sir, and your reply asked me to attend as soon as I could."

Sarah held up the letter. "Yes, I remember – I wrote this for you, Papa."

"I set off immediately I had I worked my notice for Mr Teather. It took me two days and a night, but here I am as you requested."

Chaplin nodded his acceptance of this explanation.

"Good stamina. It's no more than I expect, mind, of a young fellow like you. The drawback with you young men is that you have plenty of energy but you aren't old enough to have much experience."

George gave his standard response to this concern. "I'm getting older at the same speed you are, sir."

"Hmph. What's your background?"

"I was born into the trade. My father was a coachman. So was my grandfather, though he doesn't drive any more. He runs an inn-yard in Cheshire." He had debated in the past week how much detail he should give if Chaplin asked him. Chaplin's own background was well known – his father had been a Kentish proprietor who sent his son out to drive and learn the business from its very bottom. "So I've driven everything, from a muck cart up. Tandem when I was eleven. A team when I was fourteen."

Chaplin observed, "Anderson thinks he can drive, too. I require other skills. Tell me about yours."

"Well, sir, I don't booze, for a start. I'm quick and I'm safe. I'll keep your horses sound and your customers happy. And I want to drive for you because we both recognize quality when we see it."

Sarah nudged her father. "He has you there, Papa."

"You've a confoundedly ready tongue, young man, but you've had plenty of time to put that answer together, so here's another question. What's your duty as a coachman?"

"Whatever you tell me it is, sir."

"Hmph. That's far too glib. Have you ever had a coach upset?"

"Yes sir," he admitted.

"Your fault?"

George laid down his fork, and rummaged in the back of his memory. "The first time, sir, yes – I thought I knew the road well enough to trot through a flood, but I put the nearside wheels in the ditch, and turned her over. The second time the front axle broke going downhill."

"How long was it before you were back on the road?"

"The first time, half a hour – we took out the horses, and the gentlemen aboard helped us to right the coach, and then we put the team back in – all damnably wet, but going."

"What about the second time – when the axle broke?"

"We were lucky. Nobody took much hurt, other than being tumbled about inside – I think I came off worst because I was pitched between the wheel-horses, so I got a bit of a kicking, but nothing to speak of."

"What did you do then?"

"I had a very experienced guard. He calmed the ladies down and helped me unhitch the horses. He could mend almost anything – I've seen him splice a broken pole so well that it was stronger than before – but the job was beyond his skills, so we left the coach at the roadside. We mounted the lady passengers on the wheel horses and took the team to the next inn. The gentlemen walked, of course. There was a man and wife who didn't want to wait, but the innkeeper had a chaise, so we sent them on. It was just as well – it was more than half a day before the proprietor sent the spare coach to us."

"Hm – if an axle broke on one of my coaches, I'd be looking to my coachbuilder for compensation. Well, if I can trust you to keep a coach running – which is the best one on the road?"

George took up his fork, confident of his subject once more. "A Mail coach by Waude. Certainly not those things by Croall, I won't call 'em coaches, that carry the Mail in the North."

"Not the best-built! The best coach on the road."

"The fastest," offered George. Was this some old joke? No proprietor had ever asked him such a question before. He was too tired to enjoy being teased, and the girl watching only increased his discomfort. "Or the one that carries the most passengers." If he was wrong, that would be the end of it, and he would be put out of his misery.

Chaplin gave a bark of laughter. "That's nearer the mark. The best coach is the one that makes the most money."

"Although," remarked Sarah, "the more it makes, the better." Father and daughter exchanged a look.

"I don't eat pride," Chaplin said to Sarah. "And I won't cheat my competitors off the road, like some people."

"No, you don't," she agreed. "But I daresay we'll have to make a joke of it while Mr Horne is at table with us."

With their eyes off him George felt released, and turned his attention back to the beef and pickles.

"One final question." Chaplin stood up to look out of the window at the Mails, and spoke over his shoulder to George. "I know all my coaches from pole-head to boot – and so should you."

"I hope so, sir."

"So who looks after the spare whip – the docker – the short Tommy? Would it be you or your guard?"

The question was so unbelievable that George stopped eating. To have come so far and travelled so fast, then to be asked such a question! Anger flooded through him. Well, he might as well speak his mind plainly. It was obvious now that he'd to have to find another post. His fork clattered as he pushed the plate onto the table.

"I won't have one of those damned things anywhere it can touch a horse. I have never owned one. Never. And if you will require me to use one, I must go elsewhere. Sir."

Sarah held her fingers over her lips, he presumed with shock, but he found he didn't care, only wondered whether he'd be able to get to his feet when Chaplin ordered him to leave.

Chaplin turned to look at him. Then without any real change of expression he said, "Finish the beef. Take your time."

George had to think through the order, twice, before he realized the implications of what Chaplin had said.

Chaplin nodded to his daughter. "You tell him."

"If Papa finds such a whip on any man's coach he is instantly dismissed." She appeared to relish George's surprise as much as her father's amusement. "It's mainly due to Papa that we hardly ever see one in London. Of course," she added, "these days we only have to explain that to provincials."

Of course. He was the provincial. Of course Chaplin dismissed men instantly. He had seen the man in action. How stupid she must think him.

"Of course," George repeated, "of course," and he began to laugh uncontrollably. Perhaps that was relief taking the place of anger. He didn't know. He was so weary that he almost didn't have the strength to stop.

Chaplin picked up his hat, and Sarah tactfully busied herself with putting on her bonnet.

"I'll watch the Mails away to the Post Office. Sarah, my lamb, will you ask Mrs Baring to find Mr Davenport a bed for the night? Attend my office in the morning, Davenport. We'll have a place for you."

CHAPTER 14.

London, April 1838

George sat in the travellers' room at the Swan, trying to begin a letter to Lucy. He felt he was back in dame-school, and like a schoolboy he fiddled with the pen and glanced around for ideas. There was a framed drawing on the wall that showed the Swan with Two Necks, each facing opposite ways from a crown at its shoulders. It was more recent and more realistic than the one moulded into the wall outside, and because of its realism he found it unconvincing. The artist might as well have drawn the second neck where its tail was…

He sighed. He really should have written earlier. He was worried about Lucy, of course, but he'd been so busy – working – finding lodgings – getting to know people. Still, writing would become more difficult the longer he left it, so in a careful copperplate hand he began:

The Swan with Two Necks,

Lad Lane, London

Thursday, 26 April 1838.

One of his difficulties was that the letter must not give away too much. Although it would be sealed its postal overstamp would show the fee, which was paid on how far it had to travel, and Ma Hennessy would know that any long-distance letter to Lucy must be from him. She'd think nothing of sliding a hot knife through the seal and reading it. He would have to write carefully to evade her unfriendly curiosity.

Dear Lucy

Mr Chaplin has appointed me to drive the Liverpool Albion coach down to Stony Stratford. It is north of London by some 50 miles and we have the usual 10-mile stages. We leave at 6.30 in the evening and arrive at the Cock Hotel in Stony a little after midnight.

He bit the end of the pen and wondered whether to write about Anderson's dismissal, but he was reluctant to admit that his appointment owed so much to luck. He might tell Lucy what it was like to run into the night, nursing the four "Old Cripples," that dodgy subcontractor's team on the middle ground of his route. They had swollen fetlocks behind and scarred knees in front, and until they warmed to their work they pulled with uncomfortable, lurching gaits. Their inadequacy made him certain that he could provide better horses himself. But that would be a big responsibility for a newcomer such as himself, and he'd never had anything that could tie him down, not a horse, a dog – or even a woman – until he met Lucy. And there he was again, full circle.

Perhaps he should discuss the possibility with her when she arrived in London. He might make a mess of explaining it in the letter, and he didn't want Ma Hennessy rubbishing the idea to Lucy before he'd investigated all the risks and the potential profit. For the moment, he left it in the back of his mind, and wrote:

I take the reins of the up-coach in the early afternoon, arriving back in London at 7 in the evening – so that I might just be able to visit a theatre – but I have been too busy settling in.

The past days had been filled with finding lodgings, and places where he could eat, and arranging to get his clothes cleaned so he was smart enough for Chaplin's liking. Then there had been learning his route and getting to know his guards and his horses.

There seemed to be girls, too, everywhere he looked; that was normal at any busy inn, though the ones from Love Lane who hung around the Swan were far more gaudy and provocative than the girls in Carlisle. He noted the ones who smiled at him, but he also mentioned Lucy as a polite way to distance them. Life here was sharp and unforgiving, and he wasn't sure of himself. And Lucy might not think that fending off other women was much of an excuse for not having written. Instead, he put:

So far in the evenings I have sat in the tap room here, getting to know people. One of the older drivers plays the fiddle, so we have had some brisk music. At any rate, I am completely free until the following evening.

Free time. It was curious that it had always been something to dread – a sign that he was not doing enough, a cause for his grandfather to criticize him into action. Here at the Swan, he looked onto a busy yard, where evening sunlight still warmed the upper balconies and windows, while in the shadows, on scarlet wheels, the Mails stood in line for their evening departures. Each maroon and black body shone with gilded stars, a Post Office number and the Queen's VR written in gold, and the destination painted on the door, under the one word, LONDON. Watching, he knew the tug of ambition once more. If he could do well enough to deserve to drive a Mail…

Outside, he could see Chaplin, also watching. It was a few days since George had last seen him, but the stablemen had warned him that he shouldn't ever assume he could slack if the Guv'nor was absent. Although a good deal of the coaching business seemed to be conducted from Chaplin's home "up west" in Adelphi Terrace, no servant could be sure they wouldn't meet him, at any task, at any of the five inns he owned. His requirements were absolutely clear – keep up his standards – and since he could do every task himself, muck out a stall, strip a harness and clean it, groom a horse, put a team together and drive it well, the men gave him their respect as a horseman as well as their employer.

The drivers had stories of meeting him well outside London, where he had watched them change horses, made accurate observations on the state of their previous team and outlined precisely what must be improved. The stablemen said he had once lain hidden overnight in a corn-bin to spring out and dismiss a man known to be stealing oats. The guards agreed it was difficult to deceive him – though according to one story, a live calf had been successfully carried in the boot from Dorchester to a London butcher, because the coachman had driven so quietly so that Chaplin had fallen asleep and never heard it.

Not everyone liked him, and like all employers he suffered a string of nicknames like "Oily Billy" and "Bite-Em-Sly". They all admitted, however, that as far as it was in his power he was a fair and considerate employer. He probably didn't need to stand under the yard's gas lantern to observe his business at work – but he did it, all the same.

George too knew the drivers' activities inside out – light the whale-oil lamps against the coming dusk, throw a greatcoat up onto the seat, lean a whip across the box – those were reassuringly familiar, like the work of the guards who checked the waybills and who were responsible for the letters, the parcels and the valuables stowed under inside seats. The baggage and boxes going into each of the Mails stood in separate piles on the cobbles, while travellers hurried to the booking-office and ran back to find their coaches.

He dipped his pen and wrote:

I am watching the Mails loading. All ten of them leave for the Post Office at the same hour, half past seven, so as you can imagine, the yard is crowded. What I admire most in the evening routine is the way the ostlers bring up team after team of horses from the stables, which are underground. They lead them through all the bustle, and put them to the coaches without any roughness or shouting. It happens the same way, night after night. It is a very fine sight.

Outside he could see the "Jew boys" with their trays, working among the passengers. The youngest sold oranges or lemons while older ones specialized in personal items like sponges, combs, mirrors, razors and shaving boxes, and others offered pocket-books, pencils, sealing-wax, paper, or the whole package in a writing case. These lads made sale after sale, though he supposed that they sold little to the regular travellers, who would carry such items as a matter of course.

The passengers were allowed to board, and the insiders seated themselves, with reserve, into the cramped interior. Wherever he had worked, passengers always schemed to outwit the guard, and arranged their hand-bags and band-boxes to claim the most room for themselves. When they asked how far other people were booked to travel, they were planning to exchange their own backward-facing seat for a forward-facing one the moment it was vacated.

The occupants of the three-seater bench on each roof made conversation between themselves. Meanwhile the yard porter was taking a tip from a beautifully gloved gentleman in a greatcoat, who probably wanted the box-seat in order to talk with the driver about horses and "The Road."

George wondered whether he should tell Lucy about London. But that was such a huge subject he couldn't decide where to start. There were many more carriages than in the little provincial cities he knew. Stages and hackney cabs crowded the streets along with smart private coaches, speedy phaetons and businessmen's gigs and the occasional sporting curricle.

Heavy drays and omnibuses, and injured or collapsed horses, slowed the traffic or sometimes brought it entirely to a standstill. The carts that took the dung from the Swan stables came early, as soon as the night coaches had arrived and the morning ones had gone out. Even the finest streets smelled of horse-muck, until the vestry carts came out in an evening and scraped them, and the water carts rinsed the slurry away. And dead horses were often left lying in the streets for days, until decomposition made them easier to cut up and cart away. To that, the side streets added rotting cabbages, offal and leaking cesspits; and now that the summer was coming, although the smoke lessened as households lit fewer fires, the foul, all-pervading river sent up a miasma in its place.

There were just so many people, hundreds of thousands of people, coming into the city as he had, in search of a living. They filled every possible corner to overflowing. The narrow back streets near the Swan – Silver Street, Monkeywell Street, and Falcon Street where he and Thetford and Cherry lodged – were crowded with small businesses, tailors and drapers next to surgeons, a solicitor next to a coal merchant. Only a few streets away there were mean dead-end courts where no decent person dared venture and whose activities were better left to the imagination. Lucy wouldn't need to be told about those.

He supposed she might like to know about London's shops – and markets – and the fashions ladies wore, but the writers of fashion accounts and advertisements in the Carlisle Patriot and Journal were likely to be much better informed than he was. He assessed the space left on the foolscap sheet and decided against even trying. If he took a second sheet, the letter would cost more to post.

On the other hand, to leave the remaining space empty seemed a waste. What would go into few words? He was wary of writing endearments that Ma might read, but he could name the people he worked with.

I shall have three different guards along Watling Street, who continue with the coach when I reach Stony Stratford. Amos Clark and Tom Thetford are very quick and sober. The drivers of other coaches are friendly enough – some pretty hard drinkers and a few excellent good men.

Thetford in particular was skilful at easing his coach through the evening traffic, blowing every call just when it was needed. On the first evening run out of London, Thetford had tactfully suggested that George might follow Dick Cherry's Greyhound, which left at the same hour and shared the road for Birmingham as far as Stony Stratford. George suspected that was the reason Chaplin had put him onto the Albion without any other instruction.

As for Dick Cherry, the name fitted him well; he was a short, robin-like man, displaying a neat red waistcoat under his heavy driving clothes. He'd not only given George a lead over their common ground, he'd also encouraged him to stay at his Falcon Street lodgings. George, still slightly punch-drunk among all the new sights, sounds and sensations, had been relieved to let Cherry guide him, and he was pleased that on their return to London, plump coaching widow Mrs Bowe had been happy to rent him a room.

"She seems to look after you tremendously well," observed George the following morning, as he and Cherry walked from Falcon Street to the Swan. "Perhaps there's something I should know about you and her?"

Cherry gave a derisive snort. "That'll do, cocky. I don't dangle after petticoats. Her old man drove for Mountain at the Saracen's Head, just up there at Snow Hill – according to her the Mountain family is cousins to Mr Chaplin."

"What happened to him? Mr Bowe?"

"Ah, he was drowned, it'll be about fifteen years ago now. You know that long flat stretch along Watling Street? It floods badly in winter. The road had been washed away but he couldn't see that under the water, so the coach went over."

George pulled a face, and said nothing. His own accidents had been bad enough, but to imagine deep water – the massive cold River Ouse sweeping trees down at you – spray thrashed up by plunging horses – steel-shod hooves striking out – heavy coats and boots that held water and pulled you down, making it impossible to swim… He shuddered.

"The passengers got out without being much hurt," said Cherry, "but Bowe would try to cut the hosses free. Mrs B will tell you the story, including the funeral, right down to the collection and the hearse feathers."

Her situation reminded George of the misfortunes of Johnnie Yates' family. He recounted them to Cherry, who shook his head.

"Did you get up a subscription for 'em?"

"Yes. I mean, a couple of the other fellows did, and I subscribed. I don't know how much it collected. It's Molly's boys I'm worried for, going into a mill…or down a mine. My Da had an accident – he used to get as drunk as our old friend Anderson – and for a while we thought we'd all have to go into the workhouse. We learned soon enough where we might end up, girls as well as boys. There's collieries that go out under the sea. Brats aren't worth a candle down there, you know, they have to work in the dark."

"You done that?" asked Cherry.

"No." Even though George recognized the soft heart under Cherry's perky exterior, he was reluctant to admit that memories of that time woke him at nights. He said offhandedly, "It didn't come to that. Granda started me with the horses and I've done it ever since."

"I'm glad to hear it. Well, we can all have accidents, drunk or not," said Cherry. "That's why I've joined the Benevolent Whip Club. It's a guinea a quarter and it pays two guineas a week if you can't work. And if worst comes to worst it pays funeral expenses."

"Yes, I might do that."

"It works fine so long as nobody tries to cheat. Of course there's some that does, but they catch 'em. Maybe you won't have heard about Vaul? He drives for Sherman. He claimed ten pound expenses for his wife's funeral. Only he forgot to tell 'em, he doesn't have a wife."

George laughed aloud.

"The case comes up this week. Though it ain't that funny," said Cherry, "when you think about it. We co-operate so we don't starve in hard times, and bastards like him manage to rob the fund. It makes a mock of the whole idea. I hope he gets hard labour."

Remembering the conversation, George wrote now to Lucy:

Today there is some gossip: a coachman has been arrested for fraud. One of our booking-office clerks forged a marriage certificate to help him, and has also been arrested. Everyone is of the opinion that both are guilty. It is quite a scandal. Mr Chaplin has put his daughter Miss Sarah into the office in Sharpe's place, until the trial. She is high and mighty, but the men say she works very quickly, and better than Sharpe ever did.

By now he had almost filled the sheet of paper. He wondered whether to suggest Lucy came up to London, but decided against it, partly on the grounds of space, and partly because he didn't want to alert Ma, who would certainly read the letter first. He folded down the top and bottom of the paper, and there was enough space left for him to conclude:

I hope you are recovering from the influenza. Write as soon as you are able. I do not know how long I will stay at my present lodgings – so for now, write to me here at the Swan. If I can find a place that is cheaper, or will be more suitable for you, I may remove there.

Your truly affectionate

George

He had taken so long over his letter that the Mails were clattering out into the lane, trotting away towards St Martins le Grand with all the guards blowing their horns. Half past seven, punctual to the minute. With that burst of activity over, the Jew boys packed up and left. No more coaches would leave the Swan until early morning, so business opportunities were at an end. Cherry had told him that a few returned with the dawn, but George had already discovered that Cherry was much more of an owl than a lark, and only half believed him. The boys would reappear for certain the following afternoon.

He folded in the sides of his letter and tucked one into the other, then directed the smooth back of the sheet to Miss Hennessy, Blue Bell, St Cuthbert's Lane, Carlisle. He lit a taper at the fire and heated wax to seal the join of his letter, an infrequent task that pleased him, so the seal dimensions became ostentatious before he regretfully blew the flame out. If Lucy wrote straight back, he might hear from her next week, Wednesday at the earliest.

"Finished, have you, boy?" The question made him jump. The heavy-set traveller spoke mildly enough, but there was no humour in his manner. "When you've done daydreaming, I've a letter to write."

"By all means, sir." He slid the letter into his pocket, and gave up his place. Perhaps he ought to buy a writing case from one of the Jew boys.

CHAPTER 15.

London, May 1838

The week dragged through to Thursday with no reply from Lucy, and that evening George was so fierce with his bay horses that they snorted and pranced and shied all the way out of London, to the terror of passengers and pedestrians alike. On the hills to the north, where the weight of the coach should have steadied them, he drove so hard that he overtook Dick Cherry and the Greyhound before the end of the first stage.

When Tom Thetford climbed down to help with the change he found himself ducking reins and traces as George flung them off and hustled the exhausted team away.

"What's the matter with you, boy? Eh? You could get away with racing if it was a bit o' fun – but this ain't fun," Thetford snapped. "You've about bottomed these nags – they're pumped-out – and them the nicest team you'll ever lay hands on."

George snapped back, but he knew the old man was right, that it made no sense to wear out a fine team. He was grinding his teeth waiting to hear from Lucy. He had to admit it: he was worried. Worried about Lucy's health, troubled by her odd relationship with her mother, worried about whether she could ever get away, and if she did, whether he could support her. Chaplin himself had hinted his position in London was short-term. The pay was fair, but perks weren't turning out nearly as good as he'd hoped, and whichever way he drove along Watling Street, out of London or back, he saw the Birmingham rail-road being tidied for its opening and was reminded of the threat it posed.

Under Thetford's stern eye, he tried to settle down for the horses' sake, to drive the rest of his ground with consideration. It was ironic that when he brought the final team in to the yard of the Cock Hotel, the near wheeler should be lame. He reported it to the head horseman, and went indoors for his meal. Being after midnight, there were few customers still awake, apart from some of his own passengers who were breaking their northward journey, and a stout farmer who stared as if challenging him to question why he was in town so late.

The coffee room was lined with old-fashioned stalls along each wall. They were separated by little dark-red curtains, and held narrow tables paired with hard wooden-backed benches. The waiter compelled most of the travellers to take seats at a communal table in the middle, where the wreck of previous meals lay like flotsam on a beach, and was swept away at similarly long intervals. However the fat girl who served alongside the waiter looked favourably on the coachmen, and with the expenditure of no more than a wink and a grin George had no difficulty in securing a stall.

Dick Cherry arrived not long after and joined him, and when they finished eating they sat quietly in the lamplight while the travellers left the central table to seek their beds. Dick called for two glasses of sherry. In spite of the lateness of the hour the fat girl smiled at the order, but George was still deep in his own worries, and couldn't be bothered to respond.

"Oi oi," said Cherry, "she fancies you."

"Who?"

Cherry's hands outlined the fat girl's exaggerated curves. "Mary."

"Oh! Not for me. You're welcome to it." At the slight shake of Cherry's head, George snorted. "You're all gob and no action."

"I reckon it's what you're short of."

"You'd probably need a map to find it."

"You good lookin' ones can be terrible unkind," said Cherry with a chuckle. "The poor maid's been turning in her bed, just aching for you."

George managed a short laugh. "She needn't bother. I've got one of those at the other end of the road."

"You must be a fast worker."

"Don't be daft! I mean my lass in Carlisle! I've yet to see a London bird I'd touch without gloves. Except maybe that French judy – the dark-eyed one, what do they call her – Jan, Jeanie? She's a bit of a dasher, that one."

"Jeanne," said Cherry, identifying her without difficulty. "You should go up West, where the toffs live. There's plenty like her go promenading out that way." He winked. "Know what I mean?"

"For God's sake shut up. I can do without expensive women."

"You could go and watch the hosses being sold at Tattersall's. There's some bang-up tits go through that ring."

George laughed at the double meaning. "And they'll be high-priced, too, I'll bet."

"More than either of us could afford," said Cherry. "There's a lot of class on parade there."

"I've no need to buy trouble."

"Of course not!" agreed Cherry in good-humoured astonishment. "But even if you got something nice at home, it don't stop you looking. You just keep your hands in your pockets."

When Mary had brought the sherry and gone reluctantly back to her work, Cherry proposed a game of cribbage, their usual "twice round the board before bed." Considering his cards, he observed, "You say you ain't looking for women. That's all right by me. But when I mentioned hosses, I didn't hear no protests."

"Well, I'm thinking. There must be a better team for the Albion than those Old Cripples. If I could horse the coach for that stage, I'd be, like, driving my own team. It might make my fortune, the way some of the old boys did."

"I thought so myself, once. But ask yourself why the Guv'nor and Mr Nunn won't keep a hoss once it's over nine year old."

"What d'you mean? I've driven some that sailed with Noah in the Ark."

Cherry put down a card, and moved his peg along the board. "Fifteen-two. Ah, old nags end up on stages where there's no gentry to see 'em, but you wouldn't want to work there, would you? Driving through the night and sleeping through the day. Not your style at all."

"You can talk. You'd sleep all day right enough."

They played on. Cherry reached an exact thirty-one, turned the used cards over and pegged forward another two points.

"Now, there's a ten for you. Make it fifteen." George couldn't, and played a seven. Cherry said, "The trouble, see, with hosses, isn't the buying – it's the keeping. Worn out hosses eat, but they don't work too well."

"You don't reckon I'd make anything of it, then."

"Not if your arithmetic's anything like your cribbage," said Cherry. He laid down a rectangle of used cards. "Look! Here's your coach – four wheels, right?" He tapped each in turn. "This wheel has to pay the licence plate, the coachbuilder and the road tolls. This one pays for forage, the ostlers, the farrier and the horse doctor. This one pays you and Thetford, and the last one is your profit – if there is any."

"But if I drove my own horses, I'd take two wheels – by your reckoning."

"That's why I worry about you." Cherry collected the cards. "You wouldn't get the full two wheels, because you'd have to pay Thetford. Count up now."

"Not much in it," said George gloomily, glancing at his hand and moving the peg in pursuit of Cherry's. "You're running away with it."

"Nah. Deal! You might catch me yet."

George dealt, set down the pack, and began to sort the fresh hand. "Well, if I'm to beat you with this lot, I'll need a damn good whip."

"And that's another thing. We'd hardly got off the stones before you passed me this evening. I know you don't hit 'em much, but would you drive your own team as hard as that? I wonder."

"I don't know." George discarded two cards to his crib, and surveyed the remaining four with resignation. "Anyway, I suppose the Guv'nor would only let me horse a stage that didn't pay."

"Now you're seeing sense," said Cherry, and cut the pack for George to turn over the top card. "There! two for his heels! Maybe your luck's turning."

George lost the game fairly rapidly after that.

"Sorry. Time I went to bed."

"Not to worry," said Cherry, sweeping the pennies off the table and into his pocket. "Fat Mary, eh?" He winked. "What a lucky girl!"

"Ooh, no. No, thank you very much. Goodnight."

She was lurking, though, in the passage outside the coffee room. When she saw him she giggled in pretended surprise. There was nothing accidental in the way she used the available space, so that he had to brush against her breasts and belly as he passed – she all the while staring at him with those great soft cow's eyes. He knew the exercise she was offering would send him to sleep all right, but he still smiled and kept going. He didn't trust her enough to share his bed – even if there had been room for her.

CHAPTER 16.

He slept shallowly, fighting off worries about Lucy that never quite descended into nightmare. He rose late with a pounding head and a dry mouth. Perhaps when he got back to London, he might find there was a letter, at last.

When he went out to the stables to check the team, he was relieved to find that the lame wheel-horse was to be replaced with a young brown mare. He asked if the ostler knew anything about her.

"The Guv'nor got her for a few sovs because she ran away and smashed up a gig. Though what vicar were doing, driving a gig…he ain't fit with a cob and a turnip cart, let alone a half-blood mare."

George stroked her, and when she lifted her muzzle to his face he murmured, "Now then, you wild woman. You fancy yourself as a baggage, do you? We'll have to come to an agreement about that."

Her sensitive nostrils flared at him as he looked her over. There were healing scars on her hocks which made him suspect she might be a kicker, but he liked her stamp; she was full of quality, her eye quick and interested, undimmed as yet by the demands of coaching, and her fore-legs were still clear of the "postmaster's badge" of broken knees.

"What's her name?"

"Cinnamon," said the ostler, with disgust. "Sinner, more likely."

“Put her in at the near-side.” In that position she’d have to work hard and she’d be right under his whip the whole time. And if she did kick, it would be the passenger’s boots in danger, and not his. The prospect of reforming her almost cheered him.

Cherry departed with the Greyhound shortly after mid-day, and George went round to the stables again to make sure the new mare was comfortably harnessed. His team were all turned round in their stalls, ready to go. He thought the previous wheeler’s collar fitted Cinnamon all right, and he said so, but she was bridled with the snaffle bit that was all the lame horse had needed. He called up the ostler.

“I’m not taking her down the road in that, not for the first time. Change it for a curb and a bearing rein, and make sure it all fits. Flatten the curb-chain and don’t have anything too tight.”

The man was inclined to be huffy. “Oh yes, yer honour, and shall I fix the driving rein at the duffer’s-hole, like vicar has it?”

“No. Don’t tax your brain about the details. I’ll check before I mount the box.”

He left, aware that he hadn’t made a friend.

The Albion came in on time from Towcester. As his team was being put to the coach a gentleman in a dust-coat emerged from the coffee room, and remarked that he’d given the yard porter a little something to secure the box-seat beside George, so (with a knowing wag of the head) if only he could handle the ribbons, he’d make it worth George’s while, too.

“No,” said George, who was re-buckling Cinnamon’s reins. In spite of his command the ostler had put everything on severe settings. He put the rein in at rough cheek and eased the numbingly tight curb-chain. After a moment's consideration he loosened the bearing rein one hole. Then he strode round the rest of the team to check everything was right, and without further conversation took the reins and climbed up onto the box.

He was determined to leave on the minute, if necessary without the aspiring "whip." But that gentleman came nimbly up the near-side, and took his place beside him.

George called to his guard, "All right behind?"

Thetford responded, "All right!" and blew "Start."

"Trot on!" And he started on the interesting task of making one obedient unit out of his three old-stagers and the untried brown mare.

The gentleman, ruffled but not defeated by George's bluntness, talked on. He fidgeted with his driving gloves, and clearly itched to take the reins. "Been looking forward to this, what! Are they a good team? Light-mouthed?"

"No," said George. "They are not." His attention was on Cinnamon. She seemed to look back at him over the top of her blinkers – perhaps they fitted more slackly than they ought – and whenever she caught a glimpse of the coach towering behind she crowded into the collar, then dropped back as though astonished by the weight. George thought he might have to apologize to the inside passengers for the uneven ride, but at least her anxiety made the other three horses step out with vigour, which suited his temper; the quicker the pace the better, and the less likely it was that the mare would try to kick.

"By Jove they're good to go," said the aspiring whip. "I'd like to try them. There's a guinea in it for you."

"No," said George for the third time. Cinnamon had begun to sweat, the first sign that she might be ready to face her work calmly, and the guinea he was refusing wouldn't pay for spoiling her.

"No, SIR," said the passenger, goaded at last to remind him of his manners.

George looked him up and down. "Are those gloves of yours new? Sir? They're too tight. If I let you drive, you'll get cramp."

"Why, you arrogant young pup…!"

George didn't give any sign of hearing the rest of his abuse. Over the last miles Cinnamon went strongly and well, and at the end of the stage he was glad to see the dust-coat climb back to a roof seat.

The rest of his ground was less comfortable. The dust of oncoming wagons left a taste of dried dung in his mouth and in the afternoon heat the horseflies began to bite, so that only the bearing-reins stopped the horses scratching-off their bridles. He had to bully the "Old Cripples" into the gallop that was needed to make their time, while the offended passenger continued to make audible remarks behind his back. A draper in St Albans buttonholed Thetford to complain that a batch of cloth samples and trimmings on the previous day's run had been short of several items, and Thetford wasted time explaining that he didn't have Cordock's waybill and the complaint should go to the office. In Barnet a manservant belonging to some old lady's household kept the coach standing while he insisted that George and George alone could deliver his mistress's false teeth to Town in time for dinner. Finally, the smart team that he'd over-driven last night had none of their usual enthusiasm, and he drove them back to London growing increasingly angry with himself as he felt with every stride, every hill, every down-grade, how jaded they were.

By the time he climbed down off the coach at the Swan with Two Necks, he was prepared to snap the head off anyone who crossed him.

Tom Thetford ignored his mood, and filled his arms with a load of parcels that threatened to become a landslide.

"Here, bite." Thetford poked the edge of the waybill between George's teeth, and patted him on the back. "Good boy. Hand in that lot while I fetch the rest, and I'll buy you supper."

Effectively gagged and handcuffed, George shouldered open the door of the office. He was just depositing the landslide on Foyle's section of the counter when Sarah Chaplin came over. In this last week she seemed to have grown taller. She deferred only to Mr Ibbotson the head book-keeper, and to her father.

"You owe me a shilling," she said to George.

He looked at her and frowned, the waybill still in his mouth. Why was she asking him for money? Indeed, why was she addressing him at all? Had that fool passenger been complaining? He knew that strictly he'd been right to keep hold of the reins, but taking money to let amateurs drive was a common practice, like shouldering, and maybe he'd been too short with him. Or perhaps he'd incurred some business fine that he didn't know about, perhaps for driving too fast last night or taking a personal parcel – like the old lady's teeth that were still in his pocket. Well, he'd better keep his nose clean, just in case, and make sure Foyle took proper charge of these parcels and waybill.

Sarah stood waiting. When Thetford came in, he took over the parcels, so George reluctantly moved along the counter.

"Yes, Miss, what do you say I owe you, and why?"

She repeated, "A shilling. You've been sent a letter. The postman wanted to deliver it to you personally because it's unpaid, but to save him trouble I paid for it. One shilling please." She held out her hand.

He was suspicious, since anyone else's unpaid mail would have been given back to the postman for re-delivery in the evening. "A shilling? Here."

His suspicion became exasperation when she teasingly held back the letter.

"The fee was in fact elevenpence," she said. "Will you be angry, Mr Davenport, if I keep the penny for my trouble? Or must I return it to you, along with the letter?"

"Oh, give me the letter, and be damned to your profit." Foyle's quick sideways frown reminded George to curb his tongue. "Begging your pardon, Miss. I've been waiting particularly for that letter."

"I see." Sarah laid one finger on the seal of the letter and leaned forward confidentially. "Next time you write to her," she murmured, "stick a half-sov under the seal so she can afford to reply." She straightened, spun on her heel, and went briskly back to her desk.

***

"How dare she!" George slapped the letter down between his plate and Dick Cherry's. "The snotty-nosed bitch!"

Cherry had come in half an hour ahead of him, and already finished his meal. He turned the letter over. "Your sweetheart?"

"No! Miss Sarah-who-isn't-the-eldest! Stick a half-sov under the seal! The rotten little cow!"

Thetford came to sit with them. "I'll tell you where it is, lad, I reckon she's jealous." He laughed at the expression of shock on George's face.

"No," said George. "I mean, like, the letter could be from my mother. How would she know? It could be from my – my sister. Or a friend."

"Pull the other one. She knows you wouldn't be like a bear with a sore head if it wasn't a girl you was waiting to hear from. Come on, sit down, you make the place look untidy."

"You ain't got a sister," said Cherry.

"Oh, be quiet." George sat down. "Of course it's from Lucy. But why couldn't she pay to send it? I left her money."

"Well, look on the bright side – it's red wax," said Cherry, pointing at the seal, "not black. Nobody's died. So read the blummin' thing! Then maybe you can stop driving everybody mad."

George bolted a mouthful of stew, and then broke the seal. He saw at a glance that it might be bad news because the lines of writing inside were not only close-packed, but ran in two directions, one at ninety degrees across the other. He groaned.

"Crossed, by God!" said Cherry, peering over the top of the sheet. "You'd better read that at the window or you'll never make it out."

Lucy had written:

Monday, 30 April 1838.

My dear Love

I have been watching for the postman these five days so I am most happy and relieved to have a letter from you at last. I hope that you are well and that your place is a good one. You will be relieved to know that my health is much improved and I am feeling stronger every day. I still have a cough that troubles me but God willing I shall very soon be well enough to set off for London.

Mam has rather worse to live with since you left. I am still serving ale and meals but she forbids me to walk out at all, on the excuse that my cough must not be troubled by the street air. I will tell you more when I see you.

I shall have to ask Mariah to post this letter. I have given her a half-crown to pay for it at the Post Receiving Office. I suppose that she will keep what remains, and I shall have to take on trust her account of the postage fee.

Well, that answered the question about the lack of a payment stamp. Mariah had clearly thought of better uses for the half-crown, and he was amazed that she had even taken the letter to the office.

Perhaps I might have asked Mr Farrimond or Mr Armstrong to take it, but they are so regularly drunken that I dare not, and in any case I do not wish to be beholden to either of them.

You will be wondering why, things being as they are, I do not set off at once, and why I did not write immediately to explain. It is because I have been trying to solve a mystery,

Here, George had to swivel the page to decipher the crossed lines:

… and having not managed to solve it, I must admit, to my sorrow, that I no longer have your £5, nor the sweet ring you gave me. They were in the drawer, as you remember, but when Mam said I must move back to my own room so she might let yours again, both the money and the ring were gone. I do not know when they were taken or who to blame, and so I cannot accuse anyone.

I have asked Mr Brydon, who drives a Manchester coach, to discover for me the likely cost of travelling to London. I still have my small savings and your brooch, but even if I were to pawn the brooch, I do not know yet whether that money would be sufficient. I am ashamed to have lost the means of coming to you, and beg your forgiveness.

When George relayed this information, Cherry agreed that Lucy had probably made the right decisions.

"She sounds sensible enough – for a woman. So why she wants to write to such a fool in the first place is beyond me!"

George slapped him round the head with the letter and got a punch in the ribs. Thetford calmed them both with a word, and George returned to the window to read Lucy's closing lines.

I pray therefore that the good Lord will keep thee safe and that if it be His will, I shall soon join thee in London to stand before Him as thy wedded wife. Write to me again as soon as may be.

I am ever thy most faithful and loving heart

Lucy

After Cherry's insult, George chose not to share this descent into the tender "thee" of the dialect. He came back to the table to finish his meal, and opened his pocket to put in the letter. He froze as his fingers met a package left over from the day's journey.

"Damnation!" he said. "I must deliver the old girl's teeth."

CHAPTER 17.

Stony Stratford, 13 May 1838

The morning was sunny and quiet in Stony Stratford, apart from a single church bell calling, and on the canal the quacking of a mallard like sarcastic laughter. This was the fourth Sunday that George had endured out in the country, where Sabbath entertainment consisted of two church services, or reading the Bible, or walking. He picked up a stone and flung it forty yards ahead, where the placid water of the Buckingham canal absorbed it with a ring of ripples.

"Could be worse," said Cherry, sidestepping to kick another stone in front of him. George snorted disbelief, and kicked it back.

"Really?"

"Really! It could be raining. I told yer, it's a devil of a place for floods."

"Cherry, this boredom is ageing us before our time. Let's go out tomorrow night. I'm fed up of sitting in the tap-room of the Swan. And I must've walked more miles than Captain Barclay."

"Well, you've had my company, haven't you?" said Cherry, hurt.

George ignored him. "I want something fresh to talk about."

"Learn a poem, try a new hair oil. Read the news. We carry enough papers, don't we?"

"Our gentlemen don't want me to spout stuff from the newspapers – Chartists wanting secret ballots, and rubbish about Spring-heeled Jack." George considered Cherry's profile and said with a touch of malice, "Even if the Chartists do get their way, you won't have a vote – you en't old enough to shave yet."

"What! Thirty-one, I am!" said Cherry indignantly.

"Gerraway! Really? You're wearing very well."

Cherry abandoned the newspaper angle. "All right then, talk to 'em about hosses. That's what you want, isn't it? To feel equal to the toffs. Tell 'em what an evil team you're driving. Let 'em see how beautifully they go in your hands – you know how to make 'em gasp a bit."

"I do, but some of 'em are such muffs, they don't know how much they don't know!"

"You know how to do it though, don't yer? Well, then, ask how their Lady Wives plan to celebrate the Coronation. That should occupy half a stage or more."

"I've done all that, too. I don't need to hear *any more* about the Coronation."

"What you need," said Cherry, "is a seeing-to. There are plenty of women making sheep's eyes at you. Just go eeny meeny miney mo."

"Ar ey, Cherry! Ninety-five out of a hundred, their mothers tell 'em, 'no matter how pretty he talks, you mustn't bring shame on us.' What good is that to a fellow? And the other five have serviced all the navvies between Stony and Birmingham."

"Oh, staying pure for our little sweetheart, are we? Nice to know." Cherry added, slyly, "I thought you was starting to forget her."

George reddened, and took off his hat to fan his face. “She’s saving up the coach fare. I want her to travel in comfort, like. And she needs to stop somewhere overnight.”

“You’ve got enough put away to have fetched her by now. Maybe you’re not in such a rush for her after all.”

“Be damned to your filthy mind. I left her money, and somebody stole it.”

George picked up another stone, and flung it harder and further. The mallard drake clattered up off the water and flew a half-circle to land on the canal behind them.

“All right, all right,” said Cherry, putting his hands in his pockets. “Consider the subject changed.”

“Good!” After a minute George said more calmly, “C’mon, I still need a night out. Let’s go to the theatre.”

“I wouldn’t mind looking at a few pretty dancers.” Cherry teetered along the towpath, a ludicrous robin in a scarlet waistcoat and shiny hat. “Give us a kiss.”

“Gerraway,” said George, laughing against his will.

“Well then, clowns and hosses at Astley’s.”

“What good is that to me, watching other people fooling about with horses? I want Theatre Royal, a drama, the kind of thing our gentlemen would go to see.”

Cherry’s eyebrows made wings that said he had no illusions about the preferences of gentlemen. “That’s flying high. It’ll mean Drury Lane or Covent Garden. The legit theatres are swell kind of places.”

“I know that! We have real theatres in the country too, you know! I’ll have a look in the Examiner and find out what’s on.”

"But the time would be a bit tight," said Cherry, "I mean to get washed and changed and have our supper."

"Now look. The roads will never be more perfect. The Town teams are fit. If we push 'em we might get in twenty minutes early, or more – and anyway, you get in before I do! Yes, if you run home and warn Mrs Bowe I'll want shaving water, I'll have time to change and we can grab a pie from that shop in Fleet Street…You don't have to come along if you don't want to. Even on a Monday, I shan't be alone."

"All right, all right, we'll go if it makes you happy." It was the first time George had seen Cherry less than enthusiastic. "It had better be worth it."

CHAPTER 18.

London, 14 May 1838

Monday evening saw George and Cherry walking with other little groups of playgoers towards the Theatre Royal. George stopped to buy an orange from a red-haired Irish girl, and she responded to his wink with a more than usually lively smile. He might have lingered to flirt, but then he saw the carriages in Catherine Street setting down ladies in full-skirted silk dresses and mantles, and gentlemen in evening cloaks, and at once he forgot her. He turned and made for the portico like a hunter hearing the horn.

Cherry went after him, saying urgently, "No, mate, not that door, that's for the Dress Circle. It's all toffs in there, and bankers and solicitors' clerks. Listen to 'em all buzzing away."

"Don't we earn as much as solicitors' clerks? And who was it wanted me to go up West and see how the toffs lived?"

"Yes, but only to – oh leave orf, George, this is serious, and I didn't shave as close as you did."

George grinned at him. "Nobody'll notice. That's not a beard, it's an apology."

"Anyway I don't know if I want to watch this Shakespeare stuff," said Cherry. "I like my fun vulgar."

"You look after the orange then." He lobbed it into Cherry's hands. "Tonight I have a fancy to be a toff."

"It's the side doors for us," insisted Cherry, giving the orange back. "The pit or the gallery."

"Ar ey, Cherry! I'm not going to sit up in the gods." He settled the matter by going in.

Within moments the press of playgoers pushed George further into the saloon, and Cherry after him. Other people displayed their tickets to the staff, then, seemingly very much at home, went on towards the doors labelled Upper and Dress Circles.

"I tell you, we can't." Cherry caught his arm. "We're not in evening dress, not properly."

"Walk as though you are, then. Come on. We're clean and we've got cash. If we buy tickets they can hardly turn us out."

A woman's voice interrupted them. "Mr Davenport!"

Sarah Chaplin stood there, a little gawky despite her tawny silk, and beside her a pretty girl in blue, who must be her older sister – Chaplin had told him her name once – Helen? Ellen? Attending them both was a young man, beautifully tailored and also, as the incoming crowd forced them all to stand closer, perfectly military with disapproval. George slipped the orange into his pocket and found space to make a careful bow. Cherry reluctantly copied him. Sarah smiled and her sister nodded and the gentleman gave no acknowledgement at all except to speak in an undertone to the sister, who said timidly to Sarah, "You shouldn't accost gentlemen in public, dearest."

"Indeed, Mr Mackeson?" replied Sarah, ignoring her and directly addressing their escort. "I most certainly will, if I know them. Eleanor may feel constrained to follow your advice on etiquette. I do not."

"You shame your parents, then, since they didn't bring you up to behave like a street girl." Mackeson's drawl was cutting, and George heard Cherry catch his breath.

"Sarah," said Eleanor gently, "Papa allowed you to come out in hopes that you would recover your composure –"

"If I wish to speak to an acquaintance," retorted Sarah, "it will do nothing for my composure if I am forced to ignore him. Mr Davenport!"

She turned to him with her chin up and a brilliantly angry smile, and behind his shoulder Cherry muttered, "Run for your bleedin' life, mate."

George stood his ground. He had craved excitement, and here it was. "Good evening, Miss Sarah. I can see you're in blazing health."

"Oh, yes, I am," said Sarah vigorously, "very well indeed, Mr Davenport! May I introduce my sister, Eleanor, and her fiancé, Mr Mackeson? Eleanor, this is Mr Davenport."

"Pleased to make your acquaintance," said George. "And this is Mr Cherry, a friend of mine." He hadn't missed the fact that Sarah had introduced Eleanor to him, and not the other way around. If Sarah had defined him by their employment, as she had done the first time they met, she would have signalled that he was a social inferior, and it amused him that Mackeson was furious because he now couldn't say so himself.

"Cherry and I were just discussing which seats we ought to buy." He ignored Cherry's faint groan. "Miss Sarah, you'll know that I have only recently come to London. I don't know this theatre. Would you advise us?"

"I might advise you to see a different play!"

"Really?" said George. "The newspaper reports suggest it's been well received."

"Oh, that may well be so. For instance, I believe the Queen has attended twice. Mind you, this theatre offers a choice of Royal boxes, so that may have influenced Her Majesty rather more than the quality of the piece." Her voice rang with a sarcasm which George felt was aimed at Eleanor and Mackeson. She continued, "Have you come to see Mr Kean? He has made quite a hit, hasn't he? Nobody thought much of him until he went off to America, but when the American people like someone they are so loud in their enthusiasm that we hear it even on this side of the ocean. And after that accolade, of course, he can do very little wrong."

"Sarah," said Eleanor, at her elbow, "do stop this. People are looking at you."

"Let them. Papa has sent us up to the theatre with instructions to enjoy ourselves in his absence. And I intend to do so. Mr Mackeson! Do me a service, please. Enquire of the clerk how many seats are booked in our name."

"Don't waste your time trying to bully me," drawled Mackeson. "You know perfectly well that your Mamma engaged a box for six. You seem determined to spoil the evening!"

"Yes, and before the play has even begun," she agreed, in a strange, brittle tone. "Well, gentlemen all, it will be very simple to smooth my temper – " She focused on the two coachmen, who were standing mute, Cherry ready to retreat, George very upright and smiling. "Would you care to watch the play from a seat in our box? It will cost you nothing, since it is already booked –"

"Sarah!" said Eleanor, in a low voice, "you are insulting."

"Miss Sarah, I strongly advise you –'

"Hold your peace, Mr Mackeson. My parents chose not to attend – showing themselves wiser than Her Majesty – and so we have vacant seats, which I'm sure Mr Davenport and his – er – friend – will be delighted to fill."

There was an uncomfortable pause. George saw how Sarah had embarrassed Mr Mackeson and Eleanor with her scorn of the play and of the Queen. She made it quite clear that although they didn't want strangers to take those seats, she did. He was highly curious about what she was up to. So as he heard Cherry draw breath to refuse, he flashed a mischievous smile at her and said, "Thank you, I'd like that very much."

Mackeson exclaimed, "Now look here, Mr Devonport!"

"Daven-port," said George, drawling a little, but not so much that Mackeson could take offence. "Old Cheshire family, don't you know. Would you care to take my arm, Miss Sarah?"

Sarah looked up at him, thin and tense, with a smiling devil in her eyes. "Most certainly! But I warn you, this team will be a handful to drive. So let 'em go, and sit tight."

CHAPTER 19.

"Well, that was a bloody terrible evening," said Cherry, when George came down for breakfast in the morning. "Next time you want a night out, we'll go to Astley's."

George broke into a laugh. "It was fun."

"You've a bloody queer idea of what's fun."

George poured himself a cup of tea, still smiling. It had certainly been a very angry night. Young Miss Sarah had taken his arm in a thoroughly improper fashion and sailed down the corridor, dragging the rest of the party along by sheer pride. Dealing with that temper had been a challenge as enjoyable as educating Cinnamon, the Stony Stratford mare.

Mrs Bowe brought in George's bowl of porridge. "Mr Cherry says you went to a play last night. Did you like it?"

"Very impressive, Mrs B." And he had liked it – the heat and smell of gas lighting, the gold and bright paint of the auditorium, the conversational buzz of tier after tier of faces, the married ladies recognizing friends, and the parties of single gentlemen eyeing those bold, brightly dressed girls who strolled along the aisles without ever taking a seat – he'd enjoyed it all. "Spectacular. We had a box, of course." He winked at Cherry, who shut his mouth on whatever comment he was about to make.

"A box!" she said, "fancy that!"

"And very pretty company."

"I wondered when you'd get to it," she said archly, and removed Cherry's empty bowl.

"Well, I'm glad someone enjoyed last night," said Cherry when she had gone. "The plays were all right – there was plenty going on, what with murders and battles and plots – but the company! Strewth!"

"If I meet Mackeson again," said George thoughtfully, "one of us will punch the other on the nose."

"You do that. And bend that poker he's got up his backside. As for little Miss Sarah, she's a right spitfire."

"She is, isn't she," said George, and started on his porridge.

Sarah had sat icily proud in her silks to watch the stage while the Duke of Gloucester murdered his way through half the nobility of England. She neither gasped, nor applauded, nor gave any clue to the cause of her furious mood.

In the interval, when Eleanor praised Charles Kean's vigorous and graceful playing of the role, Sarah had responded, "It's as well he has that to recommend him. He speaks very strangely."

"He is a beautiful elocutionist," said Eleanor, indignantly. "You can hear every word."

George drew the orange out of his pocket. He, too, had been struck by the piercing nasal quality of Kean's voice, though the incongruity of such an athlete playing Crouchback had passed him by. He peeled and split the orange, and offered it to Sarah.

Mackeson, turning his shoulder on this familiarity, said to Eleanor, "The Queen thinks very highly of Kean, so you are in excellent company when you admire him."

“So I gather,” said Sarah, as she took a segment of orange. “Thank you, Mr Davenport. Perhaps the Queen, too, speaks as though she has a permanent cold in the head.”

During the second interval, between the curtains closing at the end of “Richard the Third” and opening on the romance of “Blue Beard,” Cherry complained of the heat, and grumbled that in any other theatre there would at least be sherry to drink. He got up and escaped into the corridor. George considered following him, but decided it would be more fun to observe the entertainment inside the box. Eleanor was carrying on a *sotto voce* conversation, evidently prompting Mackeson to talk over Sarah's silence. The result was a patronizing, town-mouse-to-country-mouse enquiry as to whether George admired the lighting effects of Drury Lane.

George stared back in his best high-nosed manner.

“Pleasant enough, I daresay. Coal-gas is always superior to candles, if only because the increased light and the variability allow of more naturalistic playing.” He saw Sarah press her fingers over her lips, as she had on that first evening, to hide a smile. “I'm pleased to inform you that these days even provincial towns have the benefit of gas-lighting.”

Mackeson withdrew in a cold rage. Eleanor attempted to distract him by discussing Shakespeare's language, which she thought “magnificent,” but Sarah mercilessly contradicted them both.

“Perhaps half the lines may have been the Bard's. The rest were supplied by Mr Cibber – possibly the first Poet Laureate to be ridiculed by all his fellows.”

“He has made a very affecting tale of it all the same,” said Eleanor, from beyond Mackeson's disapproving profile. “Oh, those poor little Princes – what a dreadful fate, to be smothered and thrown in the river. I could cry just thinking of them!"

"Hear hear," said Mackeson, refusing to look at Sarah. "Death in battle was too good for such a villain! It doesn't matter who wrote it, it's a dashed fine play."

"Oh, certainly," said Sarah offhandedly. "Neither Shakespeare nor Cibber has allowed history get in the way of a good story."

George chuckled over the breakfast table, appreciating again the verbal duels of the evening. He also remembered the words of King Richard, "Was ever Woman in this humour wooed?" Picturing Sarah's scornfully lifted head, George wondered the same thing.

Mrs Bowe broke his recollections with a shrill prompt to Betsy to serve their ham, and Cherry repeated, "Yes, a proper little vixen is that Miss Sarah."

CHAPTER 20.

London, 17 May 1838

"If there's one thing makes up for having to spend Sundays at Stony," said Cherry, "it's being in London on a Thursday."

George and Cherry were taking their morning constitutional, and today Cherry was leading him west through a maze of little courts and back streets that George hadn't yet had time to explore.

"And if you haven't washed behind your ears," warned Cherry, "I won't take you to watch. It's posh, is Lincoln's Inn."

George only laughed at him. All through the past week the stablemen at the Swan had been brushing and re-brushing horses, polishing harness, slicking-down edges or rubbing-up brasswork that already gleamed like gold. Today, the Mail coaches were gathered in Lincoln's Inn Fields ready to parade through London's smartest streets.

The annual Mail Coach Procession was a public affair. The major contractors received printed programmes, and a set of tickets that could be used by their families or their off-duty drivers and guards, to ride in inside seats. Each driver taking part dressed to match the guards, in new Post Office red coats laced with gold, and a man would have had to be at death's door before he yielded up the reins of his Mail on such an occasion.

At Lincoln's Inn Fields, the friends and family stood about, arguing over who would face forward and who back, noting who had been invited, and who was conspicuously absent, and lastly preferring their own finery to that of any other passengers. Although as stage coachmen George and Cherry had no role in the procession, they had no trouble working their way in to join their fellow drivers.

"In the old King's day," said Cherry, "there was twenty-seven Mails. I don't suppose there'll be so many here today. I mean, the Woodside Mail's gone – Mr Horne gave that up early in the year."

"Yeah, Mr Chaplin did mention it," said George. But the horses shone with health and good grooming, their harness was bright and supple, and each team seemed more perfectly proportioned than the last. Any regret was soon smothered by his excitement at the equine power and beauty lined up for the procession.

No gathering of coachmen could be complete without the deepest criticism of the horseflesh at the business end. George studied the greys of the Exeter and Devonport Mail, and compared them to the teams either side, before he said, "I swear these aren't Mr Chaplin's horses."

"Ah, they'll be a team out of a gentleman's stable," said Cherry,."Some of 'em like to lend hosses for the procession. Ask Ward, up on the box there. He'll tell you whose they are."

"I don't like to trouble him."

Cherry had no such qualms. "Oi, Ward!"

The young coachman looked down at him. "Hallo, Cherry. We've a fine day for it. Are you riding with anyone?"

"No," said Cherry, coming closer, "we haven't got tickets, we'll walk. This young fellow here is asking what team you've got in hand."

"How-de-do?" The two men looked each other over with much the same critical eye they applied to the horses. Ward had driven teams professionally since he was seventeen, and his skill with the ribbons was legendary. "Seen you about, but don't know your name. Are you new?"

"New enough, I suppose. Mr Chaplin put me onto the Albion last month. George Davenport."

"Ah!" said Ward, and leaned down to shake hands. "You're the man who shares lodgings with Cherry."

"Yeh, and beginning to wish I didn't. His jokes are starting to repeat, like a bad kipper." Cherry tipped George's hat over his eyes. He laughed and replaced it, and came back to ask, "So who does your team belong to?"

"Sir Henry Peyton."

"Very nice." George could fancy himself on an open road with that team in hand. "Thoroughbreds?"

"Yes. I like blood-horses, and these are admirable. You don't often find a team of greys of this quality."

"I bet they would set the pace if you let them. Makes you wonder where all those old cripples come from that we see out in the country, doesn't it?" said George impulsively, and then regretted the remark. He would have apologized, if Ward had not agreed with him.

"Even these, good as they are, won't be in as hard condition as my favourite team. But then, today is just a pretty trot round Hyde Park."

"Who's going to lead the parade? You?"

"No, I'm afraid not. The programme says Liverpool, followed by Manchester and Bristol, and then ourselves. Various horsemen in between – I suppose to lend tone to the affair." Ward shifted his whip to his rein-hand, and drew out his watch. "If you don't mind, we are close to time, I think."

George took the hint, raised his hat, and moved away. Ward's observation was supported by the fact that the proprietors' friends and families had begun to climb into their respective coaches.

"We're in posh company, you know," said Cherry. "There, that's Mr Sherman getting into the Glasgow Mail – him with the black satin shirt-front."

George blew in astonishment. "Very fancy! I can understand why they want him to ride inside – with the sun on those diamonds, we could all be blinded."

"Ah, but everyone rides inside. They're going up West, among the toffs. To have outsiders lookin' in at the upper windows," said Cherry in mincing tones, "would be – ugh – so dreadfully common! Look lively, now, George. If we cut along that side, we can watch 'em away down Long Acre."

The procession was a magnet for anyone who wasn't working, and there were crowds of people lining the route. Little groups stood outside the gates of Lincoln's Inn Fields, and others straggled away along the roadsides. George noticed two girls among them, one plump and dark, one fair and slender, who glanced back at him and swished their skirts and put their heads together as though giggling. Expensive ones, he decided – well fed and clothed, the paint on their faces subtly done, but undoubtedly whores.

Cherry, noticing his attention, said, "You keep your eyes out of Whetstone Park. They might give you a present your sweetheart won't thank you for."

"A wink costs nothing," said George. Cherry's remark was a reminder that he hadn't yet replied to Lucy's most recent letter. He excused himself, guiltily, thinking that if he was going to write to her about the procession, he'd better see as much of it as possible. But at the sound of the first post-horn blowing "Start," all thought of girls, even Lucy, disappeared.

"Here they come," said Cherry, at his shoulder.

At two dozen repeats of the bright, staccato call his throat tightened so that for a moment he could scarcely speak. He wasn't part of the Procession this year, but he knew he should be here some day. No, not "some day." Next year.

Two horsemen in livery rode ahead of the Liverpool Mail, and the Manchester Mail followed. Another rider, then the grey horses of the Bristol Mail and the Quicksilver, and at a strict trot in due order came all the other coaches, horns blowing, wheels grinding. The Mails shone black and maroon, their scarlet-spoked wheels sparkling in the sun, and the everyday drab cushions on the driving boxes were concealed under gold-embroidered hammercloths.

Cherry punched him on the arm. "Worth seeing, eh?" he shouted.

When Ward brought the "Quicksilver" level with them, by unspoken agreement they skirted the groups of spectators and ran along with the procession.

They crossed Drury Lane – and George forgot all about the theatres, possessed as he was by the spectacle of the teams and the coaches trotting down Long Acre, the horses bending to their bits and lifting their feet in an endless, thunderous, ground-shaking dance, down St Martin's Lane into Trafalgar Square, and along Pall Mall. Beautifully dressed people stood on balconies or at upper windows and looked over the crowds to clap as each Mail went by.

Opposite Carlton House, the Liverpool Mail checked and began a right turn into St James's Square. Cherry touched George's arm, puffing a little.

"Ease up here. They have to make a salute to Lordy."

"Lordy?"

"Lichfield," said Cherry. "You know, the Postmaster General. They've got to go round three sides of the square here and come out at the other corner. We can get a bit ahead of 'em. Come on!"

He set off at a run once more, and George followed. He hadn't been this far into the West End, in spite of Cherry's sardonic encouragement, so he didn't know why there were so many spectators here. The streets were very grand and wide, but even so, they were so full of people he thought the drivers might be forced to walk their horses for fear of knocking someone down. The street sellers had clearly expected the crowds. He could smell hot pies and cow heel, and if he fancied trotters or ham sandwiches, there were any number of trays for him to choose from; or fatty cakes, gingerbread or brandy-balls, with ginger beer to wash them all down. The crowd itself smelled like the cheap end of a tavern – and who were these foolish women, dithering in front of him? He touched his hat briefly and sidestepped them, trying to keep Cherry in sight.

"Well met, Mr Davenport!" A woman's voice, brisk, almost strident. A hand on his sleeve.

It was Sarah Chaplin, demure this time in a lavender bonnet and striped walking-dress, and with her maid in attendance. Why did she keep crossing his path? He wanted to just nod and take off with Cherry. And then Sarah smiled at him, her intense gaze as compelling as her fury at the theatre, and reluctantly, he stopped and took off his hat.

Sarah nodded and her elderly maid sketched a curtsey.

"Be covered, Mr Davenport. Would you help us, please?"

"How can I do that, Miss Sarah?" He put his hat back on. "I'm afraid I'm a stranger to this part of the city. You must surely be more at home than I am."

"Yes, the procession always passes very close to our house. I thought I would walk up to watch, but there is such a press –" she gestured about her – "that I'm afraid we shan't be able to see." She smiled at him again, pretending a helplessness entirely at odds with her powerful self-possession. He was mildly irritated that after her near-scandalous behaviour at the theatre, he was again being used to solve her problems. But, still, she was the Guv'nor's daughter, so he elbowed a space between a stout matron and a young fellow in sailor's uniform, and by a little step towards the roadway invited her forward. She moved confidently, much closer than he expected, her flounced skirt and its bulk of petticoats pushing against his boots. She smelled of lavender, very clean. He checked his thoughts by reminding himself that she probably had a battery of powders and perfumes to suit the colour of her dresses.

And then she said, "Ah! here they come!" and he was close enough to hear the little quiver of pride in her voice. That was unexpected. He hadn't thought her interest in the coaches would be at all deep, but there was something childish and enthusiastic in her vibrating voice and sparkling eyes, something very much in tune with his own feelings.

He said, “I saw Mr Ward this morning at Lincoln’s Inn Fields with a very fine team. Take a bet, Miss Sarah, whether he’ll be in the lead.”

The lavender bonnet flicked round and she flashed an amused glance up at him. “It would be a shame to take your money, Mr Davenport. The Liverpool Mail is to lead, and since Papa and Mamma and Eleanor and William are inside there is not a shadow of doubt that it will do so. I’m sure Mr Ward told you that. And I’m sure he will also have told you that his Quicksilver is the fastest Mail on the road. He is very proud of it being the only one that carries a name.”

“He didn’t tell me that,” said George, but he was entertained nonetheless.

“Most of Papa’s Mails will be in the first rank. Let me recite them to you – Liverpool, Manchester, Bristol, Devonport, Halifax, Holyhead – “

“Very clever, Miss Sarah. You don’t have to impress me, y’know. I’m just a driver.”

Again that toss of the bonnet, the flash of honey-brown eyes. “You sell yourself lower than you did at Drury Lane, Mr Davenport. Here is Mr Cherry. He thinks you are worth looking for, no matter how humble you pretend to be.”

Was that a compliment? He was embarrassed by her intensity.

Cherry came back, pushing through the crowd. “Davenport! I thought you’d gone and lost yourself! Oh – ah – afternoon, Miss Sarah.” He tipped his hat to her and to the maid. “Miss. I might’ve known Davenport would be teasing pretty ladies.”

"You are mistaken, Mr Cherry," said Sarah. Her voice sounded even cooler than her workaday composure. "We asked him to make room for us to see the Mails, that is all."

The black team of the Edinburgh Mail pulled up level with them, and behind it the Exeter, the Glasgow, and the Leeds, so that the parade came to a halt with its tail end still winding out of St James's Square. Cherry looked sideways at George and muttered, "Hope you're on your best behaviour, mate. We could be here a few minutes."

The leading Mail was now standing opposite the towered brick front of St James's Palace. The coaches behind it were still and the crowd went quiet.

"Lord, what's happening now?" said George. "Why don't they go on?"

Cherry only cocked his head. His attitude suggested intense listening. Sarah remarked to George, "King William used to appear at the window to review the coaches – so it's very likely…"

From the head of the procession a loud voice cried, "We salute – Her Gracious Majesty! God Bless Her!"

All the coachmen and guards took off their hats. "Her Majesty: God Bless Her!" they repeated. The crowd broke into cheering, and the maid cried with them, "The Queen, the Queen, God Bless Her!"

Sarah, demure and ironic at the same time, clapped her gloved hands, and the two men echoed her restraint. Then the coachmen and guards replaced their hats, and the parade began once more to move off.

"That's better," said George.

"Don't you want to go along and wave to the Queen?" asked Cherry.

"I don't suppose she'd know me, even if I did," said George dryly, and held his place.

Sarah remarked, "The Procession officially celebrates her birthday, but I don't think that is today. Eliza? Is it Her Majesty's birthday?"

The maid, who was drifting with the crowd towards the Palace, turned back and answered, "No, Miss Sarah, it's next week."

"Thank you. Do you remember the year when our Rosa fell ill – wasn't there almost a riot during the Procession?" She explained to George, "Rosa was one of my little sisters."

"Was?" He saw her nod. "I'm very sorry."

Eliza said, "Ah, God rest her. Fancy you remembering that."

"I'd hardly forget such a thing," said Sarah tartly.

"No, of course. Poor little soul. What I meant was, fancy you remembering the story from back then. You and Miss Marianne can't have been more than nine, and Mr Chaplin didn't let you children go to watch in those days. You see, they used to put casks of porter outside the Palace, for the coachmen to drink the King's health. The coaches hadn't hardly set off again before people was fighting for what was left."

"I expect they spilled more than they drank," said George, watching yet another splendid team trot by.

"No doubt." Sarah lifted her head, as though to shake off whatever memories had clouded her mood. "Now, we shan't be able to keep up with the Mails through Hyde Park, so I plan to walk back to Trafalgar Square and wait for them returning to the Post Office. Would you and Mr Cherry care to accompany me?" It was clear that she expected them to agree.

The horses were trotting away now up the Mall and most of the crowd seemed to be drawn after them. Sarah's choice of route went in opposition to the flow and it became difficult for the four of them to walk abreast, so George found himself beside Sarah as the last of the Mails went by, while Cherry and the maid fell in behind.

"I would very much like to drive a Mail," said Sarah at last.

"You echo my own thoughts – but I didn't know you could handle a team."

"I can't," she said, then laughed at his confusion. "Only eccentric heiresses itch to drive themselves through City streets. But I've always envied the coachmen on the Mails – *Clear the road, I'm coming through.*"

"It's grand fun. I shall hope to be back on a Mail for next year's Procession."

"Ah," said Sarah, with a change of tone. "Well! Who lives will see, I daresay."

She walked on without explaining. George found her silence more restful than the seething politeness of her theatre visit. The procession tailed off to the last of the guards and coachmen on foot, and finally a string of bugle-blowing, whip-cracking mounted postboys. After they had gone by, the streets seemed much too quiet. George tried again to engage her in conversation.

"I see there's a new booking-clerk at the Swan."

"Oh! You have noticed."

"Don't they want you in the office any more?"

"Not just at present," said Sarah. Her voice crackled, and she looked up at him, taking a deep breath as though debating whether to confide further. She said in a rush, "Papa took on the new man as soon as he heard of Sharpe's conviction. It was Mamma who told me that I was no longer needed. She said the work was not suitable for me – that I had pushed myself forward on the excuse of Sharpe being taken, and Papa had only permitted it for short time because he had not liked to disappoint me. I could hardly speak, I was so angry. She has always helped Papa! She keeps the books, and writes his letters! She even encouraged me to do so! Then she dared – dared to say that there are times when a wife may be embarrassed to work in a public office – she said I ought to look at our family and consider how she behaves. I was disgusted! Do you know that the youngest in our family is not yet old enough to be weaned? But oh, no, I should model myself on her, and confine myself to helping from home. Why? I am not a wife! I have no intention of ever being a wife!"

George cleared his throat and said, "No. Yes. I mean, I do understand." Her unladylike reference to her father's "litter of pups," as Dixon had called it, seemed to treat him once more as an equal. He glanced over his shoulder in case Cherry was listening, but he was telling Eliza one of his jokes.

Sarah continued, "Eleanor is engaged, so she is perfectly content to remain at home with Mamma. But William – he is only sixteen – yet Papa says he may take over one of the inns! It is so unfair! I'm older than he is, and no less clever! I am not content to be an ornament! I wish to be of use!"

Her frustration reminded him of how he himself had burned to drive a four in hand. That was why he'd left home– all on account of that flame, that had forced him to move on again and again to suffer with pair coaches in Manchester, to flatter visitors on the Buxton summer stage, until he earned his place on the Newcastle Mail and the Albion. It hadn't occurred to him that a woman might cherish ambitions of similar intensity, and have no means of achieving them.

"Perhaps," he suggested, trying to avoid the difficulty, "you'll marry and then the business will become less important to you."

She turned a look of real rage on him, hotter than her sarcasm at the theatre. "Don't you listen? I thought you of all people would understand! But no, all you can do is to offer me conventional platitudes, like everybody else. Eliza! We will make our own way from here. Good day, Mr Davenport! Mr Cherry."

George and Cherry raised their hats, and watched in astonishment as she strode off along Cockspur Street, cleaving a way through the crowds, with Eliza trotting every third step in her wake.

"Now what was all that about?" asked Cherry. "You don't want to cross that one, mate. She has a temper that Jehovah would be proud of."

"Don't I know it," said George. He replaced his hat and looked round the wide expanse of Trafalgar Square. "Which way d'you think we should go?"

"Ah, we can keep out of her way up Regent Street." It seemed that Cherry's mind was on other things. Eventually he said, "There's something that niggles me. You'll have seen Sherman's hosses? The black 'uns. You see he put on new harness for the procession? It's like a tradition, everybody does it. But the Guv'nor's hosses – well, you have a good look when they come by again. It's all been spit-an'-polished all right – but the harness isn't new."

CHAPTER 21.

George wrote to Lucy that night:

We have had great goings-on here. Everyone has been busy getting the Mails cleaned to parade through London.

Working hard was always a good excuse for not writing. He needn't tell her that the cleaning had nothing to do with him.

We watched the Mails salute the Queen outside St James's Palace. There were a great many people in the West End, though I am told not so many as in other years, and better-behaved. I think they came to see Her Majesty rather than the Procession but Cherry says Londoners use any excuse to have a good time. I believe you will enjoy yourself too when you come here.

I told you about Sharpe, the booking-clerk. He was tried on Monday at the Old Bailey and found guilty of forging those marriage papers. I think that in King George's time a forger would have been hanged or transported, so Sharpe was lucky to be only confined for two years – if you can call it lucky to spend two years of your life in Newgate.

I send you a half sovereign under the seal of this letter. Send any reply by Mr Walker or Mr Lloyd but do not give money to Mariah, for she did not pay the stamp for your last. Have you discovered who stole your money? Please do not feel you are at fault! Have you seen anybody wearing your ring? I am sorry that you cannot wear it, and sorrier that you cannot yet come to me here. However, the coach fares are lower now than they have ever been – I am told it is competition from the railways that has driven them down – so if I send more money in my next you should be able to afford an inside seat. That will be more agreeable for you than bearing the dust and hot sun.

I am sure you will keep my letters where neither Mariah nor your Mother may find them. Read them as I read yours, and be brave, my lovely.

your affectionate

George

He did not tell her about Drury Lane, nor explain that putting the gold under the seal was Sarah's idea. He thought Lucy might not understand.

CHAPTER 22.

22 May 1838

Chaplin rose to his feet and tapped a spoon against a glass for silence.

"Gentlemen."

The coachmen's room at the Swan was full. Window-shaped chunks of mid-day sun lit blocks of drivers and guards, leaving others in strong shadow. They were mostly sitting back after their meal, drinking their tea or porter, and waiting for the Guv'nor to explain why he'd called them together. Some wore off-duty broadcloth coats and light trousers, but George recognized men in uniform from the North of England Mails, and he knew others who drove stages to Liverpool and Manchester and places in the West of England. There were guards, too, including Clark, Thetford and Cordock off the Albion – yet this room full of men was only a fraction of Chaplin's staff.

As they sat up and quietened to listen, the burly fellow next to George muttered, "Aye-aye. This is where Billy Bite-em-Sly lives up to his reputation."

The man was a stranger, probably a coachman from one of the other inns. George, having not heard the nickname recently, looked blank for a moment, but on his other side Cherry's expression said, "Don't bother about him."

Chaplin began, "You will all be aware that the Southampton Railway has now opened for business. From this week the Mail coaches for Holyhead, Manchester,

Liverpool and Carlisle are being carried on the trucks of the Euston to Birmingham Railway. A stretch of the Great Western line between Paddington and Maidenhead is ready to open.

"Do you remember that last winter Mr Sherman pitted his Red Rover coach against the steam engines? You may be astonished to hear me acknowledge that for once, he actually won!" They laughed obediently. "If I were to take a leaf out of Mr Sherman's book, you might hear me asking you to drive ever greater lengths, at ever faster speeds, to race against the railways.

"Now, I know very well how competitive you coachmen can be! You would try to do it. I know that. I know that very well. But it would make terrible demands of you, and you would kill my teams in trying. Of course our most spirited customers, who like nothing better than a fast and jolly ride, would cheer you on. But although we honour and respect them, the Quality are not the mainstay of our trade. You all know that we are really paid by the stout publicans, the thin undertakers, the parsons, the grandmothers and the not-quite-military gentlemen who are too timid yet to travel on the rail-road – and they would faint from sheer fright!

"Go with me in thought a little further, if you will. We are told that the railways can travel, not just twice but three times as fast as we do. Would it be reasonable to demand that you drive at thirty miles in an hour? Common sense will tell you that even a team of Derby winners could never keep up such speeds. You all know that I am a man of common sense, and you won't expect me to make such demands of my servants or my horses."

"What he means," muttered George's cynical neighbour, "is that he wouldn't make any money at it, even if he tried."

"I ask you to follow me in thought now to Liverpool. A rail-road connected that port to Manchester as long ago as 1830. In that year there were over thirty coaches and Mails carrying passenger traffic between the two cities. A year later, how many were there? Only two. So we arrive an one inescapable conclusion. Railways take business from the Road. Because of the extent of my trade, the railways compete with me, wherever they are built. I have no need to wait to see what may happen, when I have a direct example, from Liverpool, that tells me what will happen. My trade will drop off until I can only sustain one coach in every ten of those I run now." Chaplin paused, then said very deliberately, "I shall withdraw coaches before that drop occurs. That is why you are here today. Your coaches have witnessed the railways being built towards Southampton, Liverpool and the West of England. It is your coaches that I must withdraw first."

A rumble of protest greeted this, and Cherry punched George's arm. "I knew it. Didn't I say so!"

George, like most of the men, shifted angrily on his chair. They had all been half expecting it, trying for the past year to ignore the accumulating evidence. Now the time had come, they would see how well or badly their Guv'nor intended to treat them.

Chaplin put up a hand, and the hubbub died down. "I regret the need for this action as much as you do, but you are all familiar with my policy. I will not run coaches where they cannot carry enough trade. Until now it has been possible to compensate by uniting two routes or withdrawing a night coach. But you can see from your own numbers here that the problem today is very much larger.

"For a little while, I foresee a rise in activity on country routes that feed the railway stations, and I can move a few of my coaches there, but I cannot find places for all of you. However, I have friends in the railway business – "

"I'll bet he has," said the cynical man.

"I can engage to find employment for you there if you are so inclined. Guards, in particular, may find the work very similar." He paused, and took a sip of wine. The men turned over the suggestions in their minds, but they waited, seeing that there was more to come.

"Mr Horne and I have also contracted to provide the Euston to Birmingham Railway with a shuttle service, using some of the coaches that we withdraw. We will run between Denbigh Hall and Rugby, covering some forty miles of ground where the railway is held up by the difficulties of the tunnel at Kilsby. We will need drivers and guards on that service, until the rail-road is complete. Three or four months perhaps." He smiled, conspiratorially. "I have no doubt there will be an immense amount of lucrative traffic to be carried towards Her Majesty's Coronation."

"Well, that's a bit more like it," said Cherry.

Chaplin had their attention again now. The faces along either side of the table, flushed with the warmth of the room, with beef and porter, and the daily toll of the weather, were all turned towards him like a border of overblown flowers.

"Your coaches will run as normal for the remainder of the week. This evening, each coach will deliver notices, detailing the changes, for all our subcontractors to distribute.

"For each of you who attends my office this afternoon, I will make what provision I can to guarantee your continued employment. So, gentlemen – I look forward to our further association, and I give you my usual toast:

"Shouldering! But don't let me catch you at it!"

The men's response was only an echo of the gleeful shout it had been in other years, and the old joke raised no smiles. Chaplin sat down between Mr Ibbotson and Mr Nunn and made quiet conversation while he watched his men digest the news.

George's neighbour drank off his porter and said, "Well, old Bite-em-Sly'll be weeding out the faces that don't fit. I ain't going to hang around his office all bloody day." He reached for another bottle, and turned away to talk to the driver on his other side.

George was subdued, studying his mug, so Cherry nudged him. "Well? Would you fancy that railway coach service?"

They both drove daily past Denbigh Hall, and they knew that a temporary station had been built next to the inn, north of Fenny Stratford. Since the railway navvies left, tents had been put up, which were going to accommodate the coach horses, the drivers and the guards. It sounded as though the men would have the rough end of the deal, as rumour had it that they were to be dispossessed of their dormitory area during the day so it could be used as a dining room. George foresaw Denbigh Hall being a place of confusion, lost luggage, and restless discontent. He made a long face at Cherry. "I don't know."

"I reckon we could make a few bob."

George shook his head, still unconvinced. He watched Chaplin stand up and leave, together with Nunn and Ibbotson, for their offices.

When they had gone George said, “We'd be worse housed than navvies. I'd rather work a regular coach.”

“Ah, now there's the rub. There's a lot of blokes here might feel the same way, and you heard the Guv'nor, he'd be pushed to place 'em all. Me, I wouldn't mind a summer under canvas. We'd all be mates together.”

“That wouldn't last long,” said George, “if the only fun is getting blind drunk.”

“Well, it'd still be work. Thank Gawd for Kilsby Tunnel, I say. They won't get that open till the autumn. The longer they take, the better, I say.”

“A coachwheel says they'll have it open for the Coronation.”

“And a coachwheel says they won't.”

The serving women were coming in now to clear tables. The drivers and guards, in ones and twos, were rising from their chairs in a general movement towards the offices.

George sighed. “I can see we might draw a few bob until they open the line, but where would that leave us? Nowhere.”

“If we don't sign up, we might find ourselves nowhere now. We'd best find out what the Guv'nor has to offer. Come on.”

As they passed the booking office door, Foyle spotted them and called out, “Davenport. There's a letter here for you.”

George paused. “Are you sure?” Nobody wrote to him except Lucy, and she could only just have had his last letter.

“I hope it's paid for,” said Cherry with a chuckle.

“Yes and yes,” said Foyle. “Here.”

George recognized the handwriting, and his heart sank. There must be some very pressing reason for Lucy to write back so soon. Perhaps she was angry, tired of the delay. The twinge of guilt only added to his worries.

"I might as well read it," he said. "We're going to have a longish wait to see the Guv'nor." He took a deep breath, pushed his thumb under the seal, and began to read.

CHAPTER 23.

In the tap-room of the Swan, George handed the letter to Cherry. The queue for Mr Chaplin's office had looked an hour long, and he'd had no trouble persuading Cherry to a couple of pints of ale.

"Well go on, read it."

"You sure?" said Cherry in surprise. "Doesn't feel right, me reading your young lady's secrets."

"Read it. You'll see why I asked."

Cherry unfolded the paper. "Her writing's a dreadful scrawl," he grumbled. "And crossed, again!"

Blue Bell, Carlisle.

Saturday, 19 May 1838.

My Dearest

Your letter arrived this morning. Forgive me for writing back so soon – it is late and I am tired, but perhaps if I write I may be able to see a way – I must settle my mind before church tomorrow. I must come to you as soon as possible. The cardinal has not visited since my illness – I have held back from telling you until I was sure – now I know I must be with child – and I cannot conceal it from Mam for very long.

Cherry gave George an old-fashioned look. "Must – must – must!" he said. "Oh dear!"

Your half sovereign arrived safely but I do not yet have enough money both to purchase an inside seat on a coach to London and to pay for a room and food on the way. Mr Mounsey however suggested that part of the journey, from Manchester to Rugby, might be undertaken more quickly and cheaply on the rail-road. He has engaged to purchase me a seat on his coach, and his guard will direct me to the rail-road station at Manchester. He advises me to stay overnight in Birmingham, but he thinks you may have better information on the best way to convey me from Rugby to London.

Cherry turned the paper sideways. "I hate trying to read these crossed things."

I do hope this plan will not vex thee. I have told him nothing, only that I wish to be with thee. Tell me how soon I may come and where I shall see thee. I will do my best to be patient until then, and I hope and pray to be a good wife to thee and a mother to our child.

I send thee kisses

thy loving heart

Lucy

Cherry put down the letter and said, "Kisses or no kisses, I reckon it's a pity you let her know where you were going."

George, slightly panicked by the responsibility implicit in the letter, had briefly thought the same thing. He had spent the last few years chasing his own ambitions and having fun; he'd never seen himself as a married man and a father. Yet Cherry's open antagonism made him look at the matter from Lucy's point of view, and the moment he thought of leaving her and the child to Ma Hennessy's tender mercies, he knew he couldn't do it. Ma would either turn her out, or abort the baby. He couldn't let it happen.

"She might be making up a story to keep a hold on you," said Cherry. "And even if it's true, the kid might not be yours."

"Shut up. You're no judge." A baby was possible, even likely.

"Oh, all right," said Cherry. "You suit yourself."

"Yes, I will, thanks! I'll do the right thing by her. Yes, I will, so don't look at me like that."

"Your best hope is that she's mistaken," said Cherry. "Do you want her hanging round your neck for the rest of your life? She'll never be out of your hair. Or your bed!"

"What on earth – ? Actually, that's quite a thought. I mean, if she's expecting, there's nothing more to worry about, is there? None of that is-she-isn't-she, do-we-or-don't-we. The bun's in the oven and that's that!"

"Wait till you're being kept awake by a howling infant, that's all."

"Give-us the letter. I wish I hadn't showed it to you now."

Cherry, with a rueful face, gave it back.

"Well," said George. There was something odd in that last exchange with Cherry, but he wasn't going to pursue it. There was quite enough to deal with in the letter itself. They sat in silence for a minute or two, letting the dust settle. "All right then. The first thing I've got to do is…"

"Find out if you've got a job," said Cherry.

"Ar, ey, I can't go and work out at Denbigh Hall, not now. I can't take Lucy to live in a field."

"She's a barmaid, isn't she? She'll cope."

"Are you stupid? You must be to make such a suggestion. She needs a home. And I've got to buy a ring – and, you know, call the banns. I'll have to find out which parish we're in at Falcon Street."

Cherry sat back as though pushing the problem away. "Oh, well if you're that set on doing it, pop into St Paul's. I'm sure they'd fix you up famously."

"Don't be ridiculous. Perhaps I should ask Mrs Bowe."

"You could get married at Stony Stratford. All three of you."

"Now you're disgusting. I'll tell her that I go to church at Stratford, but I want to get married from Falcon Street."

"Oh, yes, she'll swallow that, I don't think. You – church at both ends of the road! Ha! Why don't you keep a wife at both ends too? Fat Mary'll have you. You won't need to ask twice."

"Stop it," said George.

CHAPTER 24.

They rejoined the queue for Chaplin's office, and George shook himself out of his matrimonial problems. The men who had already seen the Guv'nor were still standing in the yard, but they huddled in little exclusive groups, and they all seemed to be from routes he didn't know. He thought the respected drivers like Ward must have already passed through and gone.

The door opened, and a man came out, shaking his head. Chaplin's voice called, "Next!" and another man went in. The interview was brief and he, too, came out with a glum expression.

"Take his offer on the railway coaches," he advised, as he passed. "There ain't much elsewhere, unless you want to turn guard on a steam engine."

Cherry made a face, but he said, "I wouldn't like to sit behind Chaplin's desk right now, giving out news like that."

"He's the Guv'nor," said George, without much sympathy. "It won't be much fun for us standing on this side of the desk, now will it?"

"Face to face, though? Over and over again? He could've given somebody else the job. You have to respect the fact that he didn't."

George shrugged.

"Next!"

The line shuffled forward. The exclamations of protest had subsided, and those still waiting now were thoughtful. They had prided themselves on being professionals who could keep time in all weathers, their horsemanship delivering Mail, parcels, newspapers, spreading the latest headlines, impressing all observers with their ten-mile-an-hour horses and three tons of coach, speeding along day after day.

"Next!"

As the man in front of him went in, George stepped up to the door. This was all a new experience for him. He had never been dismissed, always moving on of his own accord. Like the rest of the men, he was accustomed to adjustments of his work, when a coach's passenger licence changed between winter and summer, or timetables and routes were merged or split to demand. Even coaches and routes passed from one proprietor to another. He was, however, shocked to the core by the idea that the long-distance business as a whole might no longer depend on horses.

"Next!"

It was his turn. As he went into the office he noticed how the afternoon sun gleamed on the brass handles of Chaplin's desk, on the silver mounted horse's hoof inkstand, on the map of England on the wall, on the gilt-framed painting of a mail coach. The first time he'd been in that room, it had been evening and he'd been too tired to notice his surroundings, but now he appreciated, bitterly, how each item had been chosen to impress, a symbol of Chaplin's industry and wealth.

He thought it strange that the Guv'nor relaxed when he saw him. "Davenport. Did I see Cherry next in line? You'd better call him in." George obeyed. "I suppose you may have heard some good news from your guards?"

"No, sir, I haven't seen them."

Cherry came in, an enquiring expression on his face.

"Shut the door, will you? Let me put you both out of your misery. This afternoon, Mr Sherman has offered to partner me in both the Albion and the Greyhound coaches. He proposes that we continue to run towards Liverpool. There's a proviso that each coach picks up on alternate days from the Queen's Hotel, but other than that, you'll carry on as usual."

"Thank you, sir!" they exclaimed, with surprise and relief.

"Well, we'll see how it answers. However, I should warn you that Mr Sherman and I intend to practise the utmost economy. All the coachmen we retain, we are asking to drive greater lengths. So after the Coronation, Davenport, you'll have to go through to Dunchurch."

"Sir," he said. Damn. Driving on to Dunchurch would lengthen his night work. More bad horses and dodgy harness.

Chaplin continued, briskly, "Of course that means you'll arrive at the Dun Cow in the small hours, but you won't set off with the up coach until late morning so if you get your head down smartly you should have plenty of time for sleep – and at least you'll be under a roof, not a tent in a field. If you can drive two hard days you'll find the timetable gives you almost twenty-four hours off afterwards."

"I understand, sir."

"Cherry, you already drive precisely half the distance to Birmingham, so it would make no sense to lengthen your ground and shorten the other fellow's, would it! I hope you and young Davenport won't fall out over that!"

"Thank you, sir," said Cherry. Neither of them were inclined to protest. It was a far better outcome than either of them had expected.

"You both continue to draw your wages here, and you go out as usual tonight from the Swan. Now," said Chaplin, with his faint smile, "it appears you had my dinner and speech for nothing, so be off before I ask you to pay. Next!"

***

"You see, the Guv'nor hadn't forgotten us. He's a good and kind man," said Cherry, "as far as he can be."

They stood below the gas lantern, where Chaplin so often watched the Mails go out. Commercial, the first of the evening stagecoaches, was being got ready for its journey to Nottingham, with the Bristol Night coach beside it. To an inexperienced eye the yard might have seemed busy, but George and Cherry knew there were too many drivers and guards among the passengers, snapping at the Jew boys instead of joking with them, and staying longer in talk with the ostlers than they would normally do.

"They're all aggrieved," observed Cherry. There was too much emphasis in their gestures, too much edge to their voices. "It'll take more than a free dinner to turn 'em into servants of the railway."

George felt a kind of shyness, a guilty separateness in the knowledge that, for the moment, his job was safe. He thought Cherry probably felt the same. At any rate, neither of them moved to join the others.

"They'll find other places," he said, without much conviction. "Most of 'em anyway. Wouldn't you say?"

"Of course!" Cherry eased his shoulders, like a man who knows he has had a lucky break. "Y'know, I think the Guv'nor's right to knock off all those northern coaches. He should push all the dribs and drabs into one proper load, then we might pick up decent perks again."

George's expression remained sober. All his life, and all his father's life, English coachmen had been knights of the road, their skill and their teams the envy of the world. Now look at them. They were going to be ten-a-penny. Lucy was damned lucky that he still had regular work.

CHAPTER 25.

When George hesitantly told Mrs Bowe why he needed lodgings for Lucy, she was delighted.

"You done the right thing, asking," she said. "Lodgings is difficult to get, what with the people coming in to work, and the people coming for the Coronation. There'll be places cost as much as this, what isn't fit to put pigs into, let alone a gel in a delicate situation. But there's an easy answer. You give her your room, and you move in with Mr Cherry, until you get wed."

Cherry, who was sitting opposite George at breakfast, chuckled. "Hah! I'm not the marrying kind."

"That's just as well, because I wouldn't ask you," said George, with the insulting ease of friendship. "Mrs B, are you sure it's all right for her to lodge here? Is it respectable?"

"I'm sure I'm respectable enough, my dear," said the landlady, "and so are all my gentlemen, so I'll take no offence at the question, which I'm sure none was meant."

"Ar ey, Mrs B, would I even think of insulting you! But that's just it – you only take gentlemen." He winked at her out of habit, though his heart wasn't in it. "Her mother is a bit of a stickler, know what I mean."

"Such a stickler that your Lucy's got to run away to marry you? I know her kind! Don't you worry. Just let me know when she'll arrive, so I can arrange the beds."

"Do I get a reduction?" asked Cherry. "You know, for sharing?"

"I should charge you more, for providing company," she said, with a lofty toss of the head.

"Thank you, Mrs B," said George, and he caught her hand and kissed it. "You're a lovely woman. Really – you don't know what a weight that takes off my mind."

"Maybe I do know too," she said. "Me and Bowe got hitched when our first boy was on the way. We didn't say nothing of course, you'd be shamed if you did, but that was the way of it. It worked out all right, and a great strapping fellow he is now with six of his own! Pass me your plates, my dears, if you've both finished. And knowing you, I'll wager you haven't thought about where exactly you'll get hitched."

George handed over his plate and said, "Honestly, Mrs B, I don't know where to start."

"I thought as much. Are you Church of England?"

"I'm nothing in particular. Lucy is Church of England."

"Well, Betsy and me goes to St Vedast's in Foster Lane." She thrust the plates and cutlery at Betsy and shooed her out. "It'll save you a month if you tell Rector that your Lucy's been living here since Easter. Then you'll only have to wait for the banns to be called three times. Tell him that you're living at Stony Stratford, and that's why he ain't seen you afore." She nodded at George. "It'll all be right and tight. You send for her as soon as you can."

CHAPTER 26.

Stony Stratford, Thursday, 7 June 1838

In the stuffy interior of the coach, Lucy eased upright in her seat. The grey-haired lady opposite was asleep against her husband's shoulder, with her feet under the hem of Lucy's skirt, where they had wobbled at every bump over the past ten miles. The thin man next to her smelled of snuff and of trousers that had been sat in for far too long. What a blessing it would be to get away from them all, to relax and breathe fresh air and not to worry from minute to minute whether they would encounter another hilly stretch that might worsen her feelings of sickness.

There was a long-drawn out *Whhooo-oaa* from the driver above, and the rumble and grind of the wheels stopped at last. The thin man hopped out and reached under the seat for his luggage, and a swirl of warm dusty air blew in. Lucy tucked in her skirts to prevent him seeing her ankles. The grey-haired lady groaned and woke, and almost at once resumed the babble that had given Lucy a headache from Rugby to Towcester.

"Have we arrived, Alfred? Where are we? What time is it? Do you know whether there will be refreshments?"

Her husband leaned against the worn lining of the coach and so made enough room to draw out his pocket watch. "It is half past one, my dear. We have only five minutes, so if you wish to eat we had better hurry."

"Ham and spring cabbage is my fancy, but I suppose we shan't have time for that."

The thought of food was enough to make Lucy's gorge rise.

The lady looked critically at her and said, "You look very pale, child."

"I'm all right, Ma'am," said Lucy hastily. The journey had taught her how to use traveller's phrases to conceal her sickness. "I'm only a little uncomfortable, from sitting with my back to the horses. If you would draw your feet back, Ma'am, I'll take my bag."

A little elderly porter came along, rattling a hand barrow. He opened the near side door, and touched his cap. "Five minutes here, ladies and gentlemen. Good afternoon, Miss," he said, seeing Lucy with her bag in hand. "May I help you down?"

He unfolded the steps, and she got out and shook her skirts into order. "Oh, good afternoon! Is this the Cock Hotel?"

"There you are, Miss." He pointed above her head at the wrought-iron bracket that hung the painted sign halfway across the street. "Big enough for you?" He winked. It was evidently an old joke. "Now, are you sure you want to change here? If you're for London, this coach'll take you to the railway station at Denbigh Hall. You might not know that some of the coaches goes by the rail-road now."

"Oh, yes, I do know that, but I'm meeting one that doesn't."

"If you're sure, Miss, I'll take your bag."

They passed the garrulous lady and her spouse, who were buying pies from a street vendor with hurried intensity.

"I need to purchase a new ticket," said Lucy. "Where can I do that, please?"

The porter led her through the impressive doorway of the hotel to the desk where a stout, middle-aged man presided over the coach books.

"This young lady's going to London, Mr Farren."

"I intend to go by the Albion," she said.

"Ooh, no, you'll have to take the Tally-Ho. It'll be here in half an hour."

Lucy said, "I don't want the Tally-Ho. I don't know where it goes to."

"The Saracen's Head." Seeing her hesitate, Mr Farren added, "The next coach after that is the Stag, and that goes to the Bull'n Mouth, the Queen's as they call it now."

She had no idea whether these inns were anywhere near the Swan with Two Necks. "I would really like a seat on the Albion."

Outside, the guard was blowing "Start" as the coach pulled out into the street.

"It will have to be tomorrow, then," said Mr Farren, and turned the page. "Today's Albion left ten minutes ago."

She gave a little cry of disappointment.

"Only half full," added the porter, "so you wouldn't overtake it, even in the post-chaise."

"I couldn't afford a post-chaise." George hadn't waited for her, and he couldn't come back to Stony Stratford until the following evening. What on earth was she going to do? "I'm supposed to meet someone here. We arranged to meet and go up to London together. I never thought that I would miss the coach."

Mr Farren cleared his throat repressively, but the porter seemed to have taken a shine to Lucy, and suggested, "You could go by the next one, Miss, as far as Denbigh Hall. A train would get you into London in plenty of time to meet your friend."

Lucy shook her head. If she went by the railway she would have to ask her way from the station – wherever that might be – to the Swan with Two Necks. She would have to walk there and then ask for further directions, and trudge on to wherever George was lodging. If she went by coach to the Saracen's Head, she would have the same problem. In the city she would be alone, hungry and tired and very obviously a north-country girl, and she had learned early and hard not to trust strangers. She stiffened her spine. The best use of her money would be to stay here. She knew that George's timetable, which had compelled him to go, must also bring him back.

"I will stay." She thought a little show of feebleness might soften the clerk into helping her, so she brought out the lace-edged handkerchief that George had given her, and dabbed her eyes. The action made her realize that she was so tired she could easily have cried in earnest. "I know he'll come back for me."

"He?" said Mr Farren sharply. The porter seemed inclined to linger, but Mr Farren frowned at him. "You can go, Ned. I'll deal with this. Now, Miss, let me set you straight – I won't be party to anything underhand."

Lucy reminded herself that if George could have married her in Carlisle, they would already be man and wife. She said again, "I will stay."

Mr Farren breathed out dissatisfaction, but she fixed him with a steady blue gaze until he said grudgingly, "Very well. Wait here and I'll call Mrs Fox."

He shut the book and puffed away into an inner room, and Lucy sat on a bench against the wall to wait. Her hands were trembling, and she kept them busy smoothing the lace of the handkerchief. When Mr Farren reappeared behind his desk he was followed by a woman neatly dressed in black, who approached Lucy and said without preamble, "I believe you want a room."

Lucy stood up. "Yes." The woman's accent was so different from her own that it was hard to understand her, and she was not going to say "please" to someone who wouldn't address a customer politely.

"Hmph," said the housekeeper, looking her up and down. "A runaway servant, by the look of you!"

Lucy was offended by the disparagement of her sober Sunday dress, and her voice was sharp as she said, "Certainly not. I am meeting my husband."

"Really." Mr Farren sounded sceptical.

"Yes, really!" said Lucy, turning on him. "I expected to meet his coach here."

"You only said you were meeting someone. It sounds very fishy to me."

"Your name wouldn't be Hennessy, would it?" asked Mrs Fox. "Davenport's young lady? Then don't pretend he's your husband, because I know he ain't!"

"We are engaged to be married," said Lucy, blushing.

"You're a goose," said Mrs Fox. "It's Pigott who drives today's up coach to London. Davenport won't arrive till this evening."

“Oh!” said Lucy. She pressed the handkerchief to her mouth to stop herself giggling with relief. “So I’ve got them the wrong way round. Oh, how silly.”

“Indeed you are,” said the housekeeper. “Luckily for you, Davenport warned me yesterday, so I have a room ready. Come along, and bring your bag.”

As she led Lucy away, she added, “I recommend you to dine in your room. We still have a lot of roughs in town, navvies off the railway. You understand that the coach won’t be here till half past twelve tonight? I’ll send you a message when Davenport comes in.”

“How fortunate that he forestalled your mistake,” said Mr Farren, dryly, as he re-opened his book.

CHAPTER 27.

A rapping on Lucy's door woke her to a shadowed, moonlit room.

"Who's that? What's the time?"

The fat girl opened the door and said in her slow voice, "Mrs Fox says, if you want to see George Davenport you should come down now." She sniffed succulently, and waited without further comment until Lucy had got up, fastened her bodice and put on her boots. Then she led the way down two flights of stairs to the coffee room door.

"He's in there," she said, and thudded away down the passage. Lucy shook her head at the rudeness of the place, and went in.

A few late travellers sat round the main table. She couldn't see George among them, so she advanced warily to peer into each of the candle-lit curtained stalls.

When she found him he was talking to two guards, and a little fellow with corn-coloured hair who seemed to be another coachman. Her relief was so great that she wanted to kiss him, to dance, to sing. She could have kissed the guards, too, only they were all too absorbed in conversation to see her. Carefully, she moved with servant's discipline to stand just on the edge of their vision.

"Can I get you anything, gentlemen?" she asked.

"No, thank you."

She coughed. "Mr Davenport?"

George looked up – and it made her travels worthwhile to see how quickly he jumped to his feet, and to feel the warm clasp of his hands.

"Lucy, you tease!"

She gripped his fingers and laughed. Oh, what a wonderful smile he had! If only those fellows would look the other way instead of sitting there grinning, as though she were just another serving maid, and George her foolish swain.

"Did you have a good journey?" he asked. "Mrs Fox told me she'd find you a room."

"It was tiresome, but that doesn't matter now. I've had dinner and a sleep and I've found you."

She couldn't stop smiling, and when he smiled back – a sweet and kind smile, far less sardonic than she remembered – she hung on to his hand as though to let go would be to drown in all the questions she wanted to ask.

Cherry broke the tension by saying, "Bed calls. I'll be off. Come along, you fellows. We'll only be in the way of lovey-dovey talk." He stood up.

"Ah, no, Cherry – wait a moment –'

"I know your sweetheart wants you all to herself. We can all get better acquainted in the morning, can't we, Miss? Pleased to see you're all right, of course," added Cherry.

George moved aside to let the others out, then he drew her to the seat beside him, sitting close, still holding her hand. She made no effort to hide her delight. The travellers at the big table would be too sleepy to notice.

"You look thin, my lovely," he said. "Have some pie. We've made a hole in it, but there's plenty left."

She stacked the guards' plates and cutlery, while he pushed the pie and his own empty plate towards her. Now that she was properly awake, she was hungry, and it was very comforting to have him look after her when she knew how easily he could go off in his mind to horses and his driving career. She was determined to make the most of it, and said grace as rapidly as she dared.

Once she was eating he said, half as a question, "I thought you'd be hopping up and down on the doorstep waiting for me."

"Of course I was! But after I'd done that for a while, Mrs Fox told me you wouldn't be here till late, so I decided to have a lie down instead."

He laughed at that. "If I'd known you were lying down I'd have got here sooner! But I can't blame you – it's a long journey."

"But I had to come, didn't I?" She didn't tell him about the relief she had felt as she stole out of the Bell before her mother was astir, hurrying across the cold street to hide in the inn-yard and wait for the coach. "Me up there… You down here…"

"Up here. It's always Up to London."

"Really… But up or down – oh dear, what a very long way it is. I was so glad I stayed overnight in Birmingham. Did you know, the station at Rugby is only a wooden roof in a field? And when you change onto the coach the guards don't seem to know which tickets ought to be accepted. Even if I'd had a ticket all the way through to London, I might well have had to pay again. It's a shambles."

"It's the same at Denbigh Hall – or so I'm told. You'll do much better on the Albion with me and Thetford."

When she'd finished the pie, her fingers found his again. "Shall we walk out? I want to kiss thee, and I can't, not here. I know everyone around us is nearly asleep, but I daren't."

He grinned. "We can't have that, now can we?"

It was a warm night, and a full moon shone down on the dark, shuttered windows of the houses and inns along the High Street. George walked slowly beside her, until the scent of hedges and wet lowland meadows replaced the horse-smelling dust of the little town, and she paused to watch the moonlight on the river. It was cold and slow, flickering and slightly menacing. She knew that George was probably thinking of something else, but for once he didn't talk; instead he leaned against a tree and drew her to him, and in the wild drifting scent of the hawthorn he wrapped her in his arms and kissed her. She wanted nothing more than that – to stand there forever, at rest, safe and loved and at home. She was well aware that he was tame and kind because he was tired, but she was grateful all the same. So they stood quietly together, in the freedom of the night.

"Is thou happy?" she asked him, without daring to look up.

"I don't often think about it. I suppose so. For now. What about you? Was it worth coming all this way?"

"Yes. Nobody has ever cared about me before." Her arms tightened about him. "I'm happy, and I want to make thee happy. I'll do anything."

"And you won't be sorry that I asked you?"

"I'd have come anyway," she said. "Because I wanted to, because I know thou wants me." She put her arms round his neck, and kissed him again – not softly this time, but fiercely, desperately.

CHAPTER 28.

Friday, 8 June 1838

George drew out his watch for the third time and sighed.

"I hope Lucy's all right." They had finished their breakfast, and Cherry had leafed through Bell's Weekly Messenger, and still Lucy hadn't appeared.

"She's probably just tired," said Cherry. "Not used to travelling."

"If you say so."

"Well, while your little love bird gets her feathers fluffed up, I'm off to look round the market. Coming?"

George shook his head. "I'll wait."

"You're such a good boy," said Cherry, and smacked the newspaper into George's hands. "I'll see you later."

Lucy didn't come downstairs until George had read more than he cared to and was beginning to be bored. She was pale, and quite firm against his cheerful suggestions of bacon, eggs, coffee, milk, gruel. She ordered a slice of bread and a cup of weak tea, and Fat Mary set them on the table with a challenging rap and made a thumping departure.

"That girl's common," said Lucy, with an emphasis that made it a moral judgement.

"In both senses," agreed George. "You found her out soon enough."

"Well, of course! If she worked for me I'd have something to say to her."

There was a long pause, in which the sounds of the inn became magnified. Lucy ate calmly and a clock ticked with majestic indifference. A one-horse wagonette pulled up outside, took on passengers for the station, and set off again. Two coaches stopped, changed horses, and passed on. In the quiet after their departure, an auctioneer's voice droned from the corn market, a monotone broken by occasional pauses for breath and the smack of a stick on his leather gaiter. At last the conflict between Lucy's serenity and George's restlessness became intolerable.

He folded the paper irritably and put it down. "This place is too quiet."

She didn't answer, so he decided to be more direct. "It matters, you know. The trade's all going onto the rail-road. Mr Chaplin damn near turned me off. After the Coronation, he says I've got to drive through to Dunchurch. I don't suppose you know how far that is."

She looked up. "I didn't see the name anywhere."

"It's Rugby, or damn nearly. I'll only have twenty minutes' rest here at Stony, instead of a whole night."

"Oh," she said. "But that will lengthen your hours, won't it?"

"Double them, more like." He would have to drive for two days with no more than six hours' sleep. There would be no time for drinking sherry and playing midnight games of cards. "I suppose I should be thankful that the next down coach will have set off before I get back to London."

She hid a smile at his fretfulness, and said soothingly, “Well, that means thou’ll have me all to thyself the next day.”

“It isn’t going to be that easy. I shall be tired, so sometimes you’ll have to remind me how to be kind.”

“Oh, I think I shall do that all right.” She reached out and squeezed his hand. “Thou doesn’t have it in thee to be cruel. I’ve watched thee, remember – the fights thou’s had with other drivers have all been about unkindness, when men are rough with the horses they drive.”

“Of course! But that isn’t what I mean. When I do things wrong without thinking – or when I don’t do things – that’s when you must tell me. Don’t go silent and just put up with me as if I was one of your mother’s customers.”

She looked at him for a long moment as though considering whether to share a confidence. Then she said shortly, “There’s more than one set of my mother’s customers.”

He lifted his eyebrows. “Really? I would never have guessed!”

She hushed him, glancing round at the people in the coffee room. The little curtains partially closed out the other stalls, but they didn’t muffle conversation.

“Far from it. We lived in the Lanes.” She wouldn’t look at him. “I bless the preacher as showed her the power o’ God’s word. And the lasses as stood up for me.”

He knew by the dialect creeping back into her voice that the memories were painful. He wanted to sweep her into a big hug, but the room was public and he didn’t quite dare. How young had she been, and who were the girls? Why had they needed to protect her?

"I'se just glad to be free of her," she said. "I'd be shamed to tell thee more. Nay," she said quickly, when he was about to encourage her, "I cannot, I would weep. Thou wouldn't want that. If thou really wants to know… after we're married, maybe I can tell thee. When there's nobody listening. When we're easy with each other again. I promise I will."

He took her hand again and said deliberately, "I knew there was a reason why I wanted to kill the old bitch." Her fingers tightened on his, and it was the strength of her grip, as much as anything, that convinced him. "All right. I won't ask till you want to tell me."

"Now, Mr Davenport," she said, with a slightly crooked smile, "I must ask you to go and buy my ticket. I have the money ready."

"I won't let you pay, lovely."

"That's dishonest, George!" The brave Lucy of last night was back. "Mr Chaplin could dismiss you."

"Not at all. It's Tom Thetford an' me that you're doing out of the fare, and I know Thetford has a soft spot for pretty blondes. You might travel better if you ride up on the box with me, y'know, in the fresh air like, so you can see where you're going. It's much the best place to be."

"I don't think I should, when I haven't paid," she said. "And I don't like climbing up so high."

"Don't worry – nobody's going to look up your skirts!" He remembered teasing her mother about the keys of the tea caddy hidden in her petticoats. He should have up-ended the old bitch on her own fire. "We'll find a big coach apron to hide your ankles."

"No, George, I'll ride inside, please. Think how ashamed you'd be if I became giddy and fell off." He laughed at the idea, but she went on, "You can take some smelly old person on the box-seat with you, and I shall snooze inside like a seasoned traveller."

He protested, "Here! You don't think of me as a smelly old person, do you?"

"And what makes you think I think of you, at all?"

"Oh, something I found last night. I can't just put my hand on it right now but I'm sure it'll come to me." He grinned at her expression of mock-outrage. It was difficult to say something tender without it sounding like brazen cheek. But he felt that after the pain she had revealed this morning, he would insult her if he repeated the words he'd used to other girls. "Will you walk out with me again? The fresh air might settle your queasiness. We have a couple of hours before I need to get ready for the coach – and I'll behave, I promise. I often wanted to go walking with you in Carlisle, y'know, only it never seemed possible."

"Fustian!" she declared, but her smile was indulgent. "Walking wouldn't have been all you wanted. Wait till I fetch my bonnet. I'd like to visit the church."

CHAPTER 29.

The solemn calm of St Mary and St Giles oppressed him, and the shock he'd hidden earlier began to turn to rage. He had to blanket his mind with irrelevant thoughts to stop contemplating what Lucy had told him. Why did churches smell so odd? Why did marble monuments carry inscriptions that were so worthy and boring? The only gravestone he'd ever smiled at was the one that read, "Here lies John Ross. Kicked by a hoss." When Lucy knelt to pray he was willing to copy her, but he wanted to roar at the church, punch the stones, demand an explanation from the Almighty about why He allowed cruelty and avarice to flourish, and heartless old bitches like Ma Hennessy to impose misery on innocent creatures. He got up from his knees and sat studying his hat, silent and furious, while Lucy remained in prayer.

After a decent pause she rose and walked towards the chancel in steady self-possession, apparently to look at the memorials let into the walls. "Do you come to church here?" she asked, turning back to look at him.

Unable to frame an answer that wasn't bitterly angry, he avoided it by addressing a monument. "What do you think, vicar? Should I find a pretty girl to kiss? Yeh, you're right. A girl every time."

"George! Be serious."

"Of course," he said, still to the stone, "you pretended you never felt the same way as the rest of us, didn't you, vicar –

but we know better, don't we? Even vicars must feel sometimes, whether they wear skirts or no."

"You're wicked," she said. "I can see I'll have to drag you to church next Sunday morning."

"Oooh, but Cherry and I already have important business on Sunday morning."

"What's more important than listening to the word of God?"

"I'll tell you," he said. "Exercise! We do far too much sitting still on the coaches. We go to Evensong, and that's plenty. I sit at the back and snooze between the hymns."

"You're a heathen." She tapped the end of his nose. "I'd be letting myself down if I didn't go to Communion."

"Well I'd let everybody down if I ended up fat and drunk, like Armstrong." He leaned towards her. "Imagine a bit of night work with that. Choose now! Exercise or worship?"

"That's coming it a bit strong," she said. "I'm sure we should find a middle way."

"That's what the old vicar's telling me." He ran a knuckle down her midline, from breastbone to waist, where it paused suggestively. "It's a fine thing, is a middle way."

He made a snatch at her petticoats and she grabbed his hand and ran a circle, trying to hold him at a proper distance.

"No! We're in church, George, behave yourself. You promised!"

He grinned and straightened up. "Looks like you're feeling better!"

"I am, but that's no reason," she said firmly. "Now, tell me about London. Where am I going to stay?"

"At Mrs Bowe's house in Falcon Street."

"A house! What kind?" A shameful thought struck her. "Not… "

"Ar ey, no! I admit there's a low element, I mean some of the guards lodge there, but if you can overlook them it's perfectly respectable."

Her giggle was tinged with relief. "Is it comfortable?"

"I think so. You're having my room and I'm going to share with Cherry."

"Oh! That's new. I thought you preferred to sleep alone."

"I prefer to sleep with you," he said. He stopped and pulled her towards him, sharply reminded of the pleasure she gave him. "Oh, lovely. Have pity."

"Just a kiss then. None of your mucky tricks."

"As if I would," he murmured. When she lifted her face for the kiss he tightened his hold, appalled that even while he struggled to understand what had been done to her as a child, he couldn't stop wanting her. "You'll come to me, won't you? Say you will."

"George! Not if you're sharing a room with Mr Cherry!"

"Oh…but after a while you wouldn't notice him –" She lifted her hand and threatened to slap him, and he burst out laughing. "All right! I didn't mean it!"

"I am not going creeping round a strange house."

"Even if you did mistake him for me, it wouldn't do you any good. When he's had a night on the town he's useless for a week."

"George Davenport, I've never heard such mucky talk in a church before. Get out of here and spit your mouth clean."

She hustled him out under little smacks and blows that he knew were not meant to hurt, only to hide her own laughter. He went willingly enough. He could stand her rating him, if only she was well.

As they walked back up the street, she said thoughtfully, "About your timetable… if you drive up to London on a Friday, that must mean you drive down from London on a Saturday."

"Yes, of course."

"And there's no coach on a Sunday?"

"No, I kick my heels here all day."

"Oh. But I'm to lodge in London. I shan't see you from Saturday to Monday."

Her disappointment both pained and flattered him. He said, "I could apply to Mr Chaplin for a change. He's a great family man, so he might just switch me to the other coach. But you'd better be warned, he doesn't often do things for sentiment."

"What if he says no?"

"Then I suppose we'd have to settle at Dunchurch, but that would be rough on you." She hugged his arm gratefully, and he went on, "But you'll like London. There's always something going on. There'll be parades and fairs and all sorts, for the Coronation…"

"I'd rather concentrate on our wedding. The rest doesn't matter."

"Oh, yes. Once you feel at home here, we'll have the banns called."

"That's all right then," she said.

CHAPTER 30.

London, June 1838

George sat with Lucy in the front pew of St Vedast's, turning his hat in his hands. She pressed one foot against his boot and said softly, "I'm sure the vicar won't be long."

"He told us ten o'clock. We were on time, so why can't he be?"

"I expect he doesn't live his life by timepieces like you do."

He decided she meant no criticism, but he continued to fiddle with the hat, running his finger inside the sweatband, smoothing the ribbon, picking off a speck of dust and a single horsehair.

Her serene ease ought to have steadied him. He knew she was going to be happy in the house in Falcon Street. On their arrival last night Mrs Bowe had greeted them with little wordless cries of welcome and immediately sent Betsy the "slavey" to carry Lucy's bags to the room that George had cleared. He followed to make sure she liked it. It wasn't much bigger than what they had had in Carlisle, but when Lucy saw it she kissed him, much to Betsy's amusement.

The biggest relief had been that the landlady took Lucy to her bosom like a long lost daughter. As soon as they came downstairs again, Mrs Bowe laughed and teased and fed and cosseted her, starting with a command to stay in bed the next morning, later than Lucy would ever have done in Carlisle. Supper went by in a surge of female chatter. George wondered what he ought to do once the meal was over. The women's conversation showed no sign of flagging. Would it look odd if he went out? Cherry had already gone, dapper in broadcloth and clean linen for a night on the town, and joking that he expected breakfast to be waiting when he got back. George felt he was avoiding Lucy's company, and it unsettled him. And then he was uneasy about being unsettled. It shouldn't matter, but it did, and he couldn't work out why.

However, Mrs Bowe's kindness and fussing smoothed over the difficulty. She declared that Lucy must be worn out and needed to go to bed, and when Lucy stood up to obey George rose to give her a grave goodnight. He stayed patiently for a while answering Mrs Bowe's questions, but before long he made his excuses and went upstairs.

It was habit that turned him towards the bedroom that had been his, but it was devilment that made him tap at the door to see how Lucy would react.

She was slow; he heard her sigh and pad across the floor – bare feet – he pictured her pulling on a shawl. The doorknob turned, and she peered out.

"I thought I'd come and give you a goodnight kiss," he said, and leaned, smiling, against the doorpost. She opened the door a little more. No shawl. A nightdress that he was very familiar with. "On the off-chance, y'know."

She smiled tiredly. "Just a kiss. I was almost asleep." She put her mouth to his, but without letting go of the door, and when his grip tightened round her she wriggled and drew back. "Goodnight, pet."

Reluctantly, he let her go. "Sleep well."

"I shall," she said, and softly closed the door.

He drew a deep breath, and turned away to the room he would share with Cherry.

The two beds there took up more than half the floor space. A towel was draped over the foot of each, and the wash-stand squeezed between them with its chipped water ewer and a bowl, soap dish and shaving mugs. George had already agreed with Cherry about the use of cupboards and coat hooks, so he undressed, got between the fresh sheets and tried to settle down.

He knew at once that he ought to have gone out. He wasn't ready to sleep. Lucy might well be tired – she was expecting, after all, and she wasn't used to travelling – but his own day had been far too easy, and when work was easy it was worrying. The Albion had carried no more than six passengers over the whole of his ground, and a coach that paid a licence for four inside and eleven out couldn't afford to run less than half-full! He'd have to hope that as the Coronation drew nearer – and it was less than three weeks away – trade to the capital would increase. He totted up yet again how much he was getting in wages and perks, and how much Lucy's room and board were going to cost on top of his own, tapping his fingers worriedly as he subtracted one from the other. He'd get by all right, but only just, and now he wanted to buy clothes for Lucy, and give her money to buy things for the baby, and his second subscription to the Benevolent Club would be due soon. He'd have to pay that by dipping into his savings. Then there was the marriage licence to buy, and the ring, and the clergyman to pay, and no doubt Lucy would want to arrange some kind of wedding breakfast…

When he finally slept, his mind had not quietened, and fragments of nightmare drifted in and out, not full blown yet, but threatening.

He woke in moonlight, yelling himself awake. Oh God, his sisters' funeral, his mother's drunken weeping, and himself clutching his grandmother's skirts, trying to keep out the sound of earth dropping on the two small coffins in his father's grave.

Only it wasn't his grandmother he was clutching. It was Cherry.

Cherry, sitting on the bed, holding him. Cherry in his nightshirt, heady with wine fumes, slurring drunkenly, "Shh, you're all right. Calm down, me old love, me old mate, it's only a dream." An arm tight around his shoulders.

"What the hell? Cherry? What the hell!"

"Calm down, me old mate," crooned Cherry, "you was havin' a bad dream, a real bad dream. Don't like to see a mate in trouble. A bad thing to leave a mate in trouble."

George wiped his face, and sat up. "Sorry. Nightmare. Bit of a shock to come home to, eh? I should have warned you. Get off man, let me go now. I'm all right."

God, why wouldn't Cherry let go? He was worse tonight than he'd ever known him. Lucy and his old bedroom began to look like a wonderful refuge. Even if she made him sleep on the floor, it would be better than having Cherry smothering his face against his throat, one arm tightening round his shoulder, the other crawling up his thigh.

George elbowed him off but he came back, groaning, "You're the best mate I ever had."

"That's the wine talking. Time you was in bed."

"The bess mate… "

"It's bloody midnight," said George. "Get your head down and sleep it off."

"George…you're my best mate, George." Cherry shifted his hand to stroke the nape of his neck, then he drew a sudden gasping breath, and threw both arms around him.

To George, still charged with the adrenalin of his nightmare, this was horror on top of horror. His body's rejection of it came from beyond the reach of rational thought. He punched Cherry, hard, and made a grab for the water ewer. Its handle came off. He threw it away with a clatter, seized the jug bodily and dumped the contents over Cherry's head.

"Sober up, man!"

Cherry spluttered and sat up. "What d'you do that for? Y' muss know I don't chase women… "

"Ha! They chase me fast enough."

Cherry wasn't listening. "I go to a molly house sometimes …"

George shook his head, trying to understand. What the devil was a molly house? He assumed it was an ordinary brothel.

Cherry rambled on. "But s'no good, it's not f'me. You know, some of 'em, they're married – with kids … I thought you might… "

"What!" He found himself gripping the waist of the broken jug, and clanged it back into the wash-bowl with the force of exasperation.

"Jus' you and me, my best mate… "

"Are you completely crazy?"

A rapping at the door startled them both into silence.

"Mr Cherry! Mr Davenport!" It was Mrs Bowe. "Whatever are you doing?"

George could picture her out in the passageway, bulky in her nightgown and probably with her ear pressed to the door. If he'd had another jug of water at that moment, he would have gone and thrown it over her.

"Nothing!"

"You're being far too noisy for that. Be quiet or I'll fetch Mr Thetford to sort you out."

"It's all right. Go back to bed."

"If you've done any damage you'll have to pay for it! D'you hear?"

"Yes, for heaven's sake!"

"I shall see you about this in the morning."

After a moment's pause her footsteps padded away along the passage.

George seized Cherry by the elbow, and hauled him out of the puddle and onto his feet. "Listen! You're drunk, you know that? You make us both look like fools. Get into bed and go to sleep."

The moonlight showed that Cherry had suffered no worse damage than a bruised cheekbone where the punch had landed, so George pushed him across to the other bed, and covered him up. Then he sat on his own bed and watched, until Cherry was asleep.

As a result of his broken night's rest, George came down late to breakfast, and he was not surprised that Cherry sat apart with the guards. The other men seemed subdued, perhaps by the addition of Lucy to the household, and if the division between him and Cherry was noticed, nobody commented.

Mrs Bowe came in and shooed the slavey back into the kitchen. "Pots of tea, Betsy, get a move on." Her sideways glance at George didn't bode well, but she said to Lucy, "Good morning, my dear. Didn't I tell you to sleep in?"

"I felt rather flushed. I'm not used to being so warm!"

"You still look pale," said Mrs Bowe. "I hope you aren't coming down with something. The city can be cruel hard on strangers."

George thought that she looked much better, and Lucy confirmed it, assuring Mrs Bowe that she was very well. Betsy came back in, with three teapots on a tray.

"I hope you rinsed the pots with hot water," said Mrs Bowe.

"Oh yes, m'm." Betsy put one by Lucy and retreated with the others to the next table.

"I'm not used to being waited-on like this," said Lucy. "If I can be of use in the household, please tell me."

"Of course you can, my dear, and very welcome you'll be! I know you'll be steadier than Betsy, though I'm sure you'll think this is a very quiet place compared to the uproar of a coaching inn." She looked hard at George, who cleared his throat and said nothing.

Lucy replied cheerfully, "Oh, we were nothing out of the ordinary. Coachmen and guards were our trade there, just like they are here. Tell me what I can do for you."

"You can keep Betsy on the go, for a start! Such a child for wasting time as she is!"

George, feeling that Mrs Bowe was taking advantage of Lucy's willingness, said, "You need to settle in first, lovely."

Mrs Bowe agreed at once, a change of attitude that startled him after last night's asperity. "I'll tell you what, take Mr Davenport, and have a look round the shops and the street stalls. I've a regular order with Mr Howard for bread, and with Mr Cantis for ham and beef, but the vegetables and potatoes hasn't been so good recently..."

"We'll scout around, and welcome, Mrs Bowe. Won't we, George?"

"Don't include me," he said. "I only know where to buy pies. I'll be no use at all."

"Take no notice of him," said Lucy to Mrs Bowe. "He's got out of bed the wrong side this morning. Of course we'll go."

George thought that Cherry's cutlery sounded unusually busy following this remark, but he only said, "I'll tell you what, Mrs B, if Lucy's going to be of use to you, you can knock something off our rent. Or off the charges for gas and coal."

"How about I don't charge you for breakages," countered the landlady, "because in five minutes I'm going upstairs to check the wear and tear from last night! You'd be well advised to keep out of my way! You go out walking with your young lady and squire her properly while she gets her bearings. Toddle along to St Vedast's and make an appointment with the Reverend."

George sat back, resignedly, so Lucy answered, "Thank you, Mrs Bowe, we'll certainly do that." She looked inquiringly at him. "Won't we?"

"Oh, all right. I suppose now's as good a time as any." It seemed to him that the room breathed again.

When Mrs Bowe went out, Lucy asked under her breath, "Whatever have you been doing?"

He shrugged.

"Well, I'm going upstairs to fetch my bonnet. Mrs Bowe will tell me. Try to behave while I'm gone."

George went over to Cherry and laid a hand on his shoulder, and Thetford and Cordock looked at each other in silence. George suddenly saw his friendship with Cherry through the other men's eyes – men who had perhaps seen all this before and speculated about him moving into Cherry's room. He flushed, first with embarrassment, and then with anger. Did they think he knew about Cherry and shared his tastes? Had they talked of him with disgust – maybe talked of punishing him? Why had nobody forewarned him? He'd known nothing of it. He realized that last night's business had happened exactly because he'd been too ignorant to see it coming. It had been a shock – but damn it, he was marrying Lucy, wasn't he? Really, the whole business ought to be laughable.

He muttered to Cherry, "You were foxed last night. Remember?" Cherry's stillness was enough admission. George pulled a punch on him, a little harder than friendship, a good deal less hard than last night. "If you try that game again, I'll flatten you."

***

Sitting now in St Vedast's, he was startled to find Lucy watching him. "What?"

"You were grinding your teeth. Don't fret, I shan't say anything to the vicar."

He stopped rotating his hat and stared at her. "About what?"

"About the child, of course."

"Oh. Yes. Yes, once we're wed, everything will be a lot simpler."

CHAPTER 31.

July 1838

The excitement was over. Victoria had been crowned Queen of the United Kingdom, and more importantly, Lucy Hennessy had become Mrs George Davenport. She was about to write several letters to impress the importance of that fact on the people she had left behind.

The house in Falcon Street was quiet. George had been restless with no work to do, and had excused himself to go walking and ease what he called "the fidgets." The other guards and coachmen were all out, Mrs Bowe had completed her major household tasks and was taking a nap before the start of the evening cooking, and even Betsy the slavey had been sent to collect a basket of newly cleaned linen from the laundress.

Lucy had nobody to please but herself.

She pulled the washstand towards the bedroom window and spread a cloth over it, thinking that in the city's stuffy afternoon heat its marble top would make a pleasantly cool writing desk. She set out the pen, ink and paper that George had offered her from his writing case, and with a hand that trembled slightly she began to write the first and most difficult of her letters.

1 July 1838

Mother – I will call you so, though I no longer believe I have ever been your daughter in anything other than name – never in truth, by blood or by nature –

If this reminds you that I have gone, do not trouble to look for me. I know that if you had wanted to find me, you would have done so by now.

I am safe in London, but I will not give you my address, nor write again. Give thanks to God that George will not pursue you for the theft of the money he left for me, or his turquoise ring.

I never wish to see the Lanes again. May the Lord forgive you, because I never will.

Lucy

Mrs George Davenport.

Lucy folded the letter and banged it flat with her fist, several times. It was done. By marrying, she had achieved liberty. For a moment she was shaken by a desire to yell and dance and stamp her feet and laugh wildly and sob and scream. In fact she did none of those things, but the intensity of her emotion was perhaps deeper because it burned in silence.

When she recovered, she wiped her eyes and blew her nose and resolved to pull herself together.

Puzzlingly, what remained was a need to continue writing.

For the first time in her life, she had time and space to write letters like a lady of leisure, instead of in haste at her bedside, lit by a stub of candle. It wasn't the greatest of her new-found freedoms, but her back straightened as she thought how she might pride herself, perfectly legitimately, on her change of status. She wasn't a nobody any more, living in the attic of a second-rate inn and not daring to raise her eyes or take a breather from her work. She was a married woman, with a loving, good looking husband whom anyone might envy.

She would write first to Mr Mounsey who had driven the Manchester coach, because he had been kind. He had told his guard to look after her and they had both refused the perks she offered, saying she might well need the money along the road. She would write to thank him formally. If Mr Mounsey then chose to share the letter with other coachmen who lodged at the Blue Bell, and if they amused themselves by needling her mother with what they knew and she didn't, well, that would be their choice. And if they did it would serve her mother right.

She informed Mr Mounsey that she had arrived in London – though again, she was careful not to reveal where exactly – and that she was married and well and happy. After that she allowed her pen to run more freely:

We were married yesterday morning. Mr Davenport dressed very handsomely, and spoke his responses firmly. His good friend Mr R Cherry was his supporter.

It was Lucy herself who had suggested Cherry for the role of best man. She liked his neatness and self-control, and she knew George liked him too. Cherry was charming, of course. She had recognized almost at once that he wouldn't ever try anything on with her, so she felt free to spoil him and mother him a little, and occasionally confide in him. She had never spent any time in the company of his type, her experiences in the Lanes and the Blue Bell having been of a quite different nature, so it had taken a little time before she began to wonder about his friendship with George, and a little longer before she dared to ask Mrs Bowe about it. All Mrs Bowe would say was that Mr Cherry wasn't a bold lad with the girls. Then she'd patted Lucy's hand and said it didn't matter, she needn't worry, everything was all right – which was a kind of answer, without being at all explicit.

She guessed that they had had a disagreement of some sort recently. Perhaps if George asked him to be best man it might help them over it.

George had, indeed, been amused by the suggestion. "Why don't you ask him, lovely? He can hardly refuse a lady."

"Now George, it isn't the bride's place to choose the best man. He's supposed to be the red-blooded accomplice that helps you to carry me off."

"I wouldn't be too sure about that. Poor old Cherry!" George sat back in his chair and laughed. "There could be just a touch of jealousy there!"

"I'm sure Mr Cherry's too much the gentleman to cut you out," said Lucy, pretending to misunderstand. "But you should be the one to invite him. Not me."

"Oh, yes, if that's what you want. I'll catch our little cock-robin at breakfast, shall I?"

"You do that – and perhaps one of your guards would agree to give me away." She noticed that once or twice during that evening George rubbed a smile off his face, and when he did she was happy.

We made a grand little coaching party at the altar. One of Mr Davenport's guards, Mr T Thetford, stood to give me away. He is a dignified man with a trim grey beard.

Lucy was fond of Tom Thetford. Like all the friends George had made in London, beneath his dignity he was kind. On the morning of the wedding Cherry had escorted George away quite early, ostensibly to St Vedast's, and when Mrs Bowe at last said it was time for the bridal party to set off, Thetford had given Lucy his arm with such a solemn air! She had mastered her urge to toss the veil from her face and laugh and hurry and skip to church, and instead walked soberly, proud and slender, with her head high as befitted the formality of the day. Mrs Bowe and Betsy had followed, the widow's plump dignity enlivened by the constant need to check the exuberance of the girl.

As Thetford walked along beside Lucy, he said, "I shall wish yer the best of luck, Miss Hennessy."

"Thank you, Mr Thetford. I do hope we shan't need good luck."

"Ye'll be a good wife to Davenport. A young feller needs steadying. I can see ye'll do that, and once he's settled he'll look after yer properly."

"Of course," Lucy had said.

Remembering, she felt again a tiny stab of doubt about the words "once he's settled." She must try not to let it rattle her. She wrote to Mr Mounsey:

We have had only the few days of these great national festivities to celebrate our wedding. Mr Davenport I am sure would give you a most precise description of the Coronation, particularly the horses, but the best I can do is to say that he thought they were very fine, being all matched bays and mostly six to each carriage. Our landlady, who has a humorous turn of mind, says that since the Coronation has cost four times as much as King William's, Her Majesty's reign had better last four times as long, or we shall have grounds to complain of a bad bargain. Mr Davenport supposes that Mr Armstrong will be most upset about the cost, and so you will very much enjoy telling him about it.

Tomorrow Mr Davenport must begin working over a very much longer route.

Lucy knew that coachmen were always being moved onto new routes and filling-in for one another, and she got the impression that at the moment there were a lot of changes happening so this one, though it was of huge importance to her, made little difference to the larger picture. It didn't surprise her that the office had arranged George's change of timetable as soon as Chaplin approved it.

Now she would have George all to herself for four nights of the week, including Sundays, and she was full of joy and gratitude that it had turned out to be so. Cherry was clearly disappointed that he and George would be separated by the change in timetable, which meant they would travel the same road every day but in opposite directions. Lucy saw that the two work-mates would miss drinking together and playing cards, but in her happiness she gaily told Cherry that he was welcome to play cards any evening, three-handed with Mrs Bowe.

Mr Davenport sends his kindest regards to all his friends at the Bell and the Coffee House, and hopes they will write to him occasionally at the Swan with Two Necks. He also asks whether you have heard about Mr Thomas, the guard of the Manchester Mail, who has survived a bad accident at a place called Dirt House Hill north of To'ster. I understand that it was the night after the Coronation, and the Holyhead Mail had been overtaking and the two coaches smashed into one another. Mr Davenport is more upset about the horses than the people – he says there was a wheel horse killed and others much injured. Due to the harness being very old it all broke, and that was likely the reason the passengers escaped with their lives. Mr Thomas and the other guard had to separate the two coachmen who each claimed the smash was the other's fault, but we have heard that the Holyhead's lamps had been forgotten in the excitement of the Coronation, so things look uncomfortable for the stable men.

I am very sorry to say that many of the other coach drivers here have been turned off, owing to trade shifting to the railways. I hope you will not have the same troubles when they come to Carlisle. I must be grateful that Mr Davenport still has work.

No longer a servant but most grateful for your help, dear Sir, I am yours truly,

Lucy Davenport.

With that letter complete, she wondered who to write to next. There were still things about the wedding which she must glory in, and which Mr Mounsey, being male, would neither appreciate nor pass on. She would have liked to write to Maggie or Sally who had protected her in the Lanes, but she hadn't seen them since Ma shifted to the Blue Bell. They must have long ago moved away, and with luck they would have married followers and become respectable. Well, she might write to Mrs Carruthers, the cook, or possibly to Mariah – though Lucy hadn't forgotten Mariah's cheating over the postal fee of her first letter to George, and it was possible she had had a hand in the disappearance of the ring, and perhaps of the gold sovereigns, too.

She decided that it would be economical to direct the letter to Mrs Carruthers and Mariah together. What liberated her pen this time was the understanding that once she had bragged of her good fortune and her finery in all its delicious detail, she would be all square with them. Mrs Carruthers read slowly, and Mariah couldn't read at all. Lucy herself had had become literate only after Ma moved into the tenancy of the Blue Bell and, on the prompting of the clergy at St Cuthbert's, had sent her to the Central

School. However, if Mrs Carruthers read the letter aloud to Mariah, that would be another blow struck at the block of ice that Ma thought was a heart.

Dear Mrs Carruthers

Congratulate me! Mr Davenport and I were married yesterday. The men looked most handsome in church, all in their best coats, and made our party seem very grand. I have four new petticoats for my wedding dress, which is lilac, with galloon lace from Frost and Stevenson. My day-dresses are both a serviceable dark blue. I also have a new pair of lace-up boots.

I would tell you about the Coronation, and Her Majesty's wonderful procession to the Abbey, but I am sure the newspapers will have given much better accounts than I could of the gorgeous dresses, the beautiful carriages, and the shouting, and the cannon salutes, and the trumpets, and the bells ringing all over the city.

She remembered, with an inward giggle, how jealous George had been of her admiration for the Watermen as they marched by in the procession, wearing their full-skirted scarlet coats. She had made Mrs Bowe and Cherry agree that red-stockinged legs were very handsome, after which George had insulted Cherry for taking her side, and eventually Mrs Bowe had had to tease George out of his ill-humour by pretending to ration Lucy's kisses. It had been an odd incident. But then as if to apologize he bought sandwiches for them all from the street sellers, and the rest of the day had been marvellous. In the evening they had walked to Green Park, where they were able to see the most spectacular parts of both the firework displays.

The Standard had a lovely phrase, which I copy here: "In moral grandeur we may safely affirm, that it defied every approach to rivalry." There are still festivities of various kinds occurring, but many of the people who came into the city for the great day and for the Fair in Hyde Park are now returning home, and it is once more possible to walk easily along the streets.

Everyone knew that on the Friday after the Coronation the young Queen would visit the Fair, which offered every kind of entertainment from food stalls and dance floors to theatres and balloon ascents. George had dearly wanted to go, and when Lucy said she wouldn't, he immediately said he wouldn't either, but he looked so crestfallen about it that she had laughed and taken pity on him.

"Be off," she said. "This is the only time I have left to make sure I'm fit to be seen in church! Take Mr Cherry with you, and enjoy yourself."

"I'd rather take you, lovely. It isn't often I have four holidays in a row. Won't you come with us?"

She shook her head. "I overdid things yesterday. I'm going to try on my wedding dress, and Mrs Bowe is going to help me. I don't want you to see me in it until it's right."

"In fact," said Mrs Bowe, "tomorrow you won't see her at all. It's bad luck for the groom to see the bride until they meet at the altar."

Betsy chimed in, "She won't come down to breakfast, even. I'm going to serve it in her room."

"See," said Lucy brightly. "I am to be waited-on hand and foot."

"Oh! And I may die of neglect, I suppose. It's just as well the wedding's in the morning, and not the afternoon." Faced by their female unity, George went off to find Cherry.

Lucy fully expected the two of them to come back foxed, so before she and Betsy and Mrs Bowe began the trying-on, she peeked into George's room and reassured herself that his new coat and trousers were safely hung where they couldn't be spoiled.

For herself, because she had been too ashamed to tell the dressmaker that she was pregnant, she had needed to check that the wedding dress would still fit from her original measurements. If it didn't, she would have to abandon the one-piece dress, and wear one of her simpler blue day dresses which were made as a separate bodice and skirt. Mrs Bowe, seeing her hesitate over undressing, pushed Betsy out to do a couple of jobs in the kitchen.

"Go on," she said when the girl protested. "We'll call you when you can come to look."

"Yes, leave us to it for a few minutes," said Lucy. She didn't want Betsy spreading gossip. It would be best if nobody suspected anything about the baby until after the wedding. Mrs Bowe was different, of course. Her firm nod as she closed the door behind Betsy was both complicit and reassuring.

Then Lucy was afraid her stays weren't tight enough, but when Mrs Bowe lifted the dress, draped its skirt over the layers of petticoats, and fastened it up, she found she could, after all, wear it comfortably without any strain showing at the waist seam.

"Oh, that's such a relief!" She wondered whether Mrs Bowe had had a quiet word with the dressmaker, but decided that it was better not to ask. "Do call Betsy now, and let her see!"

After that there was a half hour of tweaking of skirts and patting of lace, and cooing and applauding every improvement. The lilac of the wedding dress perfectly set off Lucy's fresh colouring, and the little blue roses printed down its bodice brought out the colour of her eyes.

"Now, I need you to judge where exactly I ought to pin my brooch." It was the one with blue stones, that George had bought her in Carlisle; hidden in her bedroom, it had been a happy survivor of the theft at the Bell.

Betsy, writhing with shyness and excitement, burst out, "And if you please, m'm! I got two satin garters what I never wore yet. Will you borrow them? Oh do say you will! Then they'll be lucky for me ever after!"

When they had all agreed that everything was just right – comfortable, correct, demure, and what George would undoubtedly call "very, very fetching" – Lucy was satisfied, and at last she beamed at Betsy and Mrs Bowe.

"You know, it's hard to believe that I have so many new clothes. I am so lucky."

"You are indeed," said Mrs Bowe, "but from what I've heard nobody more deserves a bit of good luck than what you do."

Then Lucy declared that it was Mrs Bowe's turn, but the widow resisted the efforts of both girls to make her put on the dull brown taffeta she had chosen, which they assured her was the epitome of respectability.

"We shall need every inch of our dignity tomorrow," she said, as she calmly folded the dress away, "so you're next, Betsy Harper. You're not to turn out in those gaudy things you wore for the Coronation!"

Lucy sat now, pen in hand, conning over the memory of the day. Goodness only knew how much that new coat and trousers had cost George, but she thought him the most magnificent sight she had ever seen, even grander than the Watermen. As she approached the altar he'd grinned and winked at her, and Cherry had to cough and nudge him to draw his attention back to the Rector.

Admittedly, there had been moments in that quiet service when she had been anxious. The solemn requirements to "declare any impediment, why they might not be coupled together in Matrimony," were met with a bland silence from all present, although Cherry and Mrs Bowe were certainly aware of the half-truths and deliberate falsehoods it concealed. Lucy still felt a little uneasy, but she had prayed strongly both before and after the event, and she knew that none of the impediments were half as important to her as the need to marry George. And when he had at last sworn he that would take her to love and to cherish, she thought she would die of happiness.

She stopped writing when she recalled the signing of the register. Because she had never been told what her father's trade had been – or even whether Ma had known who he was – George and Mrs Bowe had concocted a story to record him as a Carlisle innkeeper, now dead. Lucy had also stated that Falcon Street was her most recent residence – that at least was true – and had given her age as twenty-one, which it most certainly wasn't. She decided it was safer not to mention these things in her letter. Although Ma was unlikely to come rushing up to London to challenge the marriage, the facts that hadn't been admitted might make ceremony void. She didn't think a marriage could be annulled once a wife was bedded and pregnant – how unfair that would be! – but she wasn't sure, and she wasn't going to give anyone – anyone – the chance to separate her from George.

She wrote to Mrs Carruthers:

The register entries showed a good many crosses, where previous brides and grooms had been unable to sign their names. I am proud to say that Mr Davenport and I were perfectly able to sign for ourselves, though if he had signed a cross I would most likely have done the same so as not to shame him. If you happen to meet Mrs Irving from the Central School, will you tell her of my good fortune, and thank her for me?

She also decided not to tell Mrs Carruthers how Mrs Bowe had agreed to a discounted rent in return for the help with the housework. None of that conveyed the air of leisure that she wanted to impress on the cook and on Mariah. It was more important to point up the little details that continued to please her about her new life:

Here I preside over both a bedroom and a sitting room, each with a fireplace, and new green wallpaper, and rugs on the floor, and a good colza-oil lamp. Mr Davenport's employer values him so well that he has changed his timetable so we can attend church on Sunday and have most of Monday together. I feel quite the lady with so much free time.

Satisfied that she had established her status without giving anything away, she added, with malicious pleasure:

I trust that Mariah enjoyed whatever it was that she bought with my half-crown. With thanks for your friendship,

yours truly

Lucy Davenport.

She need never write to them again.

Finally she struck a lucifer match to light her taper and melt wax for the seals of the three letters. She was charmed by the simplicity of lucifers – even if the smell did catch in her throat, they were so much easier than a tinderbox. She could see that in winter it would save a lot of time if she didn't have to strike sparks onto charred cotton and do all that fiddly transfer of ember to spill to candle in order to have light and fire.

It was only after the wax had set on the seals that she wondered whether George might expect to read her letters before they were sent. She must sit him down when he came in, and talk to him about how they were to deal with correspondence, and more importantly, how they would manage their home. Of course they must agree on how much housekeeping money he would allow her, but she was confident that she could persuade him to two-and-ninepence-worth of postage, for saying farewell to Cumberland.

CHAPTER 32.

Stony Stratford, Thursday, 2 August 1838

"Mary! Where are you, my little darling, my little apple dumpling?" George knew the fat girl would be hanging around the doorway of the Cock Hotel, and at his call she sidled into view, grinning hopefully at him. "I'll have a hot brandy, Mary dear, Thetford will have negus, and you shall have a kiss if you're quick about it." When she turned round he clapped both hands to her rump so that she scooted away with a delighted shriek.

He took off his gloves and his hat. Between his arrival at Dunchurch with the down coach and setting off again with the up coach to London, the hot weather had broken with such a thunderstorm that he had only managed a few hours' sleep. This morning, after a short spell in which the clouds merely threatened, the rain had begun again, to weigh down his greatcoat and make the reins more and more slippery as each stage wore on. Worse, the coach was carrying mostly parcels, the only passengers being two farmers and a hay-and-corn merchant who had all come to Stony Stratford for a sale the following day. They had been grudging about tipping him. Not that perks were much good anyway since the opening of the railway. Very few of those who travelled by coach now were the old open-handed aristocrats. They were poor customers, timid ones who distrusted the trains, cranky ones who stayed with the coaches because they were dissatisfied with the slack timekeeping of the railway companies. They grumbled when coachman and guard expected perks at the end of their ground.

George, for all his teasing of Fat Mary, was in a distinctly ill-tempered frame of mind.

Thank goodness he had twenty minutes at Stony Stratford for a meal. If he made up to Mary he'd easily get another brandy-and-water and a couple of chops put down in that time. He needed to visit the earth-closet first, though.

"Afternoon, Mr Farren," he said, as he came back in.

"Not a very good one, Mr Davenport," replied the clerk gloomily. "I daresay nobody's riding outside today, eh?"

"Three gentlemen inside, and all getting down here."

"Room for two ladies to London then."

"Certainly, certainly." One of them would be a stout and breathless widow with two bags and an umbrella – there it was in the stand beside the door – and the other would have a canary bird in a cage, which would occupy her hands when she ought to be opening her purse to tip. He sighed and went into the coffee room.

It was quiet at this time of the day, reminding him how much he missed the long late-night conversations and cribbage games with Cherry – despite his gossiping and his occasional odd behaviour. But since George had started driving this longer journey to Dunchurch, they could only exchange a brief greeting each day as their coaches passed on the outskirts of London.

George hailed the waiter and got the usual response, "Coming, sir!" as the farmers and the corn merchant were pushed towards the main table and left to seat themselves.

"Chops for two, Arthur, and make sure they aren't bullet-proof. You know my usual table."

There were two ladies sitting in the stall behind his. The nearest wore a bonnet and a dripping shapeless Mackintosh coat whose waterproofing was strong in his nostrils, but he was damned if he would move from his seat on that account – and anyway, Fat Mary had arrived with the hot drinks and her trademark sniff.

"You made me a-a-ll wet, Mr Davenport," she said, with a suggestive chuckle. "Putting your 'ands on me like that."

"Well, here, lay my gloves by the fireside – carefully! They won't dry, but they'll be a damn sight warmer next time I grab your saddle-leather. Take my hat too."

He gulped his brandy, knowing she would come back without being asked. Which she did, hovering, fully expecting to be caught round her thick waist and pulled close for a peck on the lips. "Fetch us another glass, there's a good girl."

When he released Mary, the ladies in the next box called her, and after a moment's low conversation she directed one of them out of the room.

The moment the lady had gone, her companion spoke clearly from behind the dividing curtain.

"And how many of those have you had today, Mr Davenport?" A voice he knew, brisk, astringent, like the zesty spurt when he dug his thumbs into an orange.

Sarah Chaplin.

"Don't look round," she said, before he could reply. "Eliza will be back in a moment. I'll speak to you on the coach, later."

Why the hell did she keep turning up? Blast her for catching him flirting with such a lump as Mary. Then Thetford came in grumbling and cursing the rain, and the waiter brought plates and napkins, and their chops were spring lamb that was fat and sweet and melted off the bone. Both men began to eat rapidly, George all the time conscious of Sarah at his back, behind the shabby red curtain. What was she doing here? He would get nothing out of her with Eliza dancing attendance. No doubt the mystery would turn out to be of her own making.

The farmers and the corn merchant at the main table shouted for Arthur to bring their meal. Fat Mary fetched George his brandy. He didn't touch her, and she went away looking disappointed.

He downed the brandy in one and went to the fireside for his hat and gloves.

"See you out there, Thetford." He didn't look back.

Outside, the rain was still falling, in hard straight curtains that rattled off the oil-skinned load on the coach roof and ran down the panels in little streams, with beads of water hanging from every rail and iron. The team waited under rugs thrown over their backs to keep them warm for work. A single ostler stood miserably by the wheel horses' heads, an inverted sack protecting his head and shoulders while he held the reins in raw, red hands.

Ned, the porter, watched from the shelter of the doorway and picked his teeth.

"Rain's set in for the rest of the day, I reckon. Thetford got the parcels loaded. There was nothing with an insurance note."

"Yeh. Trade's gone flat since the Coronation."

“Your new fares don’t have any baggage,” said Ned, “so they won’t tip, I suppose. I don’t know why we bother.”

“Keep smiling, Ned, it suits you.” George worked his hands into his damp gloves and walked round the team to check bits and collars. They were probably the best team he had, now. The leaders that Anderson had frightened and ruined had been sold, and these two young thoroughbreds, originally intended for the Liverpool Mail, had been put in his hands after the Mail ceased to run. He and Pigott had combined to school them into a very decent combination. Pigott wasn’t so keen on Cinnamon, but still… this was a good team now, perhaps even better than the bays he drove into London.

He drew the reins from the ostler’s hold, adjusted them to length and got up. If he fitted his coat and apron properly now, most of him would stay dry.

He heard Thetford being kindly and avuncular at the coach door.

“Can I see your tickets, ladies?” Obviously Thetford hadn’t yet recognized Sarah. “Through to London… thank you. Run between the drops, now! You’ll be nice and snug inside.”

“I am not riding inside,” said Sarah, and he heard her rattle the umbrella. “My ticket is for the roof.”

“Oh, we won’t trouble you to climb up there today, when there’s plenty of room inside – oh, it’s Miss Sarah, isn’t it!” George could picture Thetford revising his style. “Well, if you insist, Miss.”

“I do. Be so good as to fix the ladder. Eliza will take an inside seat, but I shall ride on the box.”

CHAPTER 33.

"All right behind? Trot on!" With the horses moving and the coach on the road, George glanced at Sarah and said, "You ought to be inside."

She broke into laughter at his disapproving face. "Who's in charge of these horses, Mr Davenport? And how many brandies have you had?"

"The rain soon washes it out of you."

"Well, as for that, I would hold the umbrella over both of us, but I fear we would then get equally wet."

"Oh! No. You don't need to worry about me, Miss Sarah."

She continued to smile, which he found unsettling – as though she had foreseen his rebuff, and discounted it. She watched the steadily trotting team and said, "How well they work in your hands, George."

George?

"Stop it. You're playing a very brazen game."

"No game. I am complimenting you on your driving, as I'm sure many other box-seat passengers will have done."

So many replies crowded his tongue that for a moment he was unable to speak. He remembered Lucy refusing to climb to the box-seat. And this girl assumed it by right – which he wasn't sure was true. Months ago, George had trembled at the idea of driving with William Chaplin on the box-seat. Now he had Chaplin's daughter beside him, and he wished with all his heart that her father were there instead.

"I've never had a lady compliment my driving."

"Not even your wife?"

He flushed. Then embarrassment gave way to relief. Even Sarah's advances could be held at bay by that simple word.

"No," he said. "Not even my wife."

"But you will have been told how well you drive."

"Now and then." He forced himself not to follow Sarah's hints. "You know, this could be the best team I have, maybe even better than the last stage into the city. You'll remember Anderson? He pretty well ruined the old team for this coach. These new leaders are still very green but they learn fast, and they want to please you. This wheeler on the nearside, she's half thoroughbred." Cinnamon, the wilful mare who had a piece of his heart. "We got her cheap because she ran away in single harness, but I think she's a damn good horse."

For a moment he suffered a kind of double vision – the strong game mare, the unpredictable girl. He must be tired, to confuse the two. Keep talking.

"The off wheeler is the only one of that old team that was still worth anything. Mind you, on the middle ground you have to drive all sorts," he said, "especially on the night stages. You know – the poor worn-out old things with wreckage for legs."

"I must have seen some of them in the down coach this morning. Broken knees, harness galls and all. I shall report the sub-contractor to Papa."

"It's no fun driving them, I can tell you."

Again, that shift of the umbrella, revealing the honey-brown, appraising eyes. "But it takes real skill to make a team out of wreckage. Anyone can drive good horses down a straight road."

He didn't speak for three beats of the horses' hooves, then he said roughly, "Shut up your umbrella. Put it on the footboard, behind my boots."

"Why?"

"You're going to drive."

He was getting tired of her constant challenges. He would find out whether she was thoroughbred, or just contrary.

"Hold out your left hand. These two reins go either side of your first finger. These two either side of your second finger. Curl your hand a little, so… "

He managed to transfer the reins without touching her at all. She handled the leather like a workman, no foolery, no teasing, her gloved fingers both quick and firm as they accepted control. He had to admit that although she was tense with excitement, she did as she was told. The team, released by her lighter contact, trotted faster.

"Oh!" There was that little thrill in her voice, that he had heard at the Mail Procession. "You can almost feel what they are thinking! Oh George, the power they give you!"

"Sh," he said. "Thetford will hear you. Draw your hand up a little and they will steady. There."

"Will you trust me with your whip?" Her glance flicked him. "I can drive a gig."

"Oh no, Sarah," he said, firmly. "No whip. You have enough to think about with four horses – do you see how they're running crooked? Push the two middle reins back through your fingers, back into your hand. That's good. See how they've straightened up? Well done."

He sat back a little into his seat and watched her learn. He was reminded of the thrill he'd felt when he first drove a four-in-hand himself. She lowered her hand experimentally, and when the horses responded by gathering speed she gave a delighted chuckle and drew them gently back.

"Hold them steady," said George at once. "Don't change the pace unless the road requires it. Let them keep the coach rolling at one speed. It's much less effort for them."

"Awww. You mean I mustn't spring them?"

"I do indeed."

"Why not? It's a good straight road."

"And there's a wagon ahead of us. I don't think he'd appreciate you galloping over the top of him. Can you pick up the offside reins? Bring the team over to the right – now." As a precaution, he shouted "Thetford! Blow!" and when the horn-call rang out to clear her way he saw her grin with sheer excitement and lower her hand again to let the team gain pace. The wagon fell behind, and she returned the team to their own side of the road, a move which the guard of a fast oncoming coach saluted with a quick blast of the horn.

"That wasn't half bad, was it!" she crowed.

"Beginner's luck! You give yourself away by looking at your hands."

"And how am I supposed to know which rein to pull without looking?"

"Practice. Sit up. Lower your hands. That's it."

"This seat is too flat," she said. "I would drive better if I were on your slanted box. May we change over?"

The image of her stepping across his lap was highly disturbing. He blew out his cheeks and blinked to dispel it. "We don't have time to stop."

She accepted that, but retorted, "Of course a well-bred gentleman would also say that I drive as though I were born to it."

"Why should I state the obvious? You were born to it. So was I. And both our fathers were born to it."

She gave a short laugh. "Mamma wouldn't countenance me ever trying. Her family – both our families – have taught her that a woman's place is to keep the business running, and she can't do that from the box of a coach."

"That's a shame," said George. He knew better, this time, than to suggest that driving a coach was an unsuitable job for a woman.

"Yet the rules don't apply to William. He'll be allowed to drive if he wants, or to work at the Swan, and take whatever course he chooses. It's frustrating. And there is nothing worse, for me, than frustration."

"I've noticed," he said.

"I suppose you would. I was rude to you," she continued, "when we met at the Mail Procession. You've been generous to let me drive at all."

"I've surprised myself," he agreed.

"Also, I'm sure we are behind time." Her glance teased him.

"Spoken like a coach proprietor's daughter. No, you're not going to gallop them!" He could see that the horses were apprehensive about something on the railway embankment, which converged here on Watling Street and ran over a bridge not far ahead. "Give them to me."

When Sarah didn't react he repeated, "Give them to me! Quickly! These young leaders can be a handful. See that smoke ahead? It's a goods train. Sit tight!"

He took the reins from her hand. His attention was all for his horses now, looking for the source of their anxiety. He pulled the leaders back so they couldn't affect the steering. The traces slackened and the bars at the pole-head began to chatter. "Now it won't matter too much what these young 'uns do. Cinnamon and Hero will hold us steady."

Here came the engine with its clank and hiss along the embankment, puffing smoke from its tall chimney, steam swirling down through the rain, the wheels of the trucks running *thud-thud-thud* across the joints in the rails. Sarah squinted up at it through the rain, holding on her bonnet with one hand. The sharp mix of coal-smoke and steam over-rode the stink of her Mackintosh.

The young horses shied sideways. George's voice rang off the crisp stonework, "Hup, hup, hup!" and the team dived under the bridge with a sharp echoing clatter of shoes. Then the steaming *rata-clack-chuff* was behind them, wet clouds drifting over the wagons as they trailed their *thud-thud-thud* along the embankment and faded away down the track.

"Eeeeeasy now. Trot." The team's flickering ears told him they were still running in their minds from the monster, and he kept a steady hand on the reins, waiting for them to relax. "There are some days I can get through here without meeting an engine, but there doesn't seem to be a fixed time for them on this stretch. Filthy damned things."

"Yes." Sarah rubbed tentatively at the smuts on her gloves and coat, but gave up with a sigh. "I'm afraid Eliza will have to deal with this. I'll have my umbrella, please, Mr Davenport."

He rallied her. “Have you given up driving, then?”

“Give me my umbrella,” she flashed, “or I’ll drive you harder than you can handle.”

“That’s more like your usual self.”

She laughed, and as he gave her the umbrella she smiled provocatively, and her wet glove closed over his.

CHAPTER 34.

George knew that neither Tom Thetford, sitting at the rear of the coach, nor Eliza, riding inside, could hear or see anything that happened up here on the box seat. Yet the guard's key-bugle flourished into The Young Coachman. Did Thetford guess what Sarah was up to? At once the coach window went down and the clergyman shouted, "Be quiet, out there! We'll have no bawdiness on this journey!" and pulled the window back up. There was a little pause in which Thetford, as though placidly unconcerned by the words that might be going through the minds of his hearers, played through to the end of the verse.

Sarah giggled. "How did he know it was bawdy if he didn't already know the words!"

"Don't tell me you do," said George, sternly.

"No, but it's always hushed up, so it isn't difficult to guess. I'd give a crown to hear you sing it."

"I don't sing for money."

"Oh, I see. You don't give compliments, and it seems you can't take them either."

"I know my value. So should you. So be quiet."

He drove for a little while without trying to re-open the conversation. At length he suggested, "Your bonnet and gloves must be very wet. You ought to get down and rejoin Eliza."

"Certainly not."

“Maybe you’re made of the right stuff after all,” he said, and was surprised to see that she could blush.

Sarah slept on the later part of the journey. She had put away the umbrella and found a way to lean against the side of George’s box-seat so as to shelter her face from the rain. Tucked in there, under his left elbow, she seemed innocent and as much in need of his care as Lucy, so he drove the old crippled team with more consideration than usual, and they fell in with his mood as horses sometimes will, and cantered along with their shoulders up to the collar and their ears turned away from the rain. Perhaps their compliance might only be due to the weather, but whatever the cause, he didn’t have to bully them, and there was time for him to wonder about Sarah.

She must have left very early from London to have reached Stony Stratford before him. She could have met the Albion anywhere along Watling Street without the need to spend five hours travelling out and five hours travelling back. What on earth was she doing? Especially on such a cold wet day? He hoped she hadn’t come seeking him, but the conclusion was inevitable and probably meant trouble.

Through two changes of team, and through the horn calls to open the toll gates, she leaned against him and didn’t appear to wake. She roused when he halted the coach before the steep descent into London, and when Thetford put the brake-shoe under the rear wheel the grinding noise woke her fully.

“Ugh. I’m cold. What time is it?”

“It’s half past six. We’ll be in on time.”

"Excellent.”

George said, “Your father should be pleased that we’ve added a couple of passengers at the back.”

"Perhaps."

He paid her no further attention. He was fully occupied with helping the team to control their load down the hill, and was relieved that she was no longer interfering with his rein-arm. At the bottom he stopped and reversed the coach, so Thetford could get down and twitch the shoe, steaming, back onto its hook.

"My feet are cold," she said. She wiggled her ankles beneath her wet skirt-hem, and again he had that disturbing image of the body hidden inside the waterproof so close beside him. "I suppose yours are too."

"Not at all," he said.

"Oh! But how do you keep them warm?"

He began to chuckle. "You won't believe me."

"You wear big boots and stuff them with straw!"

"It's simpler than that. I never wash my feet."

"George! That's disgusting."

"Although I do rub 'em with whale oil out of the lamps."

She broke into outright laughter.

"That's better." He could ask her now. "Sarah, what are you doing here? What are you playing at?"

She looked away across the countryside, where the grasses stood tall, their seed-heads a million arches of silver drops above the green.

"Look at all that hay still waiting to be cut. And anything that is cut will be spoiled."

"And the oldest tree in Cheshire is the Eastham yew! Come on now! If you're playing games, I'd like to know the reason."

She sighed. "I simply wanted to ride on one of Papa's coaches."

He didn't believe that for one minute, but he said politely, "You're very welcome."

"But there are also things I need to tell you – things I can only say when we are alone. This is as close to being alone as I can manage."

"Ah." That was more worrying.

She said, "This coach won't be ours much longer. Papa is selling out. Not just one or two routes, but all of them."

"Lord," he said. His hands reacted on the reins, and the horses wavered across the highway into the path of an oncoming coach. He must concentrate or they would all be capsized. The other coach was coming uphill at a gallop, and its guard blew "Clear the Road" at him. He drew the team to a halt in the nearside gutter, and shouted to Thetford to put on the brake-shoe.

"Isn't that Mr Cherry," asked Sarah, "coming up with the Greyhound?"

"Yes. He'll ask if I'm drunk." George set the team going again.

She sat up straighter and her eyes shone with excitement. Passing head on, downhill, was something to tighten the gut of even the most experienced passenger. There was no way of stopping their coach. At best, its weight was slowed by the shoe and the wheel-horses' harness. Pebbles clattered on the undercarriages and the ground shook with a thunder of shod hooves and wheels as their team and Cherry's filled the road.

Cherry shouted, "Too many damn brandies!"

George shouted back, "Speak for yourself!"

The axle-boxes cleared each other and Thetford tootled acknowledgement. Then the Greyhound was past, and the water it had thrown up washed back into the gutter.

George halted at the foot of the hill and backed the team off the shoe again.

"Thetford! All right behind? Trot on." He asked Sarah, "Is your father bankrupt?"

"Oh no. He's keeping all the property. But the leased vehicles are going back to the builders. The horses and harness will be sold. He's been planning it for months."

He thought back. She was right. Dixon had advised him to leave the Newcastle Mail. Chaplin had cut down every route that ran against the railways.

He'd been lucky to be employed for so long. He said nothing, only concentrated on his driving.

"I'm sorry," said Sarah. "Do you remember the Mail Procession? All that wonderful display? I had to come out to watch that day, because there may never be another. I wanted to tell you then, only I wasn't certain until I heard Papa talking to Mr Horne. We were withdrawing from table after dinner, and before we were well out of the room Mr Horne began to talk quite wildly about the railways and how they were going to poach his trade. Papa called him 'Benny, my boy,' and I heard him say, 'We must make friends with them, or they will hurt us a great deal, and you won't like that.' I knew Papa intended to give up the Mail contracts, but I never guessed he would do anything so absolute as selling everything! Only I suppose he must, while there is still a business to sell."

"You knew and you didn't tell me? I take that very unkindly." George drove on, silently digesting the unpleasant news, before he said, "I know a fellow that your father turned off in May. He's driving a pair-horse omnibus now."

"You could, too."

"Never!" he said in disgust.

They were coming into the city now, with all the usual horrors of the evening traffic. The team were catching-up a slower coach ahead, and he stopped talking while he estimated the relative pace of the two vehicles, then sent the horses forward to overtake.

"Oh, aren't they just a grand team! No, that fellow drives his 'bus fourteen hours a day and he hates every minute of it. There's none of this speed in heavy stop-and-start work like that. No joy at all."

"You're determined to drive four-in-hand?"

"Yes."

"Then you'll have to move away. Wales. Northern England. Scotland. Places where the railways can't build easily."

He drew in ahead of the other coach and let the horses bowl on. Scenting their home stables, they strode out eagerly, heads up and ears pricked.

"I'll go wherever I have to go. I can't give up driving teams like this."

"Please don't," said Sarah. "If you leave, I shall never see you again."

CHAPTER 35.

George drew a deep breath and tried to laugh. "How flattering. Thank you kindly, Miss Sarah."

"Don't imagine I'm hero-worshipping. I got over admiring coachmen long ago – I was born at the Spread Eagle so I've known inns and coaching men from the inside, all my life."

"Poor you," he said.

"Don't mock! I've told myself over and over again that it's impossible, but I can't change how I feel." Her voice faltered and then gathered strength. "I must tell you now, while we are still able to talk privately. I've seen your eyes on me. Have you ever wished that we might be together?"

Together? he thought. Not *together*… ?

"Don't say any more! It isn't proper – even if you don't understand what you're saying."

"But I do," she said. "Remember, I have eleven brothers and sisters and the youngest is only seven months old! Mamma is content with raising a family where I would not be. I decided years ago that I shan't ever seek a wedding band, but I do want to know what I shall be missing."

He blinked in astonishment. "You're wasting your time with me."

"I know. But you are still listening to me."

"I can hardly get away, can I?" He swallowed. He was going to have to say something more definite. It was difficult; practised though he was at keeping girls at arm's length, there were some truths he seldom spoke. "Now you listen to me. I love my wife."

"Of course," she said. "I expected no less...but I shall not steal anything that is hers. I want... one night with you... "

A night! She must be mad – possessed.

"Your family will never let you out of their sight," he said.

She heard the change in his argument, and struck home like a peregrine. "Papa and Mamma are going away. For a whole month."

He saw the trap too late.

She said in a voice that was unsteady with excitement, "They are going to the Alps. The younger children will go too, and Eleanor and Marianne and William and I are to stay in London to manage the inns while Papa is away. Officially we are under Uncle John's guidance, but I can promise you – if Papa is in Switzerland and we are here – there will be confusion. I will contrive it!"

She put her hand on his thigh.

"Please – George – I will make a chance from that."

Through all the layers between her body and his, that deliberate intimacy shocked him. There was a cool quality in it, experimental, almost calculating. He hesitated. He would have to lie to Lucy, to Mrs Bowe, to his fellow drivers, to the guards. And he realized that in listing all those people, he had been close – terrifyingly close – to giving in. In spite of the rain, he felt the sweat spring on his skin. He was forgetting how powerful touch could be.

He said hoarsely, "What you are asking is wrong, impossible. Take your hand away."

He said no more, and Sarah sat in silence. Perhaps she was sulking. He hoped so. If she was plotting some other approach he had better look out.

As he drove into the yard of the Swan with Two Necks and drew the team to a halt, she announced with decision, "I will write to you."

"Don't you dare write to my lodgings. If you do, I'll send every letter straight to your father."

"You do that at your peril," she replied. "Whom will he believe, you or me? In any case I shall wait until he has gone to Switzerland. His purpose in going away is to consider the future of the business, so he has ordered that no letters will be forwarded! You see, there is no use giving me warnings. But if you object to letters at your home, I will write to you here, to the Swan."

"You'll do no such thing. Ibbotson and Foyle know your handwriting as well as they know their own! And they both know me!'"

"That's true. I shall have to write Poste Restante, care of The General Post Office. I shall call myself Polly Peachum, and you shall be Macheath."

"I shan't collect them."

"It's only a game. Don't tell me you are afraid to play a game with me?"

He shook his head. "I've seen your games. You don't care about people being hurt."

"I certainly don't, for myself. But all I shall do is to write letters. I shan't ask you to write back. I only want you to promise that you will read them."

"Do as you please." If Sarah Chaplin wanted to write letters, he supposed she would, but he needn't promise to collect them. “Here’s Thetford with the ladder. You can sit here all night if you like, but I’m going indoors to get warm.”

CHAPTER 36.

London, August 1838

George didn't want Sarah to write to him, but all the same she had managed to make him intensely curious. What on earth could she need to write about, that rich, fierce, tricky girl? Her father had power, and George supposed she raged at being privately so chaperoned, with personal power denied to her, but he was flattered that she thought he could do anything about it. The possibilities teased him. Each evening as he walked to the Swan, the temptation nagged like an itch between his shoulder blades – to call in at the General Post Office, and enquire whether there was a letter addressed to Macheath.

He knew he ought to tell Lucy about Sarah, but no matter how he explained it she would be hurt and jealous. There were far too many difficulties in that puzzling day to make it an easy topic of conversation – glances, touches, subtle, unfinished suggestions. He was doing his best to be honest, but he knew that his anxiety about Lucy's reaction went to the heart of the matter. If he loved her truly, he would laugh off Sarah's obsession.

And he didn't.

And with that in the back of his mind, he felt guilty, no matter how technically innocent he might be.

He managed to ignore the problem, but then he heard that Chaplin and the younger end of the family had indeed gone to Switzerland. He told himself at first that it wouldn't matter – there would be no letter for "Macheath" sitting at the Post Office waiting for him. Sarah must see how ridiculous she was being, and simply not write at all, or else her letter would excuse her from going further. That would be that. But when Chaplin had been gone three days, the possibility of that letter had become painful. He would ask at the Post Office, on his way to work. It could do no harm, surely? If there was no letter, well and good, and if there were, he would take it to Dunchurch, where he could read and destroy it and Lucy would never know.

He was flattered and oppressed in equal measure when the clerk produced a letter sealed with the plain oval that had closed Chaplin's instructions to him in the spring. He got no further than the Post Office yard before he had to open it, feeling that if he left it in his pocket it might burn him through the cloth.

Sarah's letter began in a neat, slanted hand:

Macheath, I dream of meeting you. We shall be alone, somewhere dark and private and secluded…

He flushed at her audacity. Phew! He couldn't possibly read that here, amid the busy to and fro of customers – and not at the Swan, either, with his passengers crowding onto the coach and old Tom Thetford chivvying him to get onto the box-seat. He re-folded the letter with trembling fingers and put it in his inside pocket. After such an opening, Sarah might have written anything. The possibilities half blinded him all the rest of his working day.

It wasn't until he was lying on his narrow straw pallet in the Dun Cow at Dunchurch, and listening to Thetford snoring, that he drew the candle nearer to read the letter in full.

Macheath, I dream of meeting you. We shall be alone, somewhere dark and private and secluded, where we may take pleasure in each other with no-one to deny us. I burn to know what happens. When I attempted to ask Mamma she counselled patience and self-control and told me nothing. No-one will enlighten me, not even Eleanor. She pretends to me that marriage is a new dress and prayers at Mr Mackeson's side. But even the most fervent prayers, I think, do not produce a family so large as ours! What is so secret that it may only be known by married women?

Eliza once warned me that I must pay no attention to what she calls "the fallen women" who haunt such places as the Swan. Well, I cannot elude Eliza's observation – but you can. Find someone among them who will teach me.

Peachum

He let out a gasp of exasperation that blew the candle flame sideways. It was a terrible letter – shameless, insinuating, clever and extraordinarily ignorant. Did Sarah know what she was doing to him? On one level, she couldn't possibly understand – but she knew, all the same, that it was powerful, and Sarah understood power. He ought to burn her letter. If only Lucy were there, Lucy who freed him from the fascination that Sarah had for him. When he was with Lucy, he wanted no-one else. She balanced him, made him kind and kept him sane, gave their love a deep, sensual strength. But Lucy wasn't with him. Because he had kept this secret from her, he was alone, and guilty, with Sarah's words running through his body and his blood. He read them again, and a third time before he pinched out the light.

He turned over on his belly and pressed his face into the musty pillow. The ideas continued to smoulder. Through the pale summer night he lay restless, consumed with a lust that shamed and sickened him even while he gave in to it.

In the morning, he felt that breakfast with Thetford was unreal, as though he sat between two worlds, one visible, tangible, noisy, smelly and lively, and one insidiously tempting in its invisibility. During the hours along the road back to London he wondered how he might fight off Sarah's invasion of his mind. It could not be done directly. Her father would naturally defend her and attack him – in his usual fierce, subtle way. Like father, like daughter! Who would believe that George, a vigorous young man, had not made the first advances? Or encouraged Sarah?

He was convinced that Sarah's request for a meeting with a prostitute was only an excuse to write a salacious letter, but he didn't think Lucy would believe that. This situation would have been so much easier if he hadn't been flattered by Sarah's attentions – or if she had been still in the schoolroom, or plain, or old enough to be his aunt – but she was much the same age as Lucy, lively and well-dressed and far bolder. Lucy wouldn't believe that he hadn't been tempted by such a rival. She knew him too well. And if his wife wouldn't believe him, then he couldn't expect anyone else to do so.

He ought not to reply. Surely if he remained silent, Sarah might be sufficiently discouraged not to write again. But her letter burned in his brain and could not be ignored. Perhaps he should send a formal refusal to her at her home. That would put the matter to rest once and for all.

In the travellers' room at the Swan, he wrote:

Dear Miss Chaplin

I wish you will not write to me in such a fashion. Your Mamma is wise, and Eliza's advice is sound. What you ask is improper, and I will have nothing to do with it.

G Davenport

He addressed it, all the same, to Miss Peachum, at the General Post Office, and not to Miss Chaplin, at Adelphi Terrace.

CHAPTER 37.

He jerked awake in darkness, fighting off the dream. The other half of the bed was empty.

"Lucy?" The sheets next to him were still warm. He sat up, feeling the night air chill his damp skin, and listened. A faint catch of breath in the sitting room. "Lucy? What's the matter? Come back to bed, woman."

He heard her sniff, and then a shuffling sound as though she wrapped her nightgown round her and would not move. The sniffle and the silence together were bad signs. He was at a loss to know why; they had gone to bed immediately after supper and made love with all the passion of their first meetings. She couldn't possibly have guessed at the temptation he had so nearly accepted – she was too honest for her imagination to stretch that far. He slid out of bed and padded through into the dimness. Yes, definitely crying.

"Come on, lovely. Come back to bed now. You sniffle louder than Fat Mary," he said, trying to make her laugh.

"Oh George." Her voice was wobbly. "I'm so glad you've woken up."

"Ah. Yes. Come back to bed." He put his arm round her shoulders, and she gave a little sob and buried her face in the hair on his chest. "Blimey, I wish you'd wipe your nose on a handkerchief instead of on me!"

"You're such a fool," she said, half laughing.

"Come back to bed, then." When they were curled up again under the bedclothes, he asked, "What was that all about?"

"It doesn't matter."

"I don't believe you." She would tell him eventually what was bothering her, but it would come out quicker and be less damaging if he poked it from the blind side. "I know I've been a bit remiss lately. Was I that bad?"

"Oh, no!" she said, as though shocked. "I didn't mean to reproach you. You're driving such long distances. I know it's hard."

"Well if it's hard we're talking about…you can have another taste here and now." He laughed, and kissed her.

She giggled, but she pinned down his straying hand. "Later. You were having such a bad dream. Something horrible. You were shouting and struggling and the hair was standing up all along your arms. You hit me in the eye."

"Sorry. Did I hurt you?"

"Yes, but it wasn't your fault, you were asleep."

"Sorry. Sorry." He followed each apology with a kiss.

"What is it you dream about?" she asked. "Is that why you've always had a single room? You never talk about it."

"It's nothing," he said. "It's never happened before when I've been in bed with – y'know – anyone else… "

"Go on."

He hesitated. The dream had been vivid, but there were aspects of it that he must certainly not tell Lucy, and he was uncomfortable about that. What he'd told Sarah had been true: he loved Lucy, not just for her attentiveness, nor for her unswerving, uncomfortable honesty. He had known at their first meeting that she was a wounded creature who needed gentle treatment.

Since their marriage she had turned all her energy to looking after him, making sure a meal was ready for him when he came in, that his clothes were cleaned and pressed and Mrs Bowe's house polished and pretty and welcoming. She was lovingly amused by the simplest things he did, even his night-time shaving routine. She carried his baby with pride. Her adoration forced him to be strong and honourable, to give her the kind of responsible love he had received in childhood, to rediscover values that had become strange to him in the six years he had worked as a coachman. Of course those years had made on impression on him – the habit of embroidering the truth to entertain passengers remained, and made it easy to conceal the effect that Sarah Chaplin had on him – but older standards were reasserting themselves nonetheless. He felt guilty just for having been tempted.

Lucy said cautiously, "I know I'm not the first girl you ever tumbled."

There was a pause. He wondered whether the secrets that Lucy had to tell would come out now, but she lay close, and seemingly at ease.

At length, he said, "I dream about my mother, and my sisters. The girls were older than me. They died of diphtheria. We buried them in Dad's grave. That's what I dream about."

"When you're worried."

"How do you know that?" he asked, in surprise.

"I have nightmares too." She kissed his bare shoulder. "I'll tell you some other time. Not now. What about your mother?"

"She died too, lovely. Sometimes it's Mam we're burying, in the dream."

"Oh. I see. Forgive me if I don't seem to know the right thing to say... if my mother died I'd be very happy."

"That doesn't surprise me," said George. He saw her push away whatever was troubling her.

"They didn't all die, though, did they? Your family?"

"No. I didn't! And Gran and Granda are still around – at least they were. I was going to take you to visit them, but you were so ill – so I just kept going. Anyway, the old man would probably damn me to hell. He wouldn't write – I fell out with him about wanting to drive four-in-hand. And Gran never learned her letters."

"You can write, though. Your Gran must know someone who would read a letter for her. But what are you worrying about? Why are you dreaming?"

"Nothing important, lovely."

"If you're dreaming, of course it's important! Is it money?"

"No. Not exactly." He mustn't mention Sarah, even though she had only been the messenger. "I heard that the Guv'nor may sell all his coaches. If it's true, we might have to move again, out of London."

"Oh George! And we've only just got settled!"

"I know. I didn't want to worry you, what with the baby and all."

"And Mrs Bowe is so nice to us here!"

"Yes," he said. "But it may come to nothing, so don't fret. Forget about it. Your job for the next few months is to look after the baby. Think of yourself as a brood mare, or a placid cow."

She chuckled, secure in her pregnancy. "I'm certainly growing udders. I thought I felt the baby moving this morning, but Mrs Bowe said it's too early."

He rubbed a comforting hand over her belly, and kissed her forehead again. "How about calling him Matthew?"

"Why?"

He hadn't really thought. The name had just popped into his head. He improvised, "Because he'll be the first of four. Y'know, Matthew, Mark, Luke and John."

She took the reasoning in her stride, but exclaimed, "Four boys! Good heavens, George, you do count chickens before they hatch! And what if this isn't a boy. What'll you do then!"

"I'll have to brag about how pretty she is. Obviously, she'll take after me."

"Ooohh! George Davenport! You conceited toad!"

"If it is a girl I'll let you choose her name."

"Yes, you most certainly will!" She cuddled into his arms and said, "I'd like to call her after one of your sisters."

"That would be nice." His hand drifted down her body, stealthily tugging up the hem of her night-dress. "Martha sounds quite like Matthew, doesn't it."

"Not Martha," she said. "The one you shouted for when you were dreaming. Sarah. God rest her soul."

He must remember never to talk about Hannah.

CHAPTER 38.

He was free of Sarah for nearly a week.

He went about his work and saw nothing that brought her to mind, and he stopped worrying about incendiary letters at the Post Office. In fact, the whole business might have blown over. But one evening the new clerk at the Swan called him in, made a sour remark about private correspondence, and handed him a letter.

My lovely Macheath

Yes, I was afraid that perhaps you might refuse, and as I suppose you will not look for a letter at the Post Office, this goes to the Swan.

You write as though you are Oh! So proper – so careful and cold and old. I know you are not like that. Of course what I ask is improper! If it were proper, then Mamma or Eliza or Eleanor would tell me what I wish to know!

Please try to see this from my point of view. If I wished to understand why I see the rainbow, I could read of it in a book, but there is no encyclopaedia to offer me the knowledge I crave.

Girls such as I – imprisoned by our protective families – never learn what is forbidden to us until we marry – after which we have no choice.

You are married. Because you are married, you must know. Dare I ask that you teach me?

Perhaps that is impossible, but you can't stop me dreaming. You may disapprove. All the old tabbies will certainly disapprove. But help me to learn, then perhaps I will be satisfied.

Polly

She took risks that made him sweat. If Foyle or any of the staff at the Swan had seen her handwriting they would have recognized it. Her only caution had been not to use the seal from her father's office desk. George was sure he would be dismissed if Chaplin found out that he was involved in any way. That was the real danger. If he angered Sarah she would give him away without thinking, because really, the girl was outrageous.

On the other hand, he might turn her scandalous demands to his own advantage. Chaplin was about to change direction in his business and maybe Sarah's inside knowledge could be useful. That was certainly worth more than a passing thought. He could make a bargain for the information she wanted. In any case, what harm would it do if he made this meeting actually happen? He remembered, with a grin, the dark "Frenchy whore" Jeanne who frequented the Queen's Hotel and the Swan. Jeanne would do more than satisfy Sarah's curiosity – she might startle her into self-control.

That evening, instead of going straight home, he invited Jeanne into a quiet corner of the taproom. She was scornful at first at being enlisted to help a woman who already had huge advantages over her in wealth and position, but when George persisted, she scented money.

"Zis rich girl. She will pay?"

"I would say you can name your price."

"And she is *vièrge*?"

"Oh, yes! But she doesn't behave like one!"

"Ah! What we call *demi-vièrge!* You also *peut-être!*" Jeanne glanced at him, her eyes bright with malicious curiosity. "We, ser girls, we see you refuse us, and we wonder, mm?"

He was furious to feel himself blushing. These women! They saw so much and talked so much and yet told nothing unless it suited them.

"Well, you can stop wondering. You know perfectly well that I'm a married man."

"*C'est ça*. And your wife she is *enceinte*, so I understand all must be well." She gave him another of her black-eyed, considering looks that swept from eyes to groin and back. "It's very normal for a man to look at such a time for a discreet *maîtresse*, but you do not choose wisely, do you?"

"Now, now, Jeannie. I'm not trying to bed this girl."

"That is most curious, because you know she must be fast, to ask a man such a thing. It is not subtle, not discreet. It is better for a good girl not to know, unless she learn also how to look after herself. Me, I have come here to earn a *dot* – what you say, dowry, *oui*? When I go back to Bretagne, I will make a good marriage, because no-one knows I have been *putain*. For her, is not so easy. *Savoir, c'est faire.* She must be very strong to say, I know, but I will not do. If she is not so strong, she must learn how not to have a child. Her Mamma is correct. It is better for her to know nothing until she marries. And she is not subtle or discreet, so it is best to marry quickly. Tell her this."

"She says she won't ever marry."

Jeanne made a slight spitting noise. "Why do you wish to solve 'er problems?" Again that surveying glance. "You are tempted, I think, to take 'er to bed!"

"No," he said, embarrassed.

"I have a cure for that," she said. "You give me one sovereign, and take me instead. I pretend very well to be *vièrge*."

He shook his head. "What would my wife say?"

"Stupid! You would not tell 'er! But perhaps your wife, she was *vièrge* so you have no curiosity."

"That's none of your damned business!"

"Only it is strange that you talk to me and not to her."

"She'd jump to the same conclusion as you did, and that's an argument I can do without. Damn it, Jeannie! You only have to say, one way or the other, whether you'll meet the girl."

"Ah, if she has *monnaie*, then – perhaps. One afternoon. But this *vièrge*, she excites you, no? I find you safe place and you teach 'er yourself. Then perhaps you both pay me!" Her smile had an eager, predatory edge.

"Whoa, Jeannie." He stood up. "I told you, I'm not going down that road."

When she merely stared at him with that gleaming smile, he said, "I'll let you know if it suits her. Don't price yourself too high."

She watched him go, then reached for his glass, and drank the sherry he had left behind.

He went to the writing table, and composed a letter to Sarah very carefully in his head before he committed anything to paper. It had to be completed, sanded and sealed in the shortest possible time, without any crumpled drafts lying about for Jeanne to use.

Most importantly, he must not remind either Jeanne or Sarah of where he lived.

Miss Chaplin

I would be most relieved if you decided not to pursue the matter you discussed in your last letter. If you insist, however, I will introduce you to someone. You must be willing to pay her. I refuse to teach you myself.

If you wish to continue, you need to choose a day to meet her. It must be an afternoon.

I advise you not to boast of anything you may learn. Beware, though. You may not like what she says or how she says it.

G Davenport

CHAPTER 39.

London, 13 August 1838

“The glorious Twelfth,” said George, “I don’t think.” He was looking down onto Falcon Street through the rain-spattered window of the sitting-room.

Lucy was somewhere about the house, helping Mrs Bowe to turn mattresses in the other lodgers’ rooms, throwing back the bedclothes over each foot-rail. The two women had opened all the house windows, so that the street sounds came up with the hush of the rain.

Cherry lay back in one of the armchairs, immersed in a newspaper, his small booted feet stretched out in front of him.

“And all the landed gents have flitted off to shoot grouse.”

“Then thank God you aren’t out there with ’em.”

Cherry laughed. “We’ll get wet enough at work tonight.”

“You are quite like a grouse,” went on George. “Short and fat and no good at flying. That coat’s getting tight! Have you given up walking?”

“I haven’t had company to walk with,” said Cherry, lowering the newspaper. “Maybe I’ll go back to it, now I’m in town the same days as you. Anyway, it isn’t the twelfth. It’s the thirteenth.”

“Highly appropriate for the day we’re sold to the competition.”

“Sherman was a stroke of luck for us, mate.”

"You think so? I wouldn't bank on him. We struggle out of one crisis only to find ourselves in another, don't we? I'd feel safer applying for a post at the Royal Mews – at least the Palaces won't turn into railway stations."

Cherry said teasingly, "Wouldn't you look the part in the Queen's livery."

"And talking of livery, Sherman'll be sending the Greyhound and the Albion coaches to the builder, won't he, to paint them up in black-and-yellow? God knows what he'll expect us to drive in the meantime – some old bodge-ups, I suppose, with all four wheels of different sizes."

"Oh, stop grumbling. If he knows what he's doing he'll get the spare coaches painted first and swap them round when they're done. You have to admit the man's a competitor, taking on the railways."

"I don't trust him. He's no horseman, I'll tell you that for nothing. I'm not sure he's even a businessman. A showman, maybe – or a charlatan – him with his fancy shirt-front, all stuck with diamond pins!"

"You look pretty fancy yourself in that new Mackintosh," said Cherry.

The coat had turned up on Friday evening as a tight parcel in the boot of the Albion. Lucy approved of its practicality, but George was suspicious. There had been no clue to the sender, no invoice, simply a parcel with Bax's warehouse label, addressed to him, and the new coat inside. Tom Thetford had raised his eyebrows and said nothing, which allowed George to pretend to Lucy that he had bought it himself – but was it from Sarah, or from Cherry?

When George didn't answer, Cherry sighed and went back to reading.

"It says here there's been an accident on the railway."

"Mm? Which one?"

"Up at Harrow on the Hill. It says a guard's been killed, collecting fares."

"Well?" said George, shortly.

"It's shocking, making a fellow climb from carriage to carriage when the train's moving."

George pulled a face. "What about the risks we take? How many drivers make their guards take off the brake-shoe without stopping? What about that smash the night after the Coronation? Or old Bowe, drowned saving his horses? Give it another couple of years, and the newspapers won't make any more fuss about railway accidents than they do with coaches."

"As though you know anything about the future! And listen, according to this you owe me five bob. You said they'd open Kilsby railway tunnel before the Coronation, and it says here that passenger services go through next month."

"It was open!" protested George. "We met goods trains in the week before the Coronation, and your bet was that it wouldn't be open till the autumn."

"We weren't betting on goods trains. Pay up."

"It's a great shame, y'know, when a man has to split hairs just to take a coachwheel off me. I don't know what things are coming to. Here! That's more'n I owe you." He tossed a shilling to Cherry, who caught it and shook his head in resignation.

George went back to the window, and leaned there, arms folded, apparently observing a load of skins being delivered to the warehouse along the street. In reality he was listening for the town clocks to strike mid-day. Sarah's letter had told him she would meet Jeanne at the Swan at twelve, and he didn't dare check his watch with Cherry sitting there. His limited experience with "professional" girls made him curious about the kind of advice Jeanne would give her, and he was highly tempted to eavesdrop at the meeting, but he knew that his physical presence would make the whole business far too obvious, and so he wasn't going to be there. His mind and body were nonetheless charged with awareness of what might be happening at the Swan.

Sarah's reply to his note had come at the end of the week.

How can I ever thank you? I will contrive to leave Eliza in the coffee room. Are you not just a little curious? Surely you must be there. Will you? How will I know this woman, otherwise?

Peachum

He had written back to Sarah:

Jeanne will know you. Everyone knows you. She will organize everything. You will need to bring guineas – she will not talk without being paid, and she values her advice all the more highly because you are asking for it. As to how you will know her – She is French and she has black hair and black eyes. She wears a red shawl when she wishes to attract attention, and a dark green one when she does not.

Do not thank me. I will not be there. Perhaps one day I may ask a favour in return.

He caught his fingernail on the curtain, and swore under his breath.

"Davenport?"

He turned from the window in surprise to find Cherry looking at him.

"I said, Sherman ain't so daft," said Cherry. "They say he's married money more than once."

"Oh, do stop gossiping." George went across to Lucy's workbox and trimmed his nail with her sewing scissors.

"You're bloody miserable this morning," said Cherry. He put away the newspaper, and brought out his cribbage board and cards. "The weather's getting me down, too. Come on, let's play."

He began to deal the cards.

***

When George arrived for work at the Queen's Hotel, Jeanne marched up to him, the fringe of her shawl flying. Red, he noticed. She had money on her mind.

"A fine *chevalier* you are," she began, "sending that gel to me when she had no cash!" Her eyes were unfriendly, and the French accent fought with her Cockney phrases. "Three guineas you owe me. Cough up, *mon brave!*"

"The deal was between you and her," he said.

She laughed at him. "I am unconcerned. Business is business! And you did oughter add a *pourboire* for me telling her what I did!"

"I'm surprised you told her anything, if she couldn't pay."

"It was not amusing, *en effet.* She expected you to be there. She was *fâchée,* angry, crazy, and she made me to take a letter afore she would let me go. You pay me now!"

He grimaced, and dropped half a sovereign into her palm. "That's all you're getting, Jeannie. What have you done with the letter? You didn't throw it away?"

"*Quelle bêtise.* It's close to me heart," she said, patting her bodice so that her breasts quivered. "What's it worth to yer? Make me an offer."

He dropped a shilling into her cleavage, and she gave him the letter, creased and smelling of a cheap violet scent. George tucked it into a pocket and turned away, determined not to open it in front of her.

In a quiet corner of the coffee room, he read:

My darling, infuriating, impossible Macheath

I once swore I would never become hysterical, but this is beyond everything!

Jeanne demands far more money than I had bargained for, and because I will not pay her price she refuses to tell me what I want to know! I have waited for you here until now, hoping you might lend me something, but it is past three o'clock. Where the devil are you?

Also Papa has written from Luzern, saying that he is to return immediately, posting. He will be hard on the heels of his letter. Unless there is a gale that keeps the ship in Calais, he and Mamma will be home, and my freedom will be at an end! I shall not see you any more! And I am none the wiser! I shall go mad!

Polly

He folded the letter with a sigh. That was temper, not hysteria. She would never have risked approaching him if there had been any risk of damaging head or heart, and he had no fears for her sanity. So what if the game hadn't turned out the way she wanted! It wouldn't bring him any advantage now, but it was probably for the best. Chaplin was coming home, and that would put an end to it.

CHAPTER 40.

19 August 1838

Mrs Bowe said on Sunday, "You oughter take better care of your missus, Mr Davenport."

"Why?" He lowered the newspaper and gave her his politest smile. "Is she about to run off with Mr Cherry?"

"It would serve you right if she did," she replied. "I'm sure he spends more time with her than you do."

That was unfair, so he ignored her. Lucy was getting ready to attend church with him. After the service they usually went for a quiet stroll, as a couple, or sometimes with Cherry, then to church again in the evening. Today was indeed a day of rest – or it would be, if the landlady would leave him alone.

"You ain't noticed her wheezing, then? Or coughing through the night?"

"Working hard, Mrs B. I barely notice going to bed."

He shook the newspaper dismissively but Mrs Bowe had the bit between her teeth.

"That cold's settled on her chest. Mind you take care of her."

"I will, thank you." He was being careful of Lucy, wasn't he? Now that she was "Mrs Davenport in Falcon Street" she had a much easier life than "Lucy Hennessy, dogsbody at the Blue Bell." She didn't have to get up early and clean fireplaces and riddle the ashes and beat carpets. She had time to learn from Mrs Bowe how to knit and sew, to make clothes for the baby. She was only needed to help with the household tasks that Mrs Bowe found difficult on her own, and she didn't have to stay up at night, waiting for drunken customers to leave. In bed he restrained himself, being what she called "considerate."

"Well! Take a drop more water with it," said Mrs Bowe tartly, "and try listening for a change."

When he didn't answer she made a small explosive noise and went away. He moved his chair to the window, tipped the newspaper over his face to keep off the sun and wallowed in a space of pure peace.

His weekday waking hours were hard enough, the kind that only youth or physical fitness could support, and he was no longer feverish to go roving round the London theatres. He felt rather smug – not to say astonished – at his own steadiness.

The sun struck in as Lucy twitched the newspaper off his face.

"Wake up, lazybones," she said, smiling at him. "We're all ready for church, apart from you."

***

Although George's route and the stages and the horses had not altered since Sherman took over from Chaplin, the week's work seemed to get longer. The takings were mediocre, and the passengers increasingly tiresome. It didn't help either that Sherman had a reputation for late payment of his subcontractors, so that with settlement day approaching the country innkeepers were growing anxious, and their uncertainty filtered down to the yard staff, the drivers and guards, and even the horses. Yesterday Cinnamon had kicked out and narrowly missed someone's head, and on the return trip today the young thoroughbreds had tried to bolt with him. Everywhere George went, there were tempers to smooth. He decided he'd have to give up most of his break at Stony and keep the men in a good humour while they put the team to the coach, to make sure his favourite horses weren't upset.

Cordock, who had been on duty with him, wanted him to stay and drink when they finished work, but he shook his head tiredly and walked home alone.

At Falcon Street, a lamp stood lit in the hallway.

"Hullo! Lucy!"

His voice sounded weary, even to himself. These return trips to Dunchurch demanded two long days with only a few hours' sleep. Still, he had the best part of two days off now; plenty of time to catch up on sleep. He took off his hat and coat, and began to climb the stair

"Lucy? Where are you, my little sugar-plum?"

It was Mrs Bowe who came hurrying to meet him. "Oh there you are at last, Mr Davenport! Your missus has been taken ill."

"What's the problem?" His wits were wool-gathering. "Is it the baby?"

"No, no," she said impatiently. "Go in. Go in will you! Doctor Neill is with her." She set off down the stair, groaning a little with each step.

George lifted his eyebrows at her lack of explanation, and pushed open the door. Their sitting room was empty apart from an overcoat that lay on one of the chairs, so he went on into the bedroom. Lucy lay on the bedcovers with her stays loosened, and she turned her head and smiled at him. The stout, grey-haired man standing beside her bed drew out his watch and took hold of her wrist, surveying her all the while with a pleased expression.

"Ah good," said the doctor. "Your lady wife has had a poorly turn, Mr Davenport, but I think she is improving."

Lucy tried to speak, but the effort brought on her cough, and silenced her. George was shocked. He could hear the wheeze in her chest from where he stood.

"Lie quietly, dear girl," said Dr Neill, "and let me explain it to your husband – breathe slowly, my dear, breathe easily, not too deep – that's it. Good girl. Mr Davenport, your wife has a touch of bronchitis."

He looked enquiringly at George, who stammered, "Will she be all right? What about the child?"

The doctor made an irritated noise and pocketed his watch. "We must treat the mother, sir! It will be well enough provided her own health is improved." He turned to Lucy and said, "Take the Tartar and wild cherry syrup to ease your cough; a teaspoonful every two hours, preferably in hot water."

Lucy nodded, and offered a faint smile as thanks.

"Well," the doctor went on briskly, "I find your bedroom ideal – none of those old hangings that hold dust and disease – very hygienic indeed. Do you ventilate it daily? Good, good. That really is excellent. So, my dear girl, I will leave you to take your medicine from Mrs Bowe when she comes back with the hot water. Eat a light supper, and get into bed and rest. You are not to fret yourself for a day or two. I'm sure your husband will be quite as well looked after as usual. Good evening to you, and I will look in after church tomorrow. Mr Davenport – a word before I leave, sir."

He took George by the elbow and piloted him ruthlessly into the sitting room.

"Listen to me, young man. You must take good care of your wife – you're very fortunate that Mrs Bowe sets such store by her."

"It won't turn to consumption, will it?"

"No – of course not! Neither the cause nor the symptoms are the same. Don't worry on that score. Her fever is only slight. I should warn you though that it will take some time for the bronchial tubes to clear and for the irritation which makes her cough to subside. It would be easier on her if you didn't insist on your conjugal rights for a while – you take my meaning, eh?"

"Yes, sir. I do, already – well, she has enough to deal with – on account of the baby. So long as I know she will be all right…"

"Of course she will, though that if cough persists you may have to remove to a more open situation – somewhere above the city, where the air is fresher. Winter will make it worse, not because of the cold but because the smoke is always more troublesome. Combined with fog it is most unpleasant for those with weak lungs. I trust you are quite well yourself? I imagine you have no chest trouble, with all your outdoor work, eh? No? Excellent. Sound constitution, no doubt. Good evening to you."

George nodded, and as the doctor tramped down the stair he heard him taking leave of Mrs Bowe.

He sank into the armchair and ran his hands through his hair, but before he could think very deeply Mrs Bowe came in with two extra pillows.

She said flatly, "I'll help Lucy into her night clothes. I've told Betsy to serve your supper up here. It won't do you no harm to eat in the bedroom with your missus. Didn't I tell you she wasn't well? Neglect is what sends gels into a decline, in my opinion."

Well, at least he was going to be fed. It also sounded as though Mrs B had worked up a head of steam against him. As if he didn't see enough steam every day with those damned railway engines upsetting the horses. He leaned back and closed his eyes, and waited for the storm to break.

***

After supper Lucy was sleepy. She was reassured by the doctor's visit, and the syrup taken hot seemed to have eased her cough a little. George sat by the bed until she dozed off, then when he was certain that she slept soundly he pulled the blanket higher over her and half-closed the door. Then he went to the corner of the sitting room where he kept the writing case.

He unlocked it. One of Sarah's messages peeked out from under a business letter. He didn't trouble to collect her letters any more, but he recognized that as one of her less demanding efforts. He picked it out and read it again.

Adelphi,

London

Dear George,

I have been to the theatre, with Papa, Mamma, William and Marianne. We saw Mr Macready's production of Shakespeare's "King Lear," with none of the Cibber nonsense about it – hence it was I who appreciated the play and my family who were unconvinced. Perhaps you have read in the newspapers that Mr Macready is to produce "The Tempest," again using the original text. It is already predicted to be enormously successful. I shall certainly do everything in my power to see it.

I often remember our night at "Richard the Third" and how you and I together made a fool of Mr Mackeson. Do you wonder, as I do, whether this summer would have been different if we had not? I know it would have made no difference on my side, but on yours? Perhaps.

Write to me. Please.

He sighed. There was still that trace on the paper of her dangerous, clever fingers. He gathered up the others she had written, and was pinning them together when he heard a knock at the door. He called, "Yes?"

"It's me," said Cherry, coming in. "How's Mrs D?"

"Come in. Lucy's asleep. Let me put away these papers, and we can have a yarn." He locked the case. "I never thought I'd do much writing, but it seems there's always something."

"I brought a bottle," said Cherry. He had a little clutch of glasses in his other hand. "I hope you don't mind but I thought a drop of sherry might be good for her."

"Thank you – pour and I'll leave it by her bedside." George carried the glass into the bedroom for Lucy. She was still sleeping, propped with the extra pillows Mrs Bowe had brought in, the bulge of the child evident under the blankets and the bronchitis audible as a slight creak at the end of each breath. His jaw tightened. He put the sherry on the table within her reach, and moved the candle a little further away.

Cherry had poured two more glasses, and was sitting with his boots stretched to the fire.

"You're busy as a bee these days," he observed.

"True." George pushed the little case into the corner. When he came back to the fire Cherry brought out his cards and the folding cribbage board.

"You see, I'm fully equipped for merrymaking."

"So long as that's all you're making, I'm your man."

They cut for deal, and started the game. "Well," said Cherry, "I hope it turns a bit of cash for you, all this to-ing and fro-ing, whatever it is. It frets your missus, you know. She asked me if you're gambling."

George hooted with disbelief, and discarded into the crib. "Pull the other one. She's seen me play."

"She notices when you go out before me, and she knows your coach leaves later than mine," said Cherry, looking at him steadily.

"Play," said George, equally steadily.

Cherry made a dissatisfied noise, but he completed the hand before he said, "People are asking questions, Davenport."

"Let them. If I've had letters to post, it's none of their business. Nor is it any of yours, old mate. Where do you go to when you disappear?"

Cherry paused in shifting his peg on the board. "Now, Davenport, you should know better than to ask. I've seen men hanged for it. Best if you don't know too much."

"Well, what's sauce for the goose is sauce for the gander." He lifted his glass. "Here's to mystery."

After a moment, Cherry shrugged, and lifted his own glass. "You falling out with the missus, then? You didn't ought to do it. The doctor said you have to humour her, and she lives and breathes for you."

"She's well enough," said George shortly.

"Is she? I don't think she is. You ain't here much for her to love, even the ordinary way of things. There's only Mrs B and Betsy to keep her company. She wants you here, for her to make a fuss of. Like any woman."

George shrugged, and sipped sherry. "You're a fine one to talk about what women want."

"I'll tell you, I think you're up someone else's skirts, and I'm not the only one as thinks that. It ain't Fat Mary, but Frenchy Jeanne? I've seen you two whispering in corners." George fidgeted, and Cherry pounced. "That's it! It's Jeanne, isn't it? She's your mystery!"

George said, "There's nothing in that. You know I'm not likely to take up with a whore."

"No? You can't tell me there's nothing going on!"

"Keep your voice down. Lucy's asleep."

"All right!" Cherry said, exasperated. "Well, if it ain't Jeanne, and it ain't a light-frigate, what are you up to?"

"It's nothing."

"I know there's someone." Cherry shook his head. "I don't understand. Why? You should get all you need at home."

"It isn't that simple, cock robin – but I can't tell you."

"Oh, can't you! It don't show much respect for our friendship."

"Look, why do you go wandering off at a weekend? You don't tell me that, do you?"

"That's different."

"See? I'm telling you, there's nothing in it that Lucy needs to worry about."

"You ought to cut loose," said Cherry. "It ain't right."

"I would take your advice, of course, if there was anything to cut loose from."

Cherry drew breath to speak, twice, and each time thought better of it. "Really. I don't know whether I believe you any more."

"Believe whatever you like," said George. "You're in no position to judge."

"You know," said Cherry, "there's times I like you a lot, and other times I can't make you out. You punched me in the eye but I never minded that, remember? I never held it against you, because I thought, well, he's got his little wife to look after, he's settling down, doing what's right, making a proper nest with her and the baby like a good man should. You made out you were a decent bloke walking the straight and narrow. I even admired you for it. And now you're carrying on with someone – when you don't need to – before the baby's even born. You know what, Mr High-and-Mighty Davenport? That makes me sick."

He swept up the card game, and made for the door.

"That sherry's for Mrs D. Don't drink it yourself."

CHAPTER 41.

27 August 1838

On Monday Lucy insisted on getting up. She said to George, "You ought to go for a walk with Mr Cherry and get some proper exercise. Yesterday you did nothing but find fault with things in the newspapers, and this morning you grumbled about the opening of the railway so many times I could recite it all back to you."

Before George could answer there was a knock at the door, and Mrs Bowe entered with a jug of hot water, and a cloth over her arm.

"Dr Neill's sent some Jerusalem Balsam for Lucy. Give her a hand to sit over here." She put the jug down on the table, and the cloth beside it.

"I don't need help," said Lucy, indignantly.

He supported her to the table all the same, and when Mrs Bowe draped the cloth over Lucy's head and pushed the jug in front of her face, he lifted the opposite edge and grinned at them both through the steam.

"Mam used to make us do this. When we had colds. Sit at the table under an old sheet."

"Do stop fidgeting," said Lucy. "George! You're letting the steam out. I shall be perfectly all right in a day or two."

He lowered the cloth. "Right you are, lovely. Thank you, Mrs B – you're a wonder."

"You're welcome," she replied. "I'm surprised to see you still here. You've been like a cat on hot bricks about getting away to work."

It was very plain that what she'd come for was a cosy female chat. It was equally plain that George was being excluded – not only from his own parlour, but from Lucy, from Cherry, from everyone in the house.

"Oh all right," he said. "Lucy's chasing me out, too. Is Mr Cherry in his room?"

"No. And he's another one who's turned funny! He stayed home on Saturday night, and went out yesterday, and he's still not back."

"Did he miss breakfast?" asked Lucy, emerging from under the cloth. "That's not like him."

George shrugged, remembering their toast "to mystery."

"Maybe he met a friend," he said, as lightly as he could. "Well, I'm bound to run into him at the Queen's later. I'll tell him his two favourite women are worrying about him."

He gave the ladies an ironical little salute, put on his hat and coat and went to find Tom Thetford. They visited Cherry's usual haunts, the coffee houses and taverns and the Swan, but no-one had seen him. Wherever he'd gone after his disagreement with George on Sunday night, it was somewhere off the map.

George was still worrying over it when they arrived at the stables for work. Both his team and Cherry's were turned round as usual in their stalls, ready to go.

The yard porter asked with some exasperation, "What've you done with 'im?"

"Cherry?"

"Yes, blast 'is eyes. You ain't seen 'im?"

"No, not since last night. Believe me, I've been looking."

"Well, if 'e don't arrive in five minutes I'll 'ave to put Holland on the box in 'is place."

"Maybe he's just overdone the sherry," said George, more cheerfully than he felt. "He'll be sleeping it off somewhere."

But when the ostlers led out Cherry's team, it was John Holland who went out to help hitch them to the coach.

While George was standing there worrying, Frenchy Jeanne came strolling past, wrapped in her green off-duty shawl.

"Oi!" she said. "You heard about yer mate?"

"Who?"

"Him," she said, nodding towards the Greyhound, "that they are all in a tizzy about for not turning up. I think he will not be here to drive tonight. He is arrested."

"Drunk?"

Her cynical grin developed a touch of malice. "Oh no no. A much more special sin."

He pretended not to understand her. "I've no idea what you're on about."

"You want me to write it down for yer? They call it attempting an unnatural act."

"It must be a mistake," he said, trying to hide his concern. "Cherry's all right. He doesn't pick up street girls, but then, neither do I!"

"Maybe I see further than you do," said Jeanne. "It is no matter to me – he is never a follower, so I neither win nor lose. But you? Best keep quiet about being his friend, eh?" She wrapped her shawl tighter and walked away.

"I'm surprised at yer dealing with her sort," said Tom Thetford, at his shoulder. "You with that pretty Missus at home."

"Damn it all, Thetford, I don't..."

"Oh, yer don't? If you say so." Thetford's wry expression said otherwise.

"She was telling me Cherry's in gaol!"

"Oh yus, I'll believe yer." It was a moment before Thetford took in the news. Then, on the same guess as George, he made a drinking gesture and asked, "A glass too many, ah?"

"No."

The Greyhound's guard blew "Start." The team stood to their collars and the traces tightened as Holland set the coach in motion.

Thetford said critically, "He don't look like he'll enjoy the freedom of the road."

"Damn it, Thetford – it ought to be Cherry taking that coach out!"

"Ah, he's a proper artist with four reins, which Holland ain't. He mostly drives a pair, to the 'bus, so he'll be as tired as the hosses when he gets to Stratford." Thetford waited until the Greyhound had rumbled out into the street, made the turn, and clattered away northward. "Well, what's the Frenchy girl saying about Cherry?"

George made an effort to keep his voice down. "She says he's been accused of an unnatural act. Don't ask me what she meant by that. She didn't draw pictures."

"Well, we know Cherry, don't we? You work it out. Did she say where they've locked 'im up?"

"No."

"I suppose he's likely to be in Newgate, but it depends where he was took up. We can find out."

"Straight away." George couldn't bear the thought of Cherry confined in prison. "We must get him out."

"Oh, now, there's no chance of that."

"Surely, once we know where he's being held…"

"It takes influence to get bail. We don't have cash that talks that loud. No, he won't get out, not until he's been tried, and courts can be very funny things. They'd rather deal with a straightforward pickpocket or a swindler than 'one of those.'"

"Mrs B has always seemed to have a soft spot for him."

"Yes, I suppose she has, 'cos he don't make no trouble, most of the time. But you mustn't say anything to suggest she knows, understand?"

"For heaven's sake, Thetford! Of course I understand! But I can go and find out where Cherry is, can't I?"

"Not with our coach standing loaded," said Thetford. "Look George, you calm down. We've work to do. I can send Davey – see, that little varmint over there, lookin' for pockets to dip? It'll be a Christian act to distract him from his thieving activities. Won't take a moment."

"Tell him not to…" George didn't know how to phrase it without seeming weak. "Not to make things worse."

Thetford shook his head. "It's going be gossiped about – there's no way to stop that. You can't judge by Jeannie. She doesn't care two hoots, because she spends all her life in that world. But most people ye'll meet will be less broadminded. They won't say as much but ye'll find they'll be a lot more shocked."

CHAPTER 42.

28 August 1838

When George brought the Albion back to the Queen's Hotel the following evening, it was business as usual with coaches disgorging tired passengers, and the lamps being put up on the Mails as they made ready to load the evening's post. London seemed sootier than ever after his sharp day across country, and the coal smoke hung on the darkening air and made him cough.

While he was splitting the day's perks with Thetford, the boy Davey re-appeared. He edged round the groups of passengers like a scavenging dog, with a detached, calculating look in his eyes that was much older than his years.

George touched Thetford's arm, and said, "Isn't that the nipper you sent to find Cherry?"

"It is," said Thetford, with relief. "We'll hear the news, and then you an' me could have a bite of supper and chew over what to do."

"Then we'd better send Davey on to Falcon Street, to say we'll be late."

"I suppose we better had. After all, Cherry won't be going anywhere."

"Look, how would you feel about saving our perks for him?" They both knew that in prison everything had to be bought.

"Ah," said Thetford, "that's a good idea. Don't let Davey see which pocket you put it in. He'll lift it easy as winking. Cash would buy Cherry a bit of comfort – shackles off, for a start. Now, Davey boy, did you find our cock robin?"

"Took me all day, Mr Thetford. A fair old job it was finding out what's gone with him." He looked hopefully at the guard, but Thetford didn't react. "Cost me a bob or two, I'll tell yer."

"Well go on then," said George, "tell."

Davey glanced at him, saw that no money was forthcoming, and concentrated on Thetford. "Awright then. I arst a few lads if they heard anyfin. Here! There was a lot of talk about the feller being an indorser, y'know, a mandrake. Is that right?"

George's eyebrows went up at these terms, but Thetford just nodded.

"Gorblimey!" said Davey, "if I'd-a thought…"

"Go on, boy, we don't want to know what yer thought. No more cash till we know where 'e is."

"If you say so, guv. Anyways, I found out he's in Newgate – but, this is where it cost me, yer too blummin' late."

"Too late for what?" asked George.

Davey's thin shoulders rose and fell. "Well, he ain't there no more, cos he's dead." He looked from George's frozen expression to Thetford's and added defensively, "That's what the man tole me. He was one of the blokes what cut him dahn. And I had to pay him before he'd say as much as that."

"Are you saying Mr Cherry hanged himself?" asked Thetford hoarsely.

"Yes, o'course. He ain't bin tried nor nuffin. They found him this arternoon."

"Gawdstrewth. You hear tell of it but I never thought he was the man to do such a thing. Never would have thought it. Gawd rest his soul." He took off his hat.

Passengers from the coaches pushed by with baggage and shawls, too weary to pay any attention to two silent men and a ragged boy. George couldn't think of anything except Cherry. He couldn't imagine how that little dapper man would have felt, shackled in Newgate's squalor and despair.

In the short time since George had understood Cherry, he had learned that it was still possible to be hanged for "unnatural" behaviour – and that even if Cherry wasn't sentenced to death, he might endure years of confinement in the ancient gaol. The men whom Cherry met in the world of molly houses and secret rendezvous couldn't help, for fear of becoming prisoners themselves. Facing loneliness and indignity as well as disgrace, many a stronger man would have broken, and Cherry had chosen death – foolish, funny Cherry who had shown him the city, played cards, got happily drunk and loved unwisely. Cherry was gone. There would be no more wandering round the town with him, criticizing horses and drivers and cheerfully exchanging insults. And their last disagreement could never be settled. George felt he must go home, at once, before he became seven years old again, screaming *No! No!* He needed Lucy and her steady good sense, her sympathy and kindness.

"Is that whatcher wanted to know?" asked Davey, unmoved. "It cost me two bob. There's only a tanner left of yer cash and I'm keeping that, right?"

Tom Thetford swiped Davey with his hat and shoved him away. George had already run for home.

***

George stumbled up the stairs to the landing. Lucy was at the table setting cutlery out for his supper. She looked round and smiled.

"You're early!"

He stood there with his head in turmoil and his heart hammering.

"What's the matter, pet?" she asked. He didn't dare say anything. She took his arm, and led him into the sitting room, to the sofa. When she touched his face, her fingers slipped through the wetness on his cheek. "George! What is it?"

"It's Cherry." His voice came out as a croak. Then he wrapped his arms around her, hugging the firm bulge of the baby, his face against the ribbed wool of her dress.

"Is he hurt? Has there been an accident?"

He heard her asking questions but he was only conscious of the faint wheeze that her chest still made, in time with his own breathing. He could make no sense of anything she was saying. He heard Betsy come upstairs; she bounded in and put a plate on the table and Lucy hushed her and sent her away. The smell of stewed beef revolted him.

Minutes after that, Tom Thetford was there, hoarse and anxious. "I'm sorry to intrude, Missus."

"Oh, Mr Thetford, whatever's happened? Is Mr Cherry hurt? Tell me! I can't get any sense out of George."

Thetford must have replied with a gesture, because Lucy's arms tightened. After a moment the old man coughed and said, "Well, I'll be off then. I just wanted to be sure – well, look after each other, won't ye?"

George heard him clumping down the stair to his own room. He was thankful for Thetford's reserve. The facts were horrible enough without having to put them into words.

He stayed where he was, clasping Lucy, comforted by her hand stroking his cheek, letting her hold him close. He didn't know whether Lucy had ever grasped the truth about Cherry. So long as Mrs Bowe kept silence the rest of the household never discussed him. Now George had no idea where to start. While he struggled with the guilt and the grief swirling inside his mind Lucy began to talk again, and as the words flowed over him he began to hear the dialect phrases that she used only in times of stress.

"Mr Cherry was a good man, and he was fond o' thee."

The softly whispered "thee," that she used only to him, held infinite shades of comfort and love.

"For all thy cleverness, thou knows more about hosses than about people. Thou's such an innocent, thou thinks I don't understand. I knew thou had a fight with him weeks back. There was summat in it that t'wasn't decent to talk about, but Mrs Bowe tellt me t'was nowt to worry over. Didst thou fight again while I was poorly, or did he fight wi' thee? Whativver – thou couldn't-a seen what would come of it."

He shook the idea away.

"Don't fret now. There's some things best nivver known," she said. "Or best forgotten. And maybe good comes of it in the end. Listen. I nivver tellt thee this yet – but I promised I would, and maybe it'll comfort thee."

She held him close. She talked to him about Carlisle, about the years before they met, about the narrow little house and its stale, over perfumed rooms and how the men came after dark for Ma's girls. He felt Lucy's tears falling on him, and when he clung to her the baby pushed and wriggled in protest. What did Ma Hennessy have to do with Cherry's death?

"Wouldst-a have been so kind when thou first met me, if thou'd known?" She whispered, "I nivver tellt thee how I much wished thou could-a been my first."

In the silence that followed, the words echoed and grew, until he had to sit up and look at her.

"What are you saying?" He pulled out his handkerchief and wiped his face.

"When I was small," she said, "I used to sleep hidden in Mam's bed."

"Hidden? Why?"

"T'was t'only place the men didn't go. But then someone must-a seen me about, and asked for me. And Ma nivver turned away trade."

"No!"

"Oh! Yes," she said, with a breathless catch in her voice, half laughter, half scorn. "When thou's that young thou doesn't know what's right or wrong. Remember thy Mam telling thee to breathe fumes of Jerusalem Balsam, and how thou put thy head under t'cloth because she told thee to? That's how it was. I didn't like it, but I knew no different."

"No," he said again.

"The only wonder is she didn't start on me sooner. Business is business, that's what she said. Thou sells what thou's got. Everything around me said, you got no choice. All t'other girls took money from men. T'was how I was fed and clothed."

"Good God, Lucy. You ought to have run away! Somebody would have taken you in!"

"There's always an ought to. But I was too young to think of it. When I was a bit older I thought I might've found a place in a respectable house, like as a scullery maid, but I didn't know anybody to give me a character. That's the only reason I stayed. T'was only Jesus who could have saved me. I truly believe that. It was when Maggie and Sally dragged us out to hear a street preacher." She swallowed, the dialect fading as she grew calmer. "He talked and talked. Oh, how he could talk! All about hell-fire and the torments of the sinners – he tellt us how the whole world lay in the hands of the Wicked One, and we were all on the verge of ruin. He frightened us nearly to death! We knew we were sinners and damned! But after that he tellt us about Jesus, how He was willing to save all as would come unto Him, and He would wash our sins away."

George had no heart for his usual mockery.

"I clung to that idea," she said, "I don't know whether Mam believed him, but I did, that the Lord was a sin-pardoning God. The preacher said Jesus could give me hope. And it was true, wasn't it? We moved to the Bell, and Mam pretended she'd never been in the Lanes. I suppose she thought it was more respectable to sell ale than girls. I even went to school! I give thanks every day for the changes God arranged for me. My bedroom was right up in the attics, where no man could find me. Safe, do you see? I never wanted any man near me again, not until you came. But you did. You see? Everything came right, and I thank God for it."

He said helplessly, "I'm sorry." It was all he could think of. To him, God still seemed as irrelevant as ever, but if Lucy's faith had kept her sane in Ma's household perhaps it was no bad thing. He wouldn't challenge her beliefs again.

He realized too that there was a good deal he couldn't tell her. Sarah's relentless pursuit of him and her search for information had been mere adolescent fancies, but they had led to the misunderstanding with Cherry that had sent him away angry on Sunday night. George could never be sure now that anger wasn't the cause of Cherry's reckless behaviour, and his arrest. And although there were several ways that George might try to explain his own stupidity – as a married man trying to hold off the infatuation of an adolescent, or as a servant putting up with the wiles of a rich unmarried girl, or as an ambitious coachman hoping to use inside knowledge for his own advantage – he had always been playing with fire. How could he start to explain? It would be no use declaring to Lucy that he loved her and only her, and that he would honour his vow to look after her. He would mean it now all the more truly, but there was too much that would sting in the telling. Beneath the regret at his own recklessness, the sorrow for his lost friend and for Lucy's damaged childhood, he began to understand that keeping secrets was sometimes the only way to protect the people you cared for. What was it Lucy had said? *There's some things best forgotten.* He must say nothing.

He held her tightly, and neither of them spoke.

Gradually a sound forced itself on his consciousness, the faint tick-tick-ticking of a mouselike pulse that beat faster than the watch in his pocket. He recognized it at last as a heartbeat, the life of his own child. It lay there in its warm and secret world, protected and utterly self-absorbed in its determination to grow and survive. He pressed his face against it. The baby kicked him in the eye, and he felt Lucy laugh, even while her tears ran down his neck.

CHAPTER 43.

30 August 1838

The next day there was a doleful little gathering in the sitting room at Falcon Street.

"We shan't see Cherry again." Tom Thetford told them. "There won't even be a funeral. Them that goes down with the gaol fever, or takes their own life, they bury 'em in Newgate."

"We mustn't go into full mourning," said Mrs Bowe. "It would look very odd. People would talk, and we don't want that."

"But he was a friend," said Lucy. "Poor man. It would be too odd if we didn't show our respect! I can reline one of my bonnets and add some black to my mantle. Can't I? That won't be too ostentatious! I'll buy George a black cravat, and a bit of black ribbon to wear as an armband when he goes to work."

It was some time before Mrs Bowe would agree.

"I wouldn't say too much about it, if I were you," she advised, with an old-fashioned look. "There's a lot won't bear inspection, and you don't want to draw attention to yourself."

"That's right," said Thetford. "We knew him, but most people will just be horrified when they hear the story. They won't try to understand and they'll want to know why we didn't refuse to have him in the house. You might find they stop visiting – maybe cut you when they meet you in the street. It's best not to talk."

"Ridiculous!" said Lucy crossly, and whisked away to stand beside George. He slipped an arm round her as much for his own consolation as for hers. He was frustrated because there was no way to say goodbye to Cherry, and no way to close the argument of the last night they had spoken to each other. He didn't even know whether Cherry had any family who should be told of his death.

That evening, taking heed of Thetford's advice, he delayed setting off to work. He was going to arrive exactly on time, jump onto the box of the Albion and go. It was a risk, because it cut down his time for inspecting the horses and harness, but in his present mood it was the only way he could think of to escape sly remarks and off-colour suggestions, because if he punched someone that would only make things worse. Besides, he didn't want to see Holland's ham fists on the reins of the Greyhound coach, nor reminders of the face that was missing from his landscape.

He had meant to ask Thetford to warn the yard porter that he wouldn't be early, but somehow they had missed each other, so when he arrived at the Queen's he wasn't at all surprised to find Jonathan Morris pulling on his driving gloves and making ready to mount the coach in his place. He slapped Morris on the shoulder.

"I'm here now, Jonathan."

Morris started, and then looked away at the horses, as though embarrassed. "Oh, hullo, George."

"It's all right. You can stand down," he said, trying to make light of his hunger for the freedom of driving. "Have you looked them over? Everything all right?"

Morris said awkwardly, "You'd better go and see Mr Sherman."

"Oh, he knows I'm never late. Come on, give me the reins, I'm here now."

"Can't do, old son."

"Why not? What's the problem?" The bay team seemed calm and alert as usual.

"Sherman told me to drive whether you turned up or not."

George stared at him. "Whether I turned up or not? What does that mean?"

"I don't know."

"This isn't to do with Dick Cherry, is it?"

Morris considered the question before he replied. "No. I don't believe it's anything to do with – er – with that. I don't know what it is, to be honest. You'd better ask the Guv'nor." He turned away and climbed up to the box of the coach.

George fought down the urge to use his fists. What the hell was going on? Those were his horses – his coach. He ran for the booking office.

"Where's the Guv'nor?"

The senior clerk waved him aside. He said again, "Where's Sherman? Morris is driving my coach!"

One of the juniors jerked a thumb towards the inner office. "Mister Sherman is there. Expecting you, I'd say." A knowing smile accompanied the information, and George's hackles rose further.

"What d'you mean?"

"I couldn't say, I'm sure. Suppose you ask him!" The clerk lifted the flap of the counter to let George through. "Take your hat off."

George snatched it off and strode through to hammer on the door of Sherman's office.

"Yes," came the call.

Inside, Sherman's opulent black satin shirt struck George as an insult. Black should be decent, restrained, for business and formal occasions, like the funeral Cherry couldn't have.

His voice was sharp as he demanded, "What's Morris doing on my coach?"

Sherman sat back and looked at him. George returned the stare, his jaw tight with anger. Trust him to have a monstrously padded, swivelling, showy chair and to lounge offensively in it.

Sherman said, "Morris is doing what I told him to do and nothing more. Here." He tossed a folded paper across the desk.

"What's that?"

"It's a reference. You'll need it to find another job."

"You're dismissing me?" He couldn't believe it, but Sherman's unsympathetic face was enough of a reply. "What the hell for? I'm one of the best drivers you've got!"

"Plenty of men as good as you are looking for work. There's a week's pay at the front desk, in lieu of notice."

"Don't give me that. I know you're short of a driver – you had to put John Holland on the Greyhound …'

Sherman overrode his protest. "Out. And don't slam the door."

CHAPTER 44.

1 September 1838

The following evening, George sat at the table in Falcon Street, with the writing case lying open under the light of the lamp. To begin with his anger at his dismissal had been straightforward. He had fumed over the manner of it, and more, he missed his teams and fretted about whether the Old Cripples would ever be replaced, and how the young thoroughbreds and the wilful Cinnamon would behave in Jonathan's hands. That mood had changed today when the coaching businesses he approached for work had been startlingly offhand. Mr Nelson, Mrs Mountain and Mr Horne had turned him away as though he arrived clanging a leper's bell. Now more than ever he missed Cherry and his chirpy, down to earth advice.

"George?" Lucy stood by the door in her nightgown, her question hardly more than a whisper. "Aren't you coming to bed?"

He jumped, and shut the case.

"Why have you got up?" He softened his voice, realizing it had been too sharp. "Come on, lovely, back to bed. You're supposed to be having an early night."

"I can't sleep. Why aren't you driving?" When he shrugged, she added, "You've been writing letters all day."

"Bed, do you hear me?"

"Not until you tell me what's wrong. Has Mr Sherman dismissed you?"

"I'll tell you if you'll go back to bed. You're shivering."

She gave in, but once she was under the covers she held on to his arm and said, "Come on. I'm worried, pet. I hate it when you keep secrets."

"All right." He sat on the edge of the bed. "Sherman has turned me off."

"Why didn't you tell me?"

"I didn't want to upset you. I thought I'd surely find another post, and I'd tell you all about it then." He had spent the afternoon asking for work at the smaller London inns, to no avail, and he'd begun to worry about how long he and Lucy could afford to live in Falcon Street.

She shook her head at him, mock-censorious. "That's just like you. What had you been up to?"

"I don't know. I've never been dismissed before and I can't work out what I did wrong. Sherman wouldn't say. I'd done everything by the book, as far as I know."

She asked, on a note of alarm, "He didn't turn you off without a reference, did he?"

"No. It's the oddest thing. He had it ready drawn up to give to me."

"You'll find other work, then," she said, with relief. "Did he pay you? Have we enough money to get by?"

"He paid me for the week, and the Whip Club will probably cover the doctor's bill. You'd best go to sleep now – don't wait for me to come to bed. I'm writing to every proprietor I know."

She nodded, and lay back against the pillows. He returned to the sitting-room, and he knew that her gaze followed him until he was seated and had begun to write again. He hadn't told her that the Whip Club would only pay for medical relief, and there was no compensation for a man dismissed; and neither of them had talked about where new work might take them.

***

Over the next week he asked for work at every yard inside London Wall, and most of those beyond, but even the ones whose drivers were most bleary-eyed and badly dressed could offer him nothing.

At last he swallowed his pride and enquired at the omnibus companies, though he'd done enough of that kind of driving in Manchester, with only a pair of horses to draw his passengers through miles of crowded streets. The 'bus companies had all turned him away. Perhaps his reluctance had been too obvious. Perhaps there were too many coachmen looking for work. Perhaps the best had already taken the available places. Perhaps he was simply too late. The uncertainty made it feel like a conspiracy.

Coming home, he was accosted by a man selling whips, who recognized him as a coachman and tried to make a sale. He refused, but as a kind of consolation he stayed to talk, finding that the man was another driver out of place, a countryman who said he had come into the city hoping to drive a cab. George enquired if he knew of any openings there, but the answer was discouraging.

"Ye have to know London like the back o' yer hand or they won't give ye the licence – y'know, this new licence to drive in the city. I can't do it, but them as do says yer on the go from six in the morning to past midnight. I'd rather buy a bunch of whips like these and sell 'em where I can. I don't earn much from it, and that grinds yer down, but at least it's only me that starves and not some poor brute of a horse."

In the past week, Lucy had started to lay out the day's letters on the table ready for George coming home. It had become a little ceremony, begun in anticipation but so far ending always with disappointment. Today, the first two letters regretted, as usual, that their business had no place for him. Lucy waited with her hands tightly clasped while he slipped his finger under the seal of a third.

King's Arms Hotel and Posting House

Stricklandgate

Kendal

2 September 1838

Dear Sir,

Mr Croft of Preston has recently forwarded a letter from you enquiring for a position as a coachman to drive four horses.

I need a man to take the place of one of my older coachmen. His ground is some 45 miles, from Kendal to Preston where we collect the Mail at the railway terminus.

You state that you have a character reference from your previous employer, which I shall wish to see. The details of your duties and remuneration are to be agreed on your arrival should you prove suitable.

yrs truly

John Jackson

"Now this is worthwhile. A Mail! I knew I must have good news eventually. It will be a good deal easier than the old Albion's run down to Dunchurch." He re-read the letter.

"Mr Jackson doesn't say whether he could accommodate us at the hotel. I'll have to ask him about that." He gave Lucy's belly a cheerful pat. "Are you listening in there, young Matthew? Papa's going to drive a Mail again!"

He was surprised when Lucy withdrew and perched on one of the chairs opposite.

"I don't want to go so far," she said.

"Ar ey, lovely! Think of the time I've spent looking for four-in-hand work in London. Believe me, if it was there I'd find it, and there's nothing."

"I don't want to go north," she repeated, and sat down, staring at the heap of letters. "I want to stay here, with Mrs Bowe and Betsy, and I want Doctor Neill to look after me when the baby comes."

He blew out his cheeks, and let the air escape in a big sigh. He was sorry to upset her, but really, she couldn't make this demand. If he allowed her heart to keep him here, they might both be starving before he found work – that would do the baby no good, and she would certainly be ill.

"Winter's coming. You know what Dr Neill said about fogs and bronchitis."

She sat mute and defiant, rocking her pregnant belly.

"It's all very well you sitting there," he said. "I know you want to stay till the baby's born, but it isn't going to be possible."

"I shall be lying-in in January," she said. "We can't go on a coach journey in the middle of winter with a new baby."

She stopped rocking, as though perfectly satisfied with her argument. He said, "But we can't go on like this either – living on my savings and hoping something will turn up. We'll have to move, and sooner rather than later."

"But I like it here," she said, in a trembling voice.

"So do I, lovely! So do I! But the figures don't add up! Businesses in the city pay their drivers thirty bob a week. Come on now. You know how much we pay Mrs B for these rooms – is it more or less than that?"

"It's more," she admitted, and began to rock again.

"Thank God for honesty," he said. "It makes no sense to work a fourteen hour day that won't even pay for our lodgings. We'd have to move from this place, so why don't we make a clean break and just leave London altogether?"

"I understand what you're saying…But, oh – George! Kendal's too near to Carlisle. There'll be Mr Brydon, and Mr Eade, and their guards…"

"I know. That'll be part of the fun. We'll have some rare chinwags."

"Not with George Eade," she said, "unless they've found a cure for deafness. But they all know Mother. They'll tell her where I am. She'll come and take me away from you!"

"She won't! I'll see her dead first!"

"She knows I'm under-age. She'll drag me back to Carlisle. And I can't – what will become of Matthew…"

"Don't upset yourself with what she might do. She'd have to leave the Bell, and when did she ever step onto a coach? I mean, you'd never travelled anywhere until you ran away, had you? She won't, either. She won't even think of it. Trust me."

"But George – why do we have to go North?"

"It's work, Lucy!"

"It's only because you're determined to drive four in hand. You don't have to."

"Oh, no. No, I'm to spend all my waking hours drudging up and down the streets with a half starved cab-horse or couple of underbred vanners, just to please you. You'll want to live decently, won't you? And the kid as well. I can only do that if I'm driving a coach. Anywhere else, I'm wasted." His frustration was too strong to be bottled up any more. "I want speed! I want good horses! I want the open road!"

There was a knock at the door and Thetford poked his head in. Seeing the heated expressions on their faces, he was about to retreat, but George exclaimed, "Wait there, Thetford! I'm in desperate need of sherry and news. You couldn't have picked a better time." He turned back to Lucy. "Now then lovely – you think it over. I'm sure you'll see reason. Thetford and I will be at the Swan if anyone wants us."

He grabbed his hat, and steered Thetford out.

Lucy stared at the door, rocking, a hand pressed to her side. A little while later she got to her feet, and went down to tap on Mrs Bowe's door.

"Good evening!" said the landlady, in surprised tones. "Is something the matter? Come in, do. Tell me what's wrong."

Lucy's eyes filled with tears.

"Oh Mrs Bowe! I think I've come to say goodbye."

CHAPTER 45.

Friday, 7 September 1838

George came home in a fog of sherry. He and Thetford had linked arms and steadied each other from the Swan up to Falcon Street, and they hadn't separated until they reached the top of the stair.

In the sitting room the lamp was out and the fire had burned low. The argument with Lucy still nagged at him. The bedroom door was shut, and he fumbled it open, wincing at the noise of the catch.

"Shh little door, shh, don't wake mother."

Perhaps Lucy was waiting in there with an upraised rolling pin or a frying pan! He peeped in cautiously, but she was in bed, only her shoulder and her plaited hair visible. He couldn't judge whether she was asleep, but she didn't respond when he whispered her name.

"Let sleeping wives lie." He suppressed a chuckle, and closed the door again.

A plate lay on the table with a bowl inverted over it and a knife and fork beside it. He investigated, the bowl clattering as he moved it. Cold mutton and potatoes? Well, that was better than nothing. He couldn't be too deep in Lucy's bad books, or she'd have told Betsy to leave it downstairs.

When he finished eating he felt less fuzzy headed. He lit the lamp and put a few lumps of coal on the fire, then he pushed the crockery to the far end of the table and drew out his letters. He re-read Mr Jackson's offer of a coach out of Kendal. Then he put the writing case on the table, succeeded in putting the key in the lock at his second try, and began, very deliberately, to compose an acceptance.

After he'd folded his reply, he realized he still had a letter unopened. It was unusually bulky, but he recognized the handwriting at once, and the oval seal. He sighed. Sarah Chaplin was still writing to him – and now she was addressing her letters directly to Falcon Street, not to the Poste Restante.

You have not collected my last from the Post Office. I enquired for it and so it is enclosed with this.

He rubbed his face, trying to think more clearly before he went on reading.

Do you not have money to post letters? I would put a coin under the seal if it would help you, because if you have to choose between paying for lodgings and paying for postage, I know I shall never hear from you. I have nothing of you here except your letters. Write to me. Please write to me. How insane it is that we live scarcely a mile apart and yet never meet.

I am plotting how to make things right for you. I could find a position for you. I have a basket full of suggestions! Shall I come knocking at your door, crying my wares?

In hopes

Polly

He let the letter drop on to the tablecloth, feeling hunted. London was a big city, but it wasn't big enough to prevent Sarah coming to find him, dragging the disapproving Eliza in her wake. As she had pointed out, they lived scarcely a mile apart. If she had gone to the lengths of re-posting a letter just because he hadn't collected it, she was capable of walking across the city to arrive on his doorstep. He could picture her over-riding Mrs Bowe and Betsy, coming upstairs to patronize him, to queen it over Lucy. The idea was intolerable.

Perhaps he shouldn't open her other letter, but it was better to know what she was up to. Frowning, he slipped his finger under the seal.

My darling George

I have learned that Papa has paid Mr Sherman to dismiss you. I am so, so sorry. Did I tell you he dismissed Eliza, too? And she has been with our family since the Flood!

Papa has come back from Switzerland with political ambitions as well as practical ones – we shall see him sitting in the House of Commons before he is done. I shall use that. Because I have outwitted him once, he knows that I can do it again. I threatened to make a scandal that would damage him – I care nothing for myself and my reputation!

George drew a sharp breath. That would have happened right on top of the business over Cherry's death! The reactions of Mrs Bowe and her neighbours could only be guessed at. He and Lucy had had a narrow escape there.

So when I asked to work, this time Papa had to permit me. You see, if I cannot have you, then I will take power instead.

Papa is in company now with Mr Horne to carry goods to and from the railway stations. I shall eventually have a guiding hand in the new firm. He says we shall build up a carrier business to rival Pickford's.

I will see what may be contrived for you. We are seeking men to drive single and pair-horse vans. It is not coaching, but it is a growing business. If I cannot persuade Papa I will approach Mr Horne, and if worse comes to worst, I will recommend you to

Pickford's. I shall write from our office as though from Papa, directly to Mr Baxendale.

Write to me with your thoughts!

with all my love,

Polly

George knew he needed to sober up. Right now he couldn't think properly, except that he was annoyed about Sarah treating him like a picture card in her little games. He would write and tell her to go to hell! It would be easy enough. He was damned if he did and damned if he didn't. Chaplin might have taken his daughter's excuses at face value but he certainly hadn't taken the slight to his family lying down. George was sure it was Chaplin who had excluded him from worthwhile work in London.

Sarah's suggestion that she could persuade Horne to give him work was dubious, and the idea that Pickford's would be deceived if she wrote as her father was pure fantasy.

He drew out a sheet of paper, uncapped the ink, and began to write.

Falcon Street

Monday

Dear Miss Chaplin – my very dear Miss Sarah who isn't the eldest!

Keep your precious money. I am sure that I could instantly raise more in ready cash than you could. My savings are sufficient to keep me and my wife.

Money is not the issue. It is the lack of occupation – the inability to use my skills – that has troubled me. Your father did me a bad turn by keeping me on when he began to cut down his coaches. It looked kind at the time and perhaps he meant it so, but this pointless intrigue of yours has put an end to his good will and now I am too late to find any work in the city. You cannot offer me work even though you suppose you can. I am sure your father has blacklisted me.

George carefully applied a full stop, then sat back and flexed his fingers.

Your attention has been flattering, but it always goes a-wry. Please stop trying to help me. You told me yourself that to move out into the provinces was the only way I could continue to drive four-in-hand once the damned railways opened. I cannot stay in London. There is my wife's health and the child to think of.

He paused, trying to focus on Lucy, her turned shoulder a mute protest beyond the bedroom door. Would she agree at last that they must go north? Had she spent the evening crying on Mrs Bowe's shoulder? Surely she would realize that there was no choice – but would she make a scene before she accepted it? She must agree. His letter of acceptance was already written. Whatever she said, he was going, and she must go with him.

He felt vaguely guilty about writing to Sarah, as though he was being unfaithful.

His only physical connection with her had been that tantalizing coach ride. The association hadn't been all bad. He owed a good deal to Chaplin, so he would make his statement to his daughter, say farewell, and close the episode with some kind of dignity.

He read back what he had written, and crossed out the word *damned.*

He wrote on, quickly, unevenly, forgetting to dip the pen so that it ran dry before he completed his sentences, and when he did he made blots, and his words regained emphasis halfway through where he had re-traced unreadable letters.

Therefore I have found work far away from the city. I am going to drive a Mail. I want to leave as soon as possible – before the end of the week. I will make an early start and leave this house with as few farewells as I can, because a friend of mine lived here to whom I can never now say good-bye –

He stopped again, fuzzily aware that he was about to betray Cherry. He must write no more, and plant no thought in Sarah's mind that would stir up trouble around his memory. Poor Cherry. His eyes filled with tears, and he blinked them angrily away. That was the sherry making him maudlin.

With extreme care, he folded the letter in on itself, and concluded:

Enjoy your power. Do not write to me again.

G Davenport

He sealed both letters without doing any worse damage to himself than to blister a finger with hot wax. In the morning, he would post them.

CHAPTER 46.

Saturday, 8 September 1838

After breakfast, George said to Lucy, "I'm going out to post these letters."

She took a deep breath. He'd risen late and reluctantly and picked at his breakfast in a way she hadn't seen except when he was debating the move to London – and all the way downstairs, all through the meal and all the way back upstairs, she had maintained a silence that was designed not to provoke sparks. But now they were in their own rooms again, and she could stay quiet no longer.

"I wish you'd talk to me. I talked late with Mrs Bowe ... she had such good advice, George…"

"Look, I've got a hammer thumping between my ears, and right this minute, I don't care what she said. I'll tell you now, I've written to Mr Jackson – here's the letter – and we're going to Kendal. If you still want to talk when I come back, I'll listen."

"Oh!" she said, uncertainly. "Very well."

"I shan't be long."

Lucy stood immobile until he had gone. So he had already written the letter! She ought to have been quicker, and grasped the chance to delay him. Was this what happened when you were a pregnant wife and no longer a lover? Your husband didn't consult you any more when he made major decisions. You had to accept whatever he chose to do, and build your life according to his wishes. She seemed to look back at a lifetime of being bullied and browbeaten. Was she to put up with it forever? She closed her eyes.

Dear Lord, strengthen me in my hour of need.

She sighed, and took her workbox to the window, where she unfolded a rectangle of linen cut from one of Mrs Bowe's old sheets. If she kept her hands busy, her mind would work more clearly. She sat at the table and began to fold and tack a hem round the sheet, making big, rather clumsy stitches. This would be bedding for the baby's crib. Her mind was not settled enough yet for fine work, but at least tacking was a step forward. It was another form of prayer.

Mrs Bowe had been a great comfort while George was out last night. She had sympathized, but she had also been careful not to encourage Lucy's worries. George, she said, would come home with a skin-full of ale, and in the morning he'd have forgotten that they had any disagreement. However, Lucy must accept that if there was no work to be had in London, George must go wherever he could find a position.

"I followed Bowe wherever his work led him," she said. "I knew what he was when I married him, and I'm sure you know the same about your husband. Bowe was a coachman first and foremost, and only after that was he a husband and a father. Men don't change, my dear, no matter what we hope for. Our first move was hard – we had a son just a year old and another on the way and the place we rented was only one room. But I was lucky after that, because Bowe didn't have more than a couple of changes of master. You get used to doing what's needed. You feed a man and see he's fit to earn a wage, and you arrange the rest of your life round that. You cope. Davenport is like my old man was – a horseman through and through. That's why Bowe died the way he did, poor man, not that I want to talk about dying when your husband's so young and strong!"

Lucy had burst out that George didn't seem to understand her fears about the baby. There were other fears, deep in her past, that even now she couldn't share, and the thought of her imminent labour was only part of them, but it would be so much easier for her if Mrs Bowe, whom she trusted, could be there when it began. She didn't quite say all that. She complained instead that although George might be as proud as a peacock about fatherhood, he didn't seem to have given any thought to the actual birth.

Mrs Bowe confided, "I'll tell you what Bowe said to me. Whenever I started worriting, he'd say, 'I've calved cows and I've foaled mares, and I can give you a hand as well, if I have to!'"

They had both laughed and wept a little.

The evening had worn away in stories and gossip, small confidences and reassurances that nibbled at the edges of Lucy's ancient terror but never quite brought the whole of it out into the light. Mrs Bowe eventually pushed her off to bed, saying that Tom could be relied on to bring Davenport home safe and sound, however much they had both drunk. Lucy noticed that little slip – not "Thetford" or even "Bowe" as she always called her dead husband, but "Tom." Well now! She had gone upstairs with raised eyebrows and a smile on her face.

The postman's double knock sounded now at the front door. Lucy put down her sewing and went to look over the banister, to see Mrs Bowe taking in the mail.

"Nothing to pay, Henry, I hope? Thank you, good morning."

"Is there anything for Mr Davenport?"

George had received so many letters these past few weeks. It was just like him to be out posting another when the man called.

"I don't think so," said Mrs Bowe, reading the addresses. Then, on a note of surprise, "Oh! but there's one here addressed to you, my dear. I'll bring it up."

"Don't trouble," said Lucy. " I'll come down."

The thought crossed her mind that someone might have written from Carlisle – not her mother of course, but possibly Mr Mounsey or one of the other regulars at the Blue Bell, or even Mrs Carruthers. Ought she to lay it out on the table with George's mail, and wait for him to come home before she read it? However, when she turned the letter over she saw it couldn't be from Carlisle. It bore a twopenny postal stamp from within the London area and the handwriting was rapid and practised, unlike her own careful hand. The seal had been set with a plain oval, like a signet ring, showing no letters or crest.

She was struck by how similar this letter was to some that George had received recently. The difference was that this one had been addressed to her, "Mistress Davenport", written in full as though the writer wanted to make it quite clear that it was the wife, and not the husband, to whom she wrote.

She smiled at Mrs Bowe to deflect her curiosity, and carried the letter upstairs. She knew nobody in London who would write to her. She was conscious that her heart was beating too fast and her thoughts were rapid and confused. She sat at the table in the sunshine, turned the letter over several times, and smelt it. She detected nothing except the clean odour of good quality paper. How did she know the writer was a woman? Yet she was certain of it.

With a sense of impending catastrophe, she broke the seal.

Your precious husband is a liar and a cheat. Do you know that? I write and write and he doesn't answer. I want you to feel the same pain that I am feeling. I dare you to read my letters. Hunt them out. He will have hidden them.

For the last three months he has been mine. Perhaps he slept beside you, but it was me he dreamed of. Your marriage lines and the child you carry bind him to you, but that is all. May that knowledge tear your soul, the way it tears mine.

Ask him who calls him Macheath. Make him choose between us.

There was no signature.

Lucy sat utterly still for some minutes. This was the same shock she had felt as a little girl in the Lanes, a kind of disbelief at the things that could happen and leave her still alive. She did not cry, only panted and held on to the table, praying that the baby would lie quiet inside her, innocent, secure against this harm, while she re-read the words again and again as though re-reading might change the hurt into something else.

The sun sparkled through the window, where beads of condensation were beginning to join into little rivers. She must find a cloth and wipe the glass, or the water would run off the windowsill and spoil the wallpaper below… No, there was something more important to do before that. Find the other letters this woman had written. Know the true depth of the jealousy that faced her.

Where had he put them? The writing case! She knew that was where they must be. It was too much of a coincidence that he had bought it three months ago and it was always locked. Why had she never asked him about that? She had trusted him, whole-heartedly. Should she wait for him to come home, then ask him to open the case? Could she bear to wait? No, that was intolerable. What if he refused? What would that tell her? Would he claim there were no letters, when she knew there must be? Would he simply say the note meant nothing, and she ought to forget what she had read? She knew that was impossible. She had fooled herself for almost a whole summer that with George she came second only to his horses. Now the pain of betrayal threatened to turn her back into the beaten and abused child she had once been. She had better force that case to yield its secrets, and then she could judge what weapons she would need to defend herself.

She pushed the lamp to the back of the table, then went quickly to the fireplace, and picked up the poker.

It was a lightweight box, and two blows were enough to smash its thin brass lock. Inside, she found the letter from Mr Jackson. There was George's reference from Mr Sherman, pinned to Mr Dixon's recommendation, the reference from Mr Teather and a letter from Mr Chaplin – those three were from back in the spring. She considered them, then put them down. She would respect those and keep them safe. Then there was a batch of letters from Chester, Liverpool, Manchester and points north – Jones & Herbert, Brotherton, Croft, Barton – all regretting that there was no work at present. Nothing from any contractor in London. She added those to the business pile.

Her own letters to George were next. The ink seemed cheap and faded, and she realized how clumsy her own writing was compared to that of the various clerks, who had fitted all the words onto the page without having to cross their lines. Underneath them, there were several letters in a distinctive style, all using the same ink on the same paper. She pounced on them. She took up the message she had opened this morning, and laid it side by side with them. The handwriting was alike. They all bore London twopenny stamp marks and a plain oval seal. She found Chaplin's letter again and put it beside them. They were all the same. They had been written by someone who was close enough to Chaplin to write on his notepaper, someone who wrote business letters for him to sign.

She sat down, fearing her legs might give way.

She counted the letters. Nine of them, the last only a week ago.

She read them all.

The first note had shocked her too much to let her feel anything, but steadily, as she read and re-read, an emotion grew whose strength she had never known before: anger. Anger that knew its own roots, that was not founded on guilt, whose cause was righteous and whose target exact. Who was this "Polly" who wrote to George? How dared she write, grabbing all the sentiments that belonged to her, to his wife? If Polly had appeared in the room at that moment, Lucy would have snatched up the poker and struck her dead. Instead she seized the note and ripped it in two. The feeling was so satisfying that she took all the others and shredded them, sheet by sheet, then scattered the heavy paper across the carpet so that the phrases lay this way and that… *take pleasure in each other…My darling George… infuriating, impossible Macheath…*

There was no signature other than "Polly" but she was sure that it was Chaplin's daughter. A clever, well-educated girl. A girl who planned, and schemed. A rich girl, with power to put behind her passions. Lucy wrapped her skirts round her belly so she could move more easily, then she clenched her teeth and screamed and stamped on the words again and again.

When her anger subsided a little, she began to feel cold.

There were so many questions she must ask before she could make a clear picture from the disjointed sharp-edged pieces of truth. George had only gone out to post a letter. Why hadn't he come back? Was he meeting Polly? What was the business with Jeanne? Had it cost him his coaching work? Lucy sat beside the splintered writing case, puzzling things out, while condensation wandered down the window like tears and spilt tiny rainbows of sunshine across the letters she had ripped apart.

She touched a lucifer to the kindling Betsy had laid in the grate, and wondered with a shiver of childish revenge what George would do if she were to burn all his letters, including the business ones. Even as she considered it, the adult part of her mind quietly prevented her. If she destroyed the papers that supported George's work, she would destroy the foundations of their life together. After all, she was his wife. She was the one with the ring on her finger, the one who was in the right. She could ride out infidelity. And there was one line in the last letter from "Polly" that gave her hope: I write and write and he doesn't answer. The knowledge brought a surprising sense of power. She would use it.

She heard him come in, whistling sweetly.

CHAPTER 47.

8 September 1838

He closed the front door and ran up the stairs two at a time. He was happy at having accepted Jackson's work. It was natural that Lucy would be upset about leaving Falcon Street, but if she'd really wanted to set herself up against him she'd have done it last night while he was out, when her disappointment had been at its worst – she'd have told Betsy to leave his supper downstairs. She hadn't done that, and she hadn't been too cold at breakfast time, either. He was sure he could talk her round.

He thought his letter to Sarah hadn't been unkind, but he had made it clear – as far as he could recall from last night's haze – that she must stop trying to entangle him. Yes, he'd done that all right… and now he'd dealt with her, his conscience and his head were clear.

He was beginning to feel pleasantly hungry. He had a future again, and work and Lucy and the child were all safe.

"Lucy! Where are you, my little sugar-plum?"

She didn't answer. Perhaps she had gone out. Well, maybe Mrs Bowe would find him the other half of his breakfast… He opened the door of the sitting room, and stopped, shocked. There was paper all over the carpet, and Lucy standing hands-on-hips, waiting for him.

"What's all this?"

"Well?" she asked. "Has-ta posted thy letter? Who did thou send it to? I bet thou won't dare to tell me."

Every syllable crackled with anger. He took in the smashed box on the table, the newly-lit fire.

"What the hell have you done? Damn it, those letters are important!"

She didn't flinch.

"They aren't business letters. They're from thy pretty horse-breaker."

"Nonsense! What are you talking about?"

"Thy molly." Her voice was full of scorn. "Thy dolly-mop. Thy smart little trollop!"

"Don't be silly." He bent to grab a handful of the scraps, and shuffled through them, examining the writing. "Where's the letter from Mr Jackson – and my references?"

She was cool, he thought, oddly composed, when all the wreckage on the floor shouted of hysteria.

"They're in the box," she said. "I told thee, they're safe."

"They better bloody had be! Look, what set this off? I only went to the Post Office!"

"It wasn't a business letter thou was posting, though, was it?"

"It was to Mr Jackson, about the job in Kendal. What the devil possessed you?"

"Polly did!" she cried. "Polly!"

"I don't know anybody called Polly," he said, uncomfortably, but he could see she didn't believe him.

"She knows thee all right! Spiteful little bitch! She'd never have written to me if she didn't know thee!"

Oh Lord – yes, there was nothing more likely. And Lucy could see that knowledge in him, even though he denied it.

"So who is she? She's one of the Chaplins, isn't she?"

"Well, you tell me, if you think you know so much! Come on! What did she say?"

"Some of the things she writes I'd be ashamed to lay my tongue to! She's more of a whore than I ever was!"

"It was nothing, honestly, lovely. Listen to me…"

"She doesn't think it was nothing. Why did thou do it? I suppose she bought thy services, with all her money! What does she think thou is, a prize stallion?"

"No, lovely – please listen – nothing happened."

How infuriating of Sarah to announce herself as a rival to Lucy! He had to admire the way she always did the uncomfortable thing. Of course, he mustn't say anything of the sort! He had no idea what Lucy might do. He had never seen her in a rage before, never guessed she had it in her. She had obviously read enough of Sarah's letters to put him squarely in the wrong. He didn't miss the irony that he'd just written to Sarah and thought he'd done with the whole business.

"I swear to you, she was the one who chased after me!"

"Oh, yes, they all run after thee, don't they! And I suppose I was just there for the in-between times!"

"Bloody hell, Lucy, that's a stupid thing to say!"

"Oh, so now I'm stupid! That's so like a man! You all think women are stupid!"

"I don't. She wanted my advice, and I didn't see anything wrong in it.'

"What on earth could thou advise her about? A rich girl like that!"

"There are things rich girls are never told," he said, awkwardly. "You know – the facts of life."

"Oh! Thou should have asked me to talk to her. I'd have told her a thing or two! And I'd have known straight away that she was leading thee on!"

"Look, she tried – yes, I admit it, she did – but… "

"And I suppose thou was flattered!"

"Well – it meant nothing."

"Does thou expect me to believe that? Thou thinks because thou married me and I'm having thy child, that I'm bound to love-honour-and-obey thee and thou needn't go to the trouble of loving and cherishing!" Her cheeks were pink and her eyes blazed, and when she lifted clenched fists he ducked. She went on, "Thou didn't hold her off very hard! If thou thinks I'm going to put up with things like this for the rest of my life, thou's got another think coming!"

Even as he retreated he realized Lucy wasn't going to strike him. Just like the time they had argued in that empty church, if she struck out she would be careful to miss him. She was telling him off this loudly because if she didn't have her say it would leave her looking weak.

"Come here," he said. She scowled and he ducked again, but she didn't move. He began to grin. "Come on, Lucy. Come here."

"Indeed I will not."

He dropped the torn pieces of the letters onto the fire, and when he put his arms around her she tossed her head but she didn't resist.

"Look, lovely, I'm sorry. I wrote over a month ago to tell her she had to let go, but she kept on writing… I didn't write back, Lucy, I swear I didn't, not till today."

"Thou wrote to her, all the same!"

"Well, her letters kept on coming! And when I didn't answer them at the Post Office she started writing here! I had to tell her to stop. That's all. I know you won't believe me."

"Thou's right! I won't!"

"Listen," he said. "It's finished."

"Is it?" Lucy breathed out, irresolute.

"Yes. That letter to you is likely to be the last thing she tries. It was a mean trick, I know, but she's desperate. She knows you've won."

"Well. Perhaps! I'm not going to trust you until – until you pick up every bit of those letters and put them on the fire!"

He cocked an eyebrow at her. "Is that all? Give us a kiss." His mouth and chest were quivering with the effort of holding back laughter.

"You may sing for it."

"Lucy?"

"Burn them!" she said.

She stood over him, rigid with determination, while he collected all the pieces of the letters.

She told him to put together the two halves of Sarah's terrible note, and he did. She told him to read what it said, and he did. He wasn't quite sure what reaction Lucy wanted to see, but Sarah's words themselves were startling enough to make him snort and screw up the paper. When Lucy spoke again her voice trembled slightly.

"Burn it!"

She stood there, vibrating like a harp string, until he had dropped the letter with the others on the fire.

"Now then," she said. The dialect began to fade as she took control of her voice. "When we move to Kendal, we'll have to find somewhere to live. Have you thought about that?"

"I don't know." He'd thought for a moment that she was going to cry, so he was relieved to be asked to discuss such practicalities. "We'll find a house to rent somewhere. I don't suppose Kendal is as crowded as London."

"I'll need help when the baby comes."

He didn't answer for a moment. It sounded like the opening to a long discussion.

"You're brewing an idea, are you? Well, spit it out."

"It's Betsy – I want her to come with us."

"God, no! The child's scatty."

"She's not that bad, George. I did say that we couldn't take her if we were just renting rooms like we do here."

"Well, I'm glad you didn't simply say Yes without discussing it."

"If we were to take a house, like you just said, she could come as a maid-of-all-work… She'd be useful."

He realized that he had underestimated Lucy. She had grown hugely stronger, even this morning. She was no longer the downtrodden damaged girl he had found at the Blue Bell.

Lucy said, "She needn't cost much."

"Who?"

"Betsy! You're not listening!"

"Yes, I am! How much is not much?"

"Six or seven pounds a year."

He was suddenly ashamed by the memory of Ma Hennessy hinting that he should pay a similar sum for Lucy.

"That's little enough. Well, with her Cockney chirpiness you won't be a stranger for long, not even in Kendal."

"Is that a Yes?"

"Oh! Yes, lovely. I want you to be happy, and if it makes you happy to have her chattering around while I'm out working, then all right, she can come with us. But take note – she's to stop in the kitchen in an evening. I suppose I'll have to buy her a train ticket. Do you think she can behave in a first-class carriage?"

"Well, I must teach her, mustn't I?"

"Ooh, listen to the expert! Tell her, if she can't hold her tongue I'll send her as a parcel, by coach."

Lucy laughed. "She'd probably enjoy that! Poor little goose!"

"Imagine how she'll squawk and flap her wings if your mother comes calling. That'll make a pretty racket."

He saw Lucy stiffen again. "Thou said she wouldn't…my mother, I mean."

"Well, I don't think she will."

"I hate her! The way she pretends to be respectable. The only decent thing she ever did was to send me to school." She added thoughtfully, "They were good, you know. Strict, but kind. I'd rather live with somebody kind than somebody clever."

"Ouch." When she didn't speak again he said awkwardly, "I suppose I haven't been very kind to you. I'm sorry."

"I love thee," she said, as if it forgave everything. "I knew from the first that thou wanted to look after me, the way thou'd take care of anything that was hurt. It's the way thou's made. Thou always wants things to be better."

He ought to have gone down on his knees before her then. He wanted to shout in exultation.

Embarrassed, he did neither.

"Don't put me on a pedestal, lovely. It's just that I've always let the girls chase me, so that's what I did with you – and Polly, too, I suppose. I thought I could turn her to my advantage. I shouldn't have."

"Thou goose!" she said. "She's been using thee." Her voice strengthened. "It's as well we're about to move out of London, because I tell thee, if I ever meet yon lass… It had better be true, that thou's ended it!"

"Yes," he said. "I'm free of her." He didn't understand why Lucy had forgiven him, and he knew he didn't deserve it, but he felt it as surely as he could feel a horse going sweetly.

Deliberately, trying out the words, he said, "I do love thee."

She stepped forward, into his arms.

"And I love thee. But take heed – I'll stand no rivals now."

CHAPTER 48.

The day they travelled north it was a sharp, bright morning, a day on which George was impatient to drive and irritable at the thought of sitting on a train with nothing to do. To make things worse, Lucy had remembered the smoked and sooted confinement of second class railway travel, and insisted he wore his oldest coat. Its shabby appearance laid another smudge across his mood.

A four-wheeled cab waited in the street with their belongings packed on the roof, the damaged writing case among them, strapped up with an old belt. However, George carried his whip as always with the long lash looped and tied.

Mrs Bowe had wrapped herself in a shawl to lead the farewells. Tom Thetford stood by with a stolid face, and observed the fussing as though determined that no-one should have hysterics while he was about, while Mrs Bowe made sure that Betsy had securely wrapped her few possessions for the journey. Betsy herself was bundled inside a secondhand coat so large it appeared to be wearing her.

"Now you girls," said Mrs Bowe, not really making any distinction between Lucy and Betsy, "look after yourselves, and make sure this coachman fellow does the same. I know what these driving men can be like. Betsy – you imp – behave yourself when you get to your new home – it's a crying shame you leaving me to instruct a new girl from scratch – but it's your good heart, I know – and I had rather see you go and look after Mrs Davenport than get yourself into trouble with young Robbie."

"I never went with 'im," muttered Betsy. She pretended to be engrossed in stepping on and off the doorstep.

"I should think not," said Mrs Bowe. "I told you, you're not allowed to have followers. You're much too young."

"E's walkin' out with Lizzie Pearson now, anyway."

"Stop fidgeting," said Lucy.

George, with a wink at her, nudged Betsy's shoulder. "There'll be a score of sturdy lads come knocking at the door when we get to Kendal."

"Only if you introduce them to me first," said Lucy firmly, "and I arrange what evenings they're allowed to call."

"There now," said Mrs Bowe, "that's very fair, that is."

"But we shan't let you hobnob with any old riffraff," added George. "They'll have to present calling cards."

"Don't be so foolish, Mr Davenport!"

"Well, how else are we going to keep track of 'em all?"

Betsy giggled, and Mrs Bowe said, "Don't give her ideas. Oh, dear, Lucy – I shall miss you! Go well and safely, my dear. Breathe deep of that north country air. I'm sure you're going to have a beautiful healthy baby."

"I'll write to you," promised Lucy, and hugged her, and all three women clung to one another.

"Damned if I'd like to be seen carrying-on in the street," said Thetford, and turned to discuss the cab horse with George. "There's been some quality there, y'know."

"Showing his age in the hind fetlocks, though."

"Ah!" agreed Tom. "Well... I daresay it's a good thing you're leaving."

George glanced at him, surprised by his quizzical tone. "I have to follow the work, if that's what you mean."

"No. Not entirely. Seems to me there's a young woman we both know, as gave a fair show of jealousy when she worked at the Swan. I recall as 'ow she come out special-like to travel with you on the Albion."

George reddened, in spite of himself. "She did."

"Kind of flattering, but I 'ope you didn't do nothing about it." The wise old eyes gave nothing away.

"I warned her off, Tom."

"I 'ope you did, for Mrs Davenport's sake."

George realized that Tom guessed what had happened, but the old man was a realist. Making a fuss over the truth would benefit no-one. As along as nobody asked him directly, he knew Tom would keep his suspicions to himself.

"Mrs Davenport knows," he said, "And as for the young lady – she'll get over it."

The cabman, his gaze fixed on the horse's ears, stolidly observed, "If yer party's wishful to be at Euston for the ten o'clock train, better get in now."

Tom took the hint, and shook George by the hand. "That proprietor in Kendal will be lucky to get you. I wish you all the best, I do, heartily, and Mrs Davenport and the baby too."

George returned his handshake, liking the old man better than ever. The two of them stood irresolute for a moment before he said, "Well, I'd better disentangle these women, or we'll be here the rest of the morning."

Mrs Bowe startled him with a hug and a hard kiss on the ear, and when he escaped to help Lucy into the shabby interior of the cab, she showered advice on Betsy.

"Remember to make yourself useful, gel! Get up early and don't be to call – you riddle the fires and sift the ashes... make life easy for Mrs Davenport..."

George settled Lucy in a forward facing seat, and put Betsy opposite, where she sat excitedly waving farewell to Mrs Bowe and Thetford, even before the driver called to his horse and they set off. Lucy held her head high and felt for George's hand, all the while staring rigidly out towards the great dome of St Paul's. He knew she was struggling not to cry, and he gave her tense fist a little shake.

He wasn't sad to be leaving London. It wouldn't be long before Sherman and Nelson and other less canny proprietors realized, as Chaplin had done, that the railway was an implacable competitor, and then they would sell out too, and the coach routes would die, and as they died he would have to seek work in more and more remote areas, and compete with more and more drivers out of place. He'd come here with an ambition to make his name, and instead he'd found that the best part of his driving career was over.

Lucy's hand in his was a trust he mustn't betray again. He wasn't an irresponsible youth any longer, who could move on at a whistle and travel light.

They passed the Queen's Hotel for the last time, and the Post Office, and somewhere in the clustered buildings behind it, the Swan. He watched as the cab bore him away, until it turned the corner into Newgate Street, and he couldn't see even the buildings any more.

The End

ABOUT THIS BOOK

No novel has ever taken me so long to write as *Coachman*.

In the 1990s I had the idea that I would chronicle the life of William James Chaplin, who was a huge force in the London coaching business in the 1820s and 30s.

The Dictionary of National Biography says of him:

Chaplin, William James (1787–1859), transport entrepreneur, was born on 3rd December 1787 at Rochester, Kent, the son of William Chaplin, a coach proprietor on the Dover road, and his wife, Eleanor. Chaplin was educated at Bromley, and on 11 July 1816 married Elizabeth Alston at St Nicholas, Rochester. They had sixteen children.

About 1823 Chaplin succeeded William Waterhouse at the Swan with Two Necks inn, Lad Lane, London, and he was to become the largest ever coach proprietor. In 1827 his coach business employed 300 to 400 horses; by 1835 this had risen to 1200. As well as three London inns, he had extensive stables at Purley, Hounslow, and Whetstone, and was said to employ 2000 people. In 1836 he had ninety-two coaches leaving London every day, serving all the main roads from the city. He horsed fourteen of the twenty-seven mail coaches leaving London each night. His annual turnover was said to be £500,000.

Chaplin's vision was so clear that when the railways came to change long-distance travel he was able instantly to step back and rebuild his business in relation to the new technology. He liquidated all his coaching assets, though he kept the inns, and he went away for six weeks to Switzerland to do his planning. Once his carrier partnership with Benjamin Worthy Horne was established, he invested heavily in railways.

The few stories about Chaplin that are recorded in books by his contemporaries all show him in an affectionate light. He was largely responsible for the abolition of heavy brutal driving whips in London's coaching trade, and despite his nickname "Bite-Em-Sly," everybody he employed seemed to like him. He was elected MP for Salisbury, and at his death his business was worth around £300,000. A thoroughly solid, sound, clever fellow.

When I realised how damn boring that story would be – Dallas with only the nice bits on display – I knew I had to invent someone whose life would touch his, so I could show what might have happened to the drivers, stablemen and horses when railways took the heart out of coaching.

My own great-grandfather was a coachman. He was in domestic service, not on a commercial route, and he lived 50 years after Chaplin's time, but his existence in my family tree gave me a name to hang my story on: George Davenport. And my great-grandmother really was called Lucy Hennessy, though she didn't live in Carlisle and my relatives will no doubt be relieved to hear that I have completely invented her unpleasant mother and their unsavoury history. The religious belief that sustains Lucy in the novel is a known factor in the emotional survival of modern victims of child abuse.

As for the rest of the cast, I am grateful to Jennie Hill, who was a neighbour of ours in Cumbria, for the information about Chaplin's family. He had a patriarchal number of children, including twin girls, Marianne and

Sarah. Sarah was the only one of his children who died unmarried (not counting Rosa who died aged 8 and Horace who died in infancy).

Jennie Hill is a direct descendant of William Chaplin. In 1994 she asked me to transcribe a letter written by Chaplin, which a bookseller had bought at auction and brought to show her. Neither of them could read his writing. I could… So some of the phrases he used about business appear in his conversations in Coachman. Jennie also gave me a copy of the family tree, and permission to write this novel.

Nothing is known of Sarah Chaplin, so I could safely invent whatever reasons I liked to account for her spinster status. I've suppressed any mention of her twin sister for the sake of simplicity. My decision to make her obsessed with power sprang from the observation of a former coachman, who remarked that Chaplin's business was founded on "systematic application ... in which the female members of the family were called to assist."

Many of the drivers mentioned in Coachman were real people in the Golden Age of Coaching, and some, such as Cross, wrote autobiographies during their twilight years for the benefit of Coaching Revivalists in later Victorian times. Their works were rich sources for this novel.

Waude's Mail coaches really were considered by drivers to be the best on the road, and Croall's versions really were fairly horrible, as attested by documents of complaint from northern Mail coach contractors held by the British Postal Museum & Archive.

Other major sources were Pigott's Directories which listed coach routes and the times when coaches were due at various inns along the road. I found no directories for 1838. That is possibly because the rapid expansion of the railways caused coaching routes to be in a state of constant flux and discouraged publishers from printing material that would be out of date before it could be put on sale. At any rate it gave me some leeway in describing the routes George drove.

Horses still work and misbehave in the same ways today as they did then. I carriage drive myself, so speeds and difficulties were not hard to imagine. To get the full flavour of riding on a coach behind a four in hand I took part in a coaching run between Newcastle and Carlisle in 2011, with the Bowman family from Penrith. To George Bowman III and George Bowman IV – my thanks – and please note that despite his name my hero is not based on either of you, although he has stolen one or two comments that you may have let slip over the years.

George Davenport's love of driving was probably typical of his profession at the time. Coachmen by this era were well dressed "artists" who conversed as easily with aristocrats as with stablehands. A young presentable man could earn well, and he might almost claim similar social status to a doctor, banker or lawyer. I have given George some rather forward-looking attitudes, such as his reluctance to be cruel to horses to get the work out of them that his timetable demanded. Such kindness was probably not typical of most men of his time, when horses were still the major means of transport and were hardly ever treated as pets like they are today.

The only aspect of coaching that I haven't really explored in *Coachman* is the fact that the men who drove and guarded each route, and the horses who drew the coach, were a large team that changed on a rota basis. For simplicity I've mostly kept Tom Thetford as George's guard on the Albion coach, although he might well have worked with two or three others, and the guards frequently travelled further than the driver did. As for the horses, I've pointed out that the teams changed with every stage, but although I've described the same teams on the same stages, in reality the work patterns varied between proprietors and routes. A common system was for the horses to work four days, spending alternate nights in stables at each end of their stage, and then to a have a day off. On shorter stages they might work twice a day, going out, resting, then coming back at night to the same stable. George might not have always had the same four horses on any particular stretch of road, and possibly not always in the same combinations. For continuity's sake and to avoid confusion I have had to gloss over this.

The Albion and the Greyhound were indeed two coaches that continued to run on the modern A5 route out of London when William Chaplin sold up. Who bought them from him? It doesn't seem to have been recorded, but the obvious person would have been Edward Sherman, whose stubborn continuation to compete with the railways nearly ruined him. I've invented the dates on which Sherman took a half-share and took over completely; but he really did dress like a showman in a black satin shirt front stuck with diamond pins!

George's visit to Drury Lane: Charles Kean did perform as Richard III on 14th May 1838. It was probably still the Colley Cibber version that was played, since William Macready's 1838 revivals of original Shakespeare texts such as *King Lear* which Sarah went to see and *The Tempest* which she hoped to see in October, were discussed by Browning and by Dickens. Macready built the theatre in Carlisle which George and his fellow coachmen would have visited.

Postage costs and habits of the time are accurate; the Penny Post was being put in place but did not come into effect until January 1839.

The last-ever Mail Coach Procession on 17th May 1838 did follow the route I outline, and the coaches did go in the order that Sarah recited to George. The cover drawing of it by John Sturgess (fl. 1864-1903) was published in *The Coaching Age* in 1885. It's therefore not a truly contemporary image but it captures the flavour of the scene beautifully.

Finally: my years of research into the running of the coaches have been hugely helped by the digitizing of old and expensive books for the Internet Archive and Project Gutenberg.

Where I describe something or rely on it for plot I've done my best to be accurate. If you do find errors in the history, they are mine.

Sue Millard

Cumbria

September 2012

Just a few of the sources where you can read more

Bates, A, 1969, Directory of Stage Coach Services 1836

Beaufort, Duke of, 1890, Driving.

Cross, Thomas, Autobiography of a Stage Coachman.

Dixon, H.H., 1895, Saddle and Sirloin.

Harper, Charles G., Stage Coach and Mail in Days of Yore

Harris, Stanley, 1885, The Coaching Age - http://openlibrary.org/books/OL6546380M/The_coaching_age

Mountford, The Coaching Age

Historical Directories (eg, Cumberland, London, Buckinghamshire): available from http://www.historicaldirectories.org/

Historical Maps (eg Carlisle, Fenny Stratford, London):

http://www.visionofbritain.org.uk/

Article: Coronation of Her Majesty Queen Victoria, The Globe, 1838, http://www.royal.gov.uk/pdf/Archives %20education%20project/Source%203%20-%20transcript.pdf

Dictionary of National Biography, http://www.oxforddnb.com/

Oxford English Dictionary online, Historical Thesaurus, http://www.oed.com/thesaurus

British Postal Museum and Archive, http://www.postalheritage.org.uk/

The Dixon family: Blencogo web site, http://www.blencogo.com/archives.html

OTHER TITLES FROM JACKDAW E BOOKS

AGAINST THE ODDS

Leaving home to work in a racing stable, Sian finds that the long hours and hard work are more than she bargained for. The only compensation is her responsibility for her favourite filly, Double Jump.

Sian is badly treated by her boyfriend, the trainer's arrogant son, Justin. When Double Jump's owner moves the filly to another yard, Sian follows so she can escape him.

At the new yard she meets stable jockey Madoc Owen, who is battling to make a National Hunt winner out of Cymru, a bored flat-race stallion. Sian and Madoc may have a future together but there will be more than steeplechase fences in their way – Justin will see to that.

GENRE: Fiction, romance, sporting, equestrian

First Published by J A Allen, London. (Now Remaindered – final few still available direct from author.) £5.00 + Postage.

2nd Edition 2018

ISBN: 978-1720047285

£10.00 + Postage.

ASIN: B00BGBIGNU

SCRATCH

Sequel to *Against the Odds*

A Woman. A Family. A Farm.

Sian and Madoc have borrowed heavily to buy a neglected farm, Stone Side, in the beautiful countryside of east Cumbria. They are land-rich now but short of cash and indebted not only to the bank but to members of their family.

Racehorses and Fell Ponies

In this sequel to Against the Odds Madoc has reluctantly had to give up his ambition to breed thoroughbreds, and instead runs the sheep farm and pre-trains young horses for National Hunt racing. Sian is a fierce mother of their three teenage children, Robbie, Cerys and Jack. In what free time she has, she buys and trains Fell ponies.

Someone is Out to Destroy Them

When Madoc's brother calls-in a big loan, the tensions begin to mount… and on the wild fellside, for someone the stakes are as high as murder.

GENRE: Fiction, family saga / thriller, sporting, equestrian. Publication date: 18 September 2018.

ISBN: 9780957361294

£12.00 if purchased direct, plus postage. £ 12.99 from bookshops.

ASIN: B07J6PWCS5

HOOFPRINTS IN EDEN

Winner of the Saint and Company Prize at the Lake District Book of the Year Awards, 2006. Based on a 2-year-long series of interviews with established breeders, this book explores the Fell pony breed and its traditions at the start of the new millennium.

Read about the Fell pony's Cumbrian background, the events of a typical year, its life on the fell, its traditional keeping and its links with hill farming, its characteristics and the work it can do.

Fully illustrated, and complete with a dictionary of Cumbrian farming expressions.

GENRE: Non-fiction, equestrian, history, farm & working animals

Published by Hayloft, 2005. ISBN 978-1-9045243-4-2 (available direct from author.) £17.00 plus postage.

Second edition, paperback, Jackdaw E Books.

ISBN: 978-1-731565969.

£12 plus postage.

ASIN: B07KPLQ9RG

A CENTURY OF FELLS

Produced for the Centenary of the Fell Pony Society in 2022, *A Century of Fells* follows *Hoofprints in Eden*. It celebrates the 100th year of the FPS, with sequenced photographs of many families of ponies recorded in the Stud Book through the years. It also prompts consideration of how the breed may develop in the next century.

GENRE: Non-fiction, equestrian, history, farm & working animals

Hardback

ISBN: 978-1-913-106171.

£20 plus postage

Paperback in preparation

PONIES WITH WHEELS

In 40 years of carriage driving I've had a lot of fun with Fell and Dales ponies - Mr T "The Yes Man", Eric "The Comedian", Sonny "The Stroppy Teenager" and his mother Ruby "The Magnificent".

A selection of my chatty posts on my blog, the Recreational Equine Driving list forum and social media, amounting to a novel in length. I've decided to retain their conversational tone, rather than tidying everything up. It's more entertaining that way.

Paperback

ISBN: 978-1-913106-22-5.

£13.00 plus postage

ASIN: B0BGCVXVMY

HORSES IN THE GARDEN

Sister volume to *Ponies with Wheels*

In 1983, Sue and her husband Graham bought a smallholding in Cumbria. In the forty years they have spent there with their animals and other family, Sue has written anecdotes about them, articles, blog posts, poems and very silly letters-to-the-editor. This collection dances, like life, between heartbreak and hilarity.

Coming soon! Keep an eye on the web site for details. http://www.jackdawebooks.co.uk

ONE FELL SWOOP

This is where it all started, with humour, history and horses.

Much-loved cartoonist Norman Thelwell was Sue's childhood hero (they both hailed from the Wirral) so when Sue moved to Cumbria and bought a Fell pony this "fellwell" book was the inevitable result.

A series of affectionate cartoons, poking gentle fun at the Fell breed and its history.

GENRE: Cartoon humour, farm & working animals.

ISBN: 978-0-9573612-7-0

£5.00 plus postage

ASIN: B008ZBPB14

THE FORTHRIGHT SAGA

Nothing ever happens in a small country town ... does it?

Nora Forthright and her grandson Wayne stumble through the fictional Cumbrian towns of Dangleby and Pullet St Mary, putting things right entirely by accident.

GENRE: Comedy thriller / cosy crime.

Published: 2012.

ISBN: 978-0-9573612-3-2

£5.00 plus postage

ASIN: B0099RQNLU

FOR CHILDREN

DRAGON BAIT

Princess Andra volunteers to act as bait for the dragon ravaging her father's lands, on condition that she is released from an arrangement to marry a foreign prince.

Unfortunately the Knight Rescuer who turns up is not the trusty old retainer she expects, but an unknown conservationist who wants the dragon, not the lady. After that very little goes according to plan.

GENRE: Comic fantasy (age 9-12). Published: 2012; 2nd edition 2021.

ISBN :978-1-913106-15-7

£5.00 plus postage

ASIN: B008K8SDWG

STRING OF HORSES

Fourteen-year-old Claire Armstrong's Mum and Dad run a country pub in the Lake District. Pony trekking is part of its attractions, and Claire's love of the ponies teaches her a great deal about herself. But it's the humans in the pub who cause her the most heartache.

A coming-of-age novel set in the 1970s.

GENRE: Coming-of-age, romance, sporting, equestrian. (Teen to young adult). Published: 2021.

ISBN : 9781913106119

£8.00

ASIN: 191310611X

ACTIVITY BOOKS

Two activity books for children relating to ponies, and Fell ponies in particular.

FELL FUN

For ages 4 to 7 years

Puzzles, counting, colouring, spot the difference, spot the same, matching, rhyming, starting letters, mazes and dot to dot, cutting and sticking – all about ponies.

GENRE: Activity book. 20 pages. £2.00 plus postage

FELL FACTS

For 7 years and upwards

Description of the Fell pony breed, what the ponies can do, where they live, crosswords, wordsearches, picture quiz, a story and lots of pictures, plus a list of other books and DVDs about Fell ponies.

GENRE: Activity book. 20 pages. £2.00 plus postage

Both books can go in one mailing for the same postage cost.

FELL FUN and **FELL FACTS** were produced at the request of the Fell Pony Society and may also be purchased from the FPS office in Appleby, Cumbria, and at shows and events run by the Society.

www.ingramcontent.com/pod-product-compliance
Lightning Source LLC
LaVergne TN
LVHW020041110826
845155LV00029B/578

* 9 7 8 1 9 1 3 1 0 6 2 4 9 *